A Question of Malice

By

Frederick Petford

Book three in the Great Tew supernatural thriller series

Published by The Claverham Press Ltd
London

Copyright © Frederick Petford 2023

The right of Frederick Petford to be identified as the author of
this work has been asserted by him in accordance with the
Copyright, Designs and Patents Act 1988.
All rights reserved worldwide.

This publication is a work of fiction, and the majority of the
characters are fictitious. Where known historical figures, real
events or places appear they are based on the author's own
interpretation of events and the requirements of the narrative.
They should not be considered in any other light.

ISBN 9798859979523

Dedicated to Gladys Mitchell and Edmund Crispin. Two of the
greats.

By the same author

The Ghosts of Passchendaele
Book one in the Great Tew supernatural thriller series

The Death of Conscience
Book two in the Great Tew supernatural thriller series

Readers can explore more about the themes covered in
A Question of Malice and its prequels on Facebook and Instagram at

Frederick Petford

Come and join us!

Prologue

The Isle of Skye, Scotland. Easter, 1921

The turf-roofed croft crouched on the shore of Loch Coruisk, as though fearful of the towering peaks of the Black Cuillin which rose steeply behind it. Peat smoke drifted from the chimney and the quartered glass of two small windows reflected a savagely beautiful view down the loch towards the little mountain they called the Peak of Pity and a waterfall that led to the sea. There were no other buildings in sight and on both sides of the glen steep slopes of scree and heather gave way to living rock that soared upwards for two thousand feet.

The sophisticated residents of Edinburgh called them black houses, and smiled and rolled their eyes at the idea of people living in such hovels – sharing the smoky space with their beasts and a peat fire that stayed alight, summer and winter. But to the people of the islands, they were a way of life that went back beyond memory. And in remote communities across the ancient landscape, many people still carved a living from their small parcels of land. A cow, a few sheep, fish, potatoes painstakingly nurtured in the dark, acidic soil, and a loom for the long winter nights.

But the sole resident of the dwelling below the Black Cuillin was not a crofter. She lived alone and every week the villagers of Elgol despatched a boat to the foot of the waterfall on Loch Scavaig. From there a party of varying size would pick its way over the rough ground by the loch carrying supplies to sustain her for another seven days.

They called her the cailleach, which means old woman or hag in Gaelic, but it was used with affection in her case. Even though she lived apart from them, she was a respected part of the little community in that remote part of Skye.

Because the cailleach had the sight.

The previous day the boat had brought alarming news back from Loch Coruisk, so early the following morning another little party made its way along the rocky shore towards the black house. There were four of them. A widowed woman in her sixties and her daughter, both dressed in plaid shawls and long dresses, the daughter's husband, a tall angular priest whose dark clothes and dog collar seemed incongruous in that wild setting, and their son, a young man in his mid-twenties.

The older woman called out as they approached the door. 'It's Morag, Mother, here with Katie and Alastair, and Cam.' They entered the single room. It was dark compared to the pristine, rain-washed light above the loch and they stood for a moment adjusting, although they all knew every nook and cranny of the simple building.

'You've come then. That's good.' The cailleach's voice sounded in the gloom, her Gaelic soft and flowing in the manner of the western islands.

She was sitting in a chair by the window and seemed somehow to have shrunk in her clothes. Morag walked over, concerned. 'Ally said you weren't well and wanted to see us.' She glanced back at her daughter. 'Put the kettle on, Katie, we'll have a cup of tea.'

Her mother nodded slowly. 'It's time to say our goodbyes, my love.'

'Och, stuff and nonsense.' Morag knelt by her feet and took her hand. 'You've a few more years in you yet.'

'Aye, no doubt about that,' added her son-in-law.

But the old woman ignored both their remarks and stared down the loch for a moment. 'I have things to say to all of you. And it must be done today. I'll be gone by the morning.'

'No, I'm sure—' Distressed now, the daughter squeezed her hand, but her mother interrupted.

'I have lived many lives and will live many more, but this one will end tonight.' She smiled gently at Morag and the others. 'Death holds no terrors for me, and you will manage perfectly well on your own. Now make the tea, and, Cameron, you take yours and wait outside, I will speak to you privately in a while.'

Ten minutes later these arrangements were put in place and, with both her daughter and granddaughter visibly tearful, the cailleach addressed them.

'I've had no need of money, but my father left me a nest egg with the Commercial Bank in Kyle. When last I checked there was over five thousand pounds.' As her family stirred in surprise, she looked at her daughter. 'Half of it is yours now, Morag, to secure your old age.' She looked at Katie. 'And the other half will go to you, my dear. To you personally.'

She moved her gaze to the clergyman and her eyes creased in gentle amusement. 'You've been a good provider for my granddaughter, Alastair Breck, with your fine priest's house and regular stipend. It's just a shame you don't believe in God, isn't it?'

He made to speak but she gently shushed him with a raised hand. 'Don't worry, your secret's safe with me. And for what it's worth, neither do I, and I know much more about the matter than the Church of Scotland ever taught you, believe me.'

7

She spoke for a further few minutes, ending with, 'Morag, you will stay with me tonight, the rest of you can return in the morning with the undertaker. It'll be the coffin road for me and I've no regrets.'

The family remained with the cailleach all day and in the evening they built a fire outside the croft and carried two chairs out to it. As the peat flames flared, she addressed her great-grandson.

'Cameron, you sit here with me for a while and the rest of you wait inside.' In the light from the fire the cailleach saw the gleam of avarice in his eyes. He had obviously been listening earlier and had heard about the money. She imagined he was expecting a share. 'Sit here. How old are you now?'

'Twenty-four.'

'And what are your plans?'

'Plans?'

'Aye, what will you do with your life? Are you ambitious?'

'Well, I hope for success of course.'

'In what field? When you came out of the navy you went away to the mainland, then came back, as I recall.'

'I like the islands.'

Her tone of gentle inquisition hardened. 'Perhaps. But you also like being looked after by your mother and three square meals a day. A bit too much.' She met his eye. 'A young man needs direction and independence. You are young and strong and healthy. It's time for you to forge your own way, Cameron Breck.'

He looked at her but said nothing, so she continued. 'I will die tonight, but before I go, I have a gift for you.'

He stiffened in the straight-backed wooden chair. 'A gift?'

She nodded. 'I imagine you think money would be useful to you?'

He grinned and nodded. 'Oh aye, great-grandma, that would be grand.'

A small smile showed on her face. 'I'm sure it would. But the gift I have for you is something even more valuable.'

'Than money? What is it then, a jewel?'

'Knowledge.'

He looked at her, clearly disappointed. 'Knowledge?'

'I want to tell you something. It is for your ears only, and it is up to you to decide what you will do with it. But it is momentous, and it will affect your life. That much I know.'

He sat still, interested now. 'What is this knowledge, great-grandma?'

With her black eyes fixed on his, she told him and as he stared back at her, astonished, six hundred miles south of Skye, in the remote and ancient village of Great Tew, a witch stirred in her sleep and opened her eyes.

*

True to her word the cailleach died that night. As the visitors kissed her goodbye, she met her great-grandson's eye and gave him a slow and knowing nod but said nothing. And then the old woman and her daughter were left alone in the highland night.

Much later as Morag sat dozing with her mother's hand in hers something woke her. Glancing up she saw an eagle high in the night sky, turning lazy circles in the moonlight directly above the croft. *Eagles don't fly at night*, she thought. She felt her mother stir and sigh, then release her hand. Her face fell gently backwards and as her mouth opened, a stream of pale smoke emerged. It rose into the air, as long and thick as a man's arm, and held there for a second before spreading across the night sky at incredible speed and disappearing. At the same time the eagle cried and a voice in her head whispered, *'Goodbye, my darling.'*

And with that her mother was gone.

But as tears formed in her eyes, her daughter felt something else. A shiver of deep awareness, as though she had jumped into a warm pool. It suffused her body and then slowly faded, but Morag knew something had changed. As though a door into another world had been opened. She looked up and saw the eagle glide out of sight behind the ridge.

And she understood. It was her mother's parting gift. In the moment of her death, she had passed the sight to her daughter.

As his grandmother mourned the cailleach's passing, Cameron Breck stood in his bedroom in the manse in Elgol and stared at himself in the mirror. He was an only child, as had been his mother, and hers, and many before. The act of birthing made the Breck women barren, they said. A curse delivered upon the family many generations ago.

He wondered if it were true. The evidence suggested so. But in reality, the question was just a distraction from the information he was carrying in his head. The astonishing news his great-grandmother had passed on to him.

It was a measure of the cailleach's reputation that he never queried or questioned what she had told him. As the clock at the foot of the stairs struck two in the morning, he closed his eyes and conjured up the scene again.

Her voice had been soft, matter of fact even, and she had refused to answer his questions or discuss the matter further. But her four words echoed repeatedly in his head, as the staggering implications sank in.

'You have a son.'

Chapter One

May Day, Great Tew, Oxfordshire. 1921

In the ringing room halfway up the tower of St Mary's church, the bellringers of the Langford estate eased down on their ropes and, led by the ancient great bell, a joyous cascade of chimes rang out over the village. The noise carried down the valley to Little Tew, where people stopped in the street, smiled and nodded to each other.

'That's them wed then,' an old man remarked.

'They've taken their time,' his wife replied. 'Good news though.'

'Amen to that,' he agreed.

In Great Tew, loud cheers erupted from the villagers who lined the path to the lychgate as Mr and Mrs Edward Spense appeared grinning at the church door and descended the steps arm in arm. Behind them, Piers Spense, the current Lord Langford, walked with his mother, followed by Rory and Elizabeth Knox, the bride's parents.

'Give her a kiss then, Mr Edward!' someone called from the crowd.

He glanced towards the voice and smiled when others took up the cry. As people flowed out of the church door behind

12

them, he turned to his new and remarkably beautiful wife and smiled.

'Is that alright?' he said quietly.

She looked back at him, eyes warm, then reached up and gently pulled his mouth down to hers. A further great cheer sounded from the villagers and someone else called, 'You got there in the end then!'

Jocelyn Dance and his wife, Eve, were just leaving the church and heard the remark. Up ahead Edward's mother turned, and the two friends exchanged a smile of mutual recognition followed by a gloriously ironic eyeroll from the Dowager Lady Langford.

'It has been quite a journey,' Eve said to her husband as she took his arm.

'Oh, it was never in doubt really. I knew they'd be together.'

She stared at him. 'Really? Both nearly killed, Edward twice, for heaven's sake. All kinds of alarms and excursions and you knew they'd get there in the end?'

'Made for each other,' the colonel replied blithely. 'I'm surprised you couldn't see it.'

Smiling, she dug him in the ribs, and they descended the steps.

*

Two hours later the wedding breakfast at Langford Hall was in full swing and showing every sign of being a roaring success. Two hundred finely dressed guests including many from noble families and the government were crammed into the ballroom where they chattered noisily to one another, and ate estate venison, and drank champagne from the cellars. Dereham the butler presided over it all with a stern but benevolent expression, keeping a close watch on the additional waiting staff supplied by a London agency, while sneaking the occasional soft-eyed glance at the top table where the family that he had served for over fifty years were celebrating another milestone.

When the meal ended the toastmaster rapped his gavel on the top table and, as silence fell, announced, 'My lords, ladies and gentlemen, pray silence for the brother of the groom.'

Lord Langford stood up and smiled down the room. He was saturnine, a little portly and beautifully dressed in formal wear. 'In my father's regrettable absence my brother has asked me to make the opening speech, an honour which I am most delighted to accept.'

Gentle cries of 'Hear, Hear' permeated the ballroom as he grinned and continued. 'Whether he will be quite so delighted when I have finished is a matter of conjecture, as my intention is to give you all an insight in the stark reality of growing up with Mr Edward Spense, his many failings, tantrums and rare ability to make the wrong choice at nearly every step.'

A ripple of laughter sounded from the tables as he added, 'Although I must say there can be no doubt whatsoever that, in asking Innes to marry him, he has got one thing gloriously right and my mother and I are both overjoyed to welcome her into the family.' He turned towards the bride and gave her a fulsome and genuine smile. She dipped her head and returned it with interest.

As a cheer and spontaneous clapping erupted, he held up his hand and added, 'Now then, back to Langford thirty years ago, and my brother's appalling behaviour regarding the rocking horse in the nursery…'

By six o'clock the formalities were complete, and guests had moved out of the ballroom and dispersed throughout the other main rooms on the ground floor as hasty preparations were made for a dance. The tables were dismounted and moved, a dance band arrived and more chilled champagne was brought up from the cellar.

In the milling good-natured crowd Innes and Edward managed to snatch a brief moment together as they passed

14

through the entrance hall going in opposite directions. 'Mrs Spense, good evening,' Edward said, 'how are you getting on?'

'It's wonderful and exhausting at the same time. There are so many people here I only know from their photographs in the papers. I can't help feeling if someone let off a bomb the empire would be left entirely rudderless.'

He grinned. 'It is a full turn out, isn't it? Thank heavens that photographer fellow has left now, although watch out, there are a few society journalists on the guest list. The public like to know what's happening behind walls like these, I'm afraid. And the politicians all adore publicity of course.' He took her hand. 'Don't worry, it won't always be like this, you've seen enough of life at Langford to know that it's pretty sleepy here most of the time and we'll soon have each other to ourselves.'

Innes gave him a look full of promise. 'That'll be lovely.'

'Has Jaikie finally gone to bed?'

'Yes, after repeated goodbyes, prevarication and, finally, tears. I'll go and see him in a minute.'

His mother appeared. 'Sorry to drag you away, Edward, but you haven't said hello to Winston yet and he's keen to see you.'

'I beat you to it there.' His new wife smiled. 'He's rather a charmer, isn't he.'

'Oh yes, I suspect the country will see a lot more of Mr Churchill before he's done,' Claire Spense replied, and with a quick smile she led her son into the drawing room.

As Innes turned to continue on her way, she met a tall and austerely handsome man in his mid-thirties who gave her a warm smile. 'Congratulations, Mrs Spense, my heartiest good wishes for your and your husband's future together.'

She smiled up at him. 'That's very kind, Mr Pentire. I'm sorry we have seen so little of you.' She gestured around and added, 'As you can see, we have been rather busy.'

'Not at all, Lord Langford and Lady Claire have been most welcoming, and I was delighted to receive an invitation to this evening's celebration. Time certainly flies. It's been three months since I arrived.'

'Crikey, that long?'

'Indeed. It was the first of February when I moved in, during that cold snap, but I must say the village is quite delightful in the spring and I'm sure May Day is an excellent choice for a wedding.'

'We'd originally thought Easter, but I was away on a course so we delayed things. In fact I'm still in London twice a week so the honeymoon will have to wait for a few weeks as well, I'm afraid.'

'That's a shame but I'm sure settling in here will be no hardship.' He gently gestured around the sumptuously decorated hall.

She smiled. 'That's a very fair point, Mr Pentire. My upbringing was in considerably more modest circumstances than these, as you may be aware. Tell me, are you enjoying the Dower House?'

The house in question had been commissioned in 1770 by Elliot Wynn Spense who had inherited the Langford title six months earlier. On the death of his father his already difficult relationship with his mother had deteriorated to the extent that their co-habitation of Langford Hall had become intolerable to both parties. Accordingly, the Dower House had been built with all despatch and she had moved in a year later to their mutual relief.

The house was an almost exact copy of a gracious three-storey Georgian property that could been seen on the Oxford road, and legend had it that the new Lord Langford was in such a hurry to uproot his mother that he took his builder and architect past it in a carriage and announced, 'Build me one of those, and do it quickly.'

Resisting his wife's pointed suggestion that a site be chosen on the far edge of the estate, as far from the hall as possible, Lord Langford nominated an area of land at the top of the village and once completed, the new building settled comfortably into its setting.

For much of the last hundred and fifty years the Dower House had been used by family members, however, since the 1890s, with Lord Colin and Lady Claire's three boys all growing up at the hall and no one else needing it, the noble lord had taken the decision to rent the property out. Mr and Mrs Mason had lived there quietly for fifteen years before Mr Mason died suddenly and his elderly wife had reluctantly left to live closer to her sister's family in Brighton. Vaughan Pentire and his man had arrived as the new tenants a few weeks later.

'I am enjoying it very much indeed, Mrs Spense. Peace and quiet are what I'm looking for and I seem to have found them here.'

Innes was a perceptive woman and sensed something behind his words. 'I'm delighted to hear it, Mr Pentire. We must try and see more of each other once things calm down a little.'

'What a pleasant thought.' He nodded towards a group of people wearing highland dress who were looking over at them. 'Friends and family, I imagine, and I've kept you to myself for long enough. Have a wonderful evening.' His eyes followed her as she crossed the hall and was absorbed into the grinning group.

Finding himself alone he stood and watched people circulating until a voice sounded behind him.

'Evening, Pentire. How are you getting on?' He turned and saw Lord Langford standing close by.

He gave him a warm smile. 'Good evening, my lord. I'm enjoying myself and have met some delightful people, thank you again for the invitation.'

'Our pleasure. Although marriage is not for everyone.'

Lord Langford's eyes met his as he said this, and the taller man returned his look, a bittersweet expression on his face. 'How very true,' he said quietly.

They held each other's gaze for a long moment before the older man asked, 'How is the village suiting you?'

'It is everything I hoped it would be.'

Lord Langford nodded slowly. 'I trust it will continue in that vein. Enjoy your evening, my dear fellow.' He touched him briefly on the arm and with that drifted off towards the highlanders.

*

Away from the sumptuous grandeur of Langford Hall *en fête*, another celebration was taking place in the Black Horse public house which was jammed to the rafters with villagers enjoying the generous allowance Lord Langford had put behind the bar. They had spilled out into the street and back garden and Stanley Tirrold and Beatrice Wray were battling to keep up with the flow of orders.

'Bert, this barrel's gone. Give me a hand to rack up another, will you?' the landlord bellowed across the sea of heads to the swarthy poacher-cum-Jack of all trades whose family had been in Great Tew almost as long as the Spenses.

Bert gestured his agreement and eased through the crowd, leaving his wife Edna pressed up against Nobby Griffin, the local wheelwright and coffin maker. 'Steady now, Edna, I am spoken for, you know.' Nobby grinned at her. 'Unless you fancy a trip to the Promised Land?'

She roared with laughter. 'It is the first of May, isn't it? But my outside courting days are long gone, Nobby, and if I remember right, you need to wait for a warmer night than this.'

'You have the advantage of me there,' he observed with a straight face and as she shrieked again, cried 'Liar!' and punched him on the arm, he added, 'you havin' another cider?'

'Go on then.' She pressed her glass into his hand, and he disappeared into the crowd, heading for the bar where Stanley and Bert were straining to lift the new barrel up onto the rack.

Suddenly a great cheer sounded, and Edward and Innes appeared in the doorway. Laughing, the groom held up his hand for silence and called, 'We just thought we'd sneak away for a few minutes to have a drink with you all and thank you for your good wishes.' Shaking hands and exchanging good-natured banter, they pushed through to the bar where Stanley Tirrold placed two full glasses before them and cried out, 'Ladies and gentlemen, a toast to the happy couple!'

Another cheer sounded as Innes looked at the smiling faces. *They really mean it*, she thought as she recalled what her new mother-in-law had said to her weeks earlier.

'Your marrying Edward will be a big relief to all the estate workers. It means children, and an heir, and things continuing the way they are. If neither Edward nor Piers had married, Langford passes to my late husband's people in Canada. The McCredies of Winnipeg. From the Scottish side of the family, all red hair and freckles, and very much an unknown quantity for the locals.'

Much later, as the last revellers rolled down the high street to their homes, a conversation took place in Nobby Griffin's cottage on the corner of Rivermead, the lane that led up the valley across Spense land.

Bert and Edna were there, tempted in by the thought of a nightcap, and Nobby's wife Bridget made up the four. As they passed round a bottle of metheglin Edna looked at Bridget and said, 'What about having a look on the board?'

Bert looked at his wife uneasily. 'Now then, we don't need any of that nonsense.'

But his wife ignored him. 'Just to have a go, Bridge, you know you can and I'm curious even if no one else is.'

Nobby said, 'I'm with Bert. Let sleeping dogs lie, I say. They've had enough trouble these last two years without knowing more is on the way.'

'Oh go on, Bridge, it'll be a bit of fun to round the evening off, that's all,' Edna persisted.

Nobby's wife, a grey-haired woman in her fifties, looked at them all and then smiled and stood up. 'I don't see why not. We'll need the kitchen table. Come through.' Shaking their heads, the two men followed the women through the low door.

Five minutes later four candles had been lit and placed at the corners of the table. Their soft light illuminated Bridget's circular talking board. It was wooden, eighteen inches in diameter, and quite roughly made. The letters of the alphabet were inscribed around the perimeter with a smaller circle inside which showed the numbers one to ten. The words Yes and No were next to each other in the centre of the board. Its surface was worn and scratched in places, the edges chipped. A diamond-shaped wooden planchet with a finely carved scrollwork lay on the board.

'How long have you had this, Bridget?' Bert asked as they took their seats, one at each side.

'It's been passed down through the family. My grandmother used it every day and was very good. She spoke to the other side as easily as I'm speaking to you. And she taught me.' In the candlelight her eyes glittered as she placed a notepad and pencil on the table.

Bert watched her, still unsure if this was a good idea. Such skills were passed down through the maternal line, mother to daughter, and it was well known in the village that Bridget Griffin could communicate with the spirit world. The Reverend Tukes of St Mary's thought of her as a witch, a rather judgemental viewpoint considering that Eve Dance with whom he was on good terms was known to have the same abilities. In fact, the chief constable's wife was considerably more adept and capable of intervention in a way that was beyond Nobby's dark-eyed wife.

Nevertheless, Bridget Griffin was a gifted medium and she instructed the four of them to hold hands and close their eyes. A long silence followed, so much so that Bert was drifting into a comfortable doze when she inhaled deeply and said quietly, 'Open your eyes and put your hands on the planchet.'

They did so, and listened as she said, 'I sense you are new to me. Will you answer my questions?' After a moment the planchet moved to the Yes on the board and Bridget continued, 'Thank you, we mean no harm and offer you our respect. What is your name?'

The planchet quickly spelt out JEREMIAH. Bert knew he wasn't moving it and realised that the speed at which it passed from letter to letter meant it would have been obvious if any of the others had been doing so. With a mental sigh, he let his last remaining doubts flow away and concentrated on the board.

'Welcome, Jeremiah. Do you have anything you wish to tell us?'

The seance continued for ten minutes as Bridget Griffin asked questions and the spirit responded. He had worked on the estate as the land agent in the later years of the nineteenth century and had various things to say to his descendants.

Finally, Bridget said, 'Jeremiah, thank you for being with us, I think it's time…'

But before she could finish her sentence the planchet started moving at high speed across the board. She hastily wrote the letters down; HUGHISHERE, then looked at the others. 'Hugh?' But before anyone could speak the planchet moved again. Spelling out SPENSE.

Sudden tension filled the room. The middle son of Lord Colin and the Dowager Lady Claire had been killed in the war and the news had devasted his mother and remaining brothers.

Bridget gathered herself. 'Welcome, Mr Hugh. Do you have a message for us?'

FOREDWARD

21

'For Edward.' Bridget paused and swallowed. Providing a service to her friends and acquaintances across the Langford estate was one thing, being privy to information relating to the big house was another thing entirely. The planchet suddenly started moving again, at high speed.

NAMDERIAHDEREHTERAWEB

Her pencil flew across the page as she got the letters down on the pad. Then she shuddered and her eyes glazed over as the candles flickered in unison. In the shadowy light she looked at the others.

'They've gone.'

'Mr Hugh. Blimey.' Nobby's words were loaded with implication. The Spense family was one of the oldest and most noble in the country, immensely well connected and influential. While they were benign masters on the Langford estate, no one in the room was under any illusions that Lord Langford could destroy their lives at a pen stroke if he so chose.

'What does it mean anyway?' asked Edna.

Bert pulled the notepad towards him and peered at the row of letters in the candlelight. 'It doesn't make any sense to me,' he said.

'Give it here.' Bridget took the pad back, picked up the pencil and, clearly concentrating, wrote a second line of letters under the first. She studied it for a moment then inserted a number of short vertical strokes between the letters. The others watched in silence until she looked up, her expression troubled.

'My grandmother told me warnings are sometimes given backwards.' She turned the pad round and Bert, Nobby and Edna craned forward. 'This is the message from Mr Hugh to Mr Edward.'

BEWARE|THE|RED|HAIRED|MAN

There was long silence.

'Beware the red-haired man. What does that mean?' asked Edna finally, giving voice to their common thought.

22

'It means we keep our mouths shut,' Bert replied firmly. 'This ain't no business of ours and they won't thank us up at the hall if we deliver this to the happy couple.' He looked at the others. 'Alright?'

'I said sleeping dogs should be left alone,' Nobby agreed and met his wife's eye. 'You keep your lip buttoned, Bridget Griffin, and no more with the board for a while. Mr Hugh was a nice fellow, but we don't want to encourage him.'

She looked at her husband uncertainly. 'The thing is, Nobby, I'm supposed to pass the message on. That's why I'm here, my old nan always told me that. "You're not the judge or jury, you're just the messenger," she'd say. Drummed it into me, she did.'

Alarm showed in Bert's eyes, and he made to say something, but his friend was ahead of him. 'Not this time, Bridge. There's deep waters up at the hall sometimes. Deep enough to drown the lot of us. Remember what they say about shooting the messenger. You keep your head down and your mouth closed, you hear me?'

She nodded silently, still absorbed in the message. 'Yes, alright.'

Nobby thought for a moment. 'We could keep an eye out though.'

'For a red-haired man?' Bert looked at him.

He shrugged. 'Just saying.'

The poacher looked at him in the glow of the candles and said, 'Yes, we could do that.'

Chapter Two

Summer was a cunning seductress that year and in the weeks leading up to the June solstice gave the village day after day of idyllic weather that seemed to slowly seep into the bones of everyone on the estate. It was a lazy golden time as crops flecked scarlet with poppies ripened in the fields and beasts grew fat on sweet green grass.

The villagers swam in the cool water of Dipper Pool and moved slowly through their days, as a profound and timeless sense of peace spread across the arcadian landscape. Only the insects worked, the buzzing of their constant labours providing a gentle backdrop for the men in the fields who, sapped of industry and purpose, dozed in the shade of the trees, luxuriating in their time of rest before the harvest.

It was high summer deep in the English countryside, the most perfect of all things.

At four o'clock on midsummer's day the Reverend Tukes surveyed the colourful stalls and booths arranged in a long double row across the common and sighed with satisfaction. St Mary's church fete, one of the set-piece events of what Lord Langford wryly called 'The Great Tew Summer Season', was thronged with people.

An hour earlier he had enjoyed a full congregation for the summer solstice service and had just collected a shilling from each of the stallholders and ten bob from Mr Hargreaves the owner of the roundabout, swing boats and helter-skelter that lay at the far side of the common. Idly jingling the money in his pocket, he smiled as the memory of his first encounter with a young Eve Dance thirty years ago drifted into his mind.

Having spent his first ten years working in a poor parish in the east end of London, when he had been transferred to the village, the Reverend Tukes had endured a distinctly lukewarm welcome from its inhabitants, who had taken one look and decided they would prefer a rural man in the rectory. After some weeks of toil for little reward, he had received an invitation to Marston House from Mrs Dance who, though not a churchgoer herself, saw no reason not to find common cause with the Anglicans when it suited her. Over a cup of tea, quickly followed by something a little stronger, she spelt the problem out for him and presented her proposals.

'I won't beat about the bush, Reverend. The villagers are pagans by and large and you're going to have trouble tempting them into your fold. My recently deceased aunt was the local witch and I'm following in her footsteps.'

Tukes had heard many alarming things during his time in London but this candid and relaxed acceptance of the presence of the occult in the English countryside was a shock. He nodded vaguely and managed a glassy smile as the petite and attractive blonde opposite him briskly continued.

'Your predecessor, who one might say died in harness as he was found stone cold in front of the rood screen, understood all this and settled down to a quiet arrangement where, for twenty-five years, he rarely bothered the villagers, and they rarely bothered him. Five souls in the congregation was a full house for old parson Banks. But I sense a missionary zeal in you which he did not possess. As my husband is away with his regiment at present and I am at something of a loose end, I wish to make a suggestion which will work to our mutual benefit.'

'And what is that?' the churchman asked, holding out his glass as his hostess wielded a bottle of her beloved's best single malt.

'The summer solstice has long been celebrated by people living around here. Since way before Christianity. They built a double circle of stones that aligns with it and, as it happens, one of the energy streams that crosses Creech Hill Ring runs right down the aisle of your church and over the altar.' She raised her eyebrows at him.

Round-eyed and unmoving, Tukes said nothing. *Energy streams?* He had been glad to leave the poverty and raw inhumanity of Limehouse, but involuntary thoughts of frying pans and fires were appearing in his mind. *Would the bishop have me back?* he wondered as Mrs Dance continued.

'I propose a midsummer celebration. A joint celebration. Let's face it, the Church of England has been pinching our festivals ever since your lot were invented. Yule became Christmas, Ostara became Easter, Imbolc became Candlemas—'

'Er, yes, quite,' Tukes interrupted, but the woman opposite was only just getting into her stride.

'In fact, it wasn't just festivals, you took our sites as well. St Mary's is built on a much older pagan sacred place and that's true of many other churches. I suppose the Romans were very practical and recognised that if people were in the habit of going to a particular place to worship that was where they'd build the churches.'

She took a generous sip and rolled her eyes at him. 'Golly, it's almost as though it was more about controlling people than faith, isn't it.'

Tukes was more than capable of addressing that point but decided to let it slide. 'Tell me again. What is it you have in mind?'

26

'A combination of church service, fete and summer solstice festival.'

The reverend sipped in turn and pondered. As something of a historian concerning the dawn of Christianity in Britain, he knew that early church services had been a potent mix of pagan and biblical beliefs. Fire, incense, ritual, even animal masks and other forms of zoomorphism had all been permitted as the clerics battled to win the day for God. The relics were still there in St Mary's, where two stone green men peered down at the altar from high above. One was grinning, the other leering. And there was reputedly a third engaged in an act wholly inappropriate for consecrated ground hidden in the organ loft.

He shuddered as an image of his church full of costumed revellers engaged in some modern-day Bacchanalia passed through his mind.

'What's in it for you, if you don't mind me asking?' he said.

'Oh, nothing really,' she said airily. 'There's a tradition of a parade as the sun rises. We all walk from one of the stones in the outer circle to the centre of Creech Hill Ring and then as the sun appears on the horizon, onwards towards another of the outer stones. West to east, you see – towards the dawn on the longest day. And as it happens the route is along the stream of energy that runs down the aisle of St Mary's.'

As the implications of what she was saying hit the vicar she leaned forward with the bottle and added, slightly defensively, 'It's really not our fault. You built the church in the way.'

Accepting another generous slug of Scotch, the Reverend Tukes met his hostess's eye. 'So just to be clear, you are asking for permission to lead a pagan ritualistic procession through a Christian church at dawn on the summer solstice?'

She grinned and nodded. 'That's the ticket. Parson Banks used to leave the keys to the church doors with Stanley Tirrold the landlord of the Black Horse the night before, and then lock

27

himself in the rectory until after breakfast. And we never make a mess.'

'Good lord.' This mild blasphemy was permitted under the circumstances, Tukes felt.

Speaking quickly, Mrs Dance continued, 'So, the idea is that we have our little parade early in the day, then you have your church service later the same day. It will be very well attended I guarantee, although I wouldn't leave it too late, it being a celebration and all, if you know what I mean. Then we'll have a fundraising fete and a bonfire on the common to finish.' She beamed at him. 'How does that sound?'

Picturing the undeniable attraction of a full church, he said, 'If I were to endorse such a celebration then there would have to be rules.'

Mrs Dance nodded fulsomely. 'Oh yes, vicar. Very clear rules indeed.'

A thought struck him. 'Am I right in thinking, by any chance, that on the twenty-first of December a "parade" takes place in the opposite direction?'

She clapped her hands in delight. 'At sunset. The winter solstice. Good heavens, Reverend Tukes, you're a natural pagan, if you don't mind me saying so.'

'Hardly.' A look of pain passed over his face, but he battled on. 'I will expect you to put the word about that in agreeing to this…' he searched for a suitable word, selected 'desecration' but couldn't bear to say it, and settled on an inadequate alternative, 'unusual request, I will expect a full and enthusiastic attendance at the service and regular worship on Sunday mornings. It's not much to ask, you know, St Mary's is their church after all.'

'Oh, absolutely. Do you drink cider, Reverend?' Eve Dance was grinning at him in delight.

Slightly befuddled by the generous glasses of whisky, he shrugged, trying to keep up with her train of thought. 'I haven't really tried it.'

'Good heavens, what an admission.' She stood up. 'Let's go to the Black Horse. I'll introduce you to Stanley Tirrold and we can give him the good news.'

The slightly built and prematurely balding churchman found himself ushered out of the front door of Marston House and escorted up the road to the pub. When, some hours later, he was carried home by Bert Williams and Nobby Griffin and laid to rest on the settee in the rectory, his reputation was secure with the residents of Great Tew.

Two days later, after a hangover of biblical proportions had finally worn off, Tukes set his alarm clock for half past three in the morning, woke to its bell and slipped down the rectory path, across the graveyard and entered his church. He crossed to the door at the foot of the tower steps and climbed the narrow, worn flight to the ringing chamber and then the wooden staircase that gave access to the room above. From there, a leaning ladder bolted into place led up to the bell chamber. Squeezing round the great bell, he grasped another ladder fixed to the wall, ascended to a trap door and clambered nimbly out onto the battlement at the summit of the tower.

As his breathing calmed, he stared out across the still, dark land. A velvet silence engulfed him as he laid his hands on the lichen-covered balustrade. And deep within him, something stirred and woke.

So old, this landscape. So much buried within it. A slow, pulsing beat, more potent and powerful than I could ever conceive.

Afterwards he would never be quite sure how long he stood there – a dark figure high in the night sky. At one point he felt as though he were breaking up into tiny pieces, joyously free to move within the earth and sky at will, an integral part of everything that had ever happened, or ever would. It was an ecstatic sensation and he realised he was smiling.

Am I in the presence of God? he wondered dreamily. Does it even matter?

Something showed in the corner of his eye, and he turned and looked towards Tan Hill. A line of light was approaching the village. It was flickering as the lanterns moved under the trees and emerged again. A rhythmic low chant reached him, as though the land itself was speaking.

They were coming.

Dallying for as long as he dared, he watched the procession emerge from the woods on the far side of the common and walk directly towards the church. He reckoned he had five minutes, no more, and quickly descended the tower. By the time the west door of the church swung open, and chanting filled the sacred space, the Reverend Tukes was concealed behind the pulpit in a dark corner that gave a good view of the aisle.

And down they came, about fifty men, women and children, pacing slowly towards the rood screen. Even a few babes in arms he noticed. Some carried lanterns on poles, others held sticks garnished with oak and holly leaves. Many were masked with animal faces and at the column's head a statuesque figure wearing a great fourteen-point stag's head led the way towards the altar.

For a moment the vicar felt a pang of fear as he realised that the chant was not in English. Or Latin, for that matter. Old English perhaps? he wondered. But then he saw that many of them were smiling. There was no threat. Not satanists, simply, as Eve Dance had told him, followers of an ancient belief system that pre-dated his own by thousands of years. It was a remarkable survival in modern-day 1921, he told himself. But even as the thought entered his mind, he remembered his curious trance-like state on the top of the tower and the sense of energy rippling across the village, like a strong tide running through an archipelago. He had definitely sensed something. Some power at work.

What is this place?

Absorbed in the theatre of it all, he watched as the final stragglers passed to the side of the altar and out through the door, heading for Creech Hill Ring and the rose-coloured light now showing behind the east window. When the door clicked shut, he rose from his position. Resisting the temptation to climb the tower stairs again and follow their passage across the landscape, he walked thoughtfully back to the rectory and made himself a pot of tea. Taking it into his study, he sat and drank it, and was still sitting there three hours later, staring out of the uncurtained window when his housekeeper Mrs Vane bustled in.

*

'Alright then, vicar?' Bert Williams' familiar voice jerked him out of his reverie, and he turned to see him standing there. Nobby Griffin was with him. A smell of cider drifted across the space between them.

'Bert, Nobby.' He nodded a greeting. 'All very well organised as usual, gentlemen, thank you.' The two villagers were the official stewards for the day and helped with the bookings and general arrangements.

'The Dean coming?'

A shadow crossed the reverend's face. 'Sadly not.' His superior the Dean of Oxford had paid a surprise visit to the service the previous year and, despite Tukes' increasingly desperate efforts to pack him off afterwards in his chauffeured car, had stayed on to 'get a feel for the celebrations'.

Late in the evening, fortified by a considerable amount of metheglin served out of a stone bottle by Nobby Griffin, the Dean had watched another couple drifting away into the warm night hand in hand and remarked, 'I keep hearing people mentioning the "promised land", Tukes. Why is that, might I enquire? Some biblical reference, one presumes?'

As the vicar had struggled to find the words, a leering Bert had stepped in. 'They're courtin', Dean. It's the name we have for the woods where everyone goes for a bit of a wriggle, if you know what I mean. Like they do all the time in the Old Testament. Although not with cousins and that. Not any more anyway.'

The faint tone of regret and heavy nudge that accompanied this loaded remark had put the senior cleric on his back and it had been a minute or two before order was restored. At which point he had called for his car and been wafted back to Oxford having resolved to give Great Tew a wide berth for the rest of his life.

'We had a bit of a panic with the fortune teller yesterday,' Nobby remarked. 'The tent was all ready and put up, but she telephoned the Black Horse to say she'd had a fall and broken her ankle.'

'Miss Zelda? Oh dear, so there's no one in there?' Tukes glanced down the stalls to where a tall Middle Eastern-style tent stood.

'Don't worry, we found someone else. Very keen he was. Stood in as soon as he heard.'

'Really, who is it?'

A cunning look appeared on Nobby's face. 'How about you get your fortune told and see if you can guess, eh, vicar? You should see him. All made up with a turban and beard. I reckon most people won't know who it is.'

'True,' Bert affirmed. 'His own mother wouldn't recognise him.'

'Harold at the coconut shy is giving us a wave, Bert. You said we'd stand a turn while he has a look round.' Nobby waved back. 'Come on, mate.'

'We'll see you later then, vicar.' And with that the two men pushed through the crowd.

Curious, Tukes walked down between the stalls until he reached the fortune teller's tent. Bert's wife Edna was standing outside. She nodded to him and pointed to a sign on the flap that read 'Please wait if shut'. It was, so he did.

After five minutes a woman called Rosemary Kennedy emerged. The parson thought she looked a little discomfited and gave her a smile and said, 'Hello, Mrs Kennedy,' but she just looked straight through him and disappeared into the crowd.

He stared after her as Edna poked her head into the tent and said, 'It's the vicar.' Then she turned to him and added, 'One moment please, Reverend.'

A minute later a bass voice called, 'Enter,' and with a smile Bert's wife pulled the flap to one side and gestured him in. Nodding his thanks he entered the semi-dark tent as the voice continued, 'Close the flap, please, and sit down opposite me.'

*

Two days later a young man called Ronnie Back was moving quietly through Lye Cross woods south of Little Tew. It was mid-afternoon and he was on the way to check his rabbit snares, but his mind was fully occupied with a snub-nosed, freckled girl with corkscrew curls. Her name was Beatrice Wray and she had given him to understand that his attentions would not be unwelcome. In fact, late on the evening of the fete, she had made it abundantly clear.

Aged twenty-three, Ronnie Back was on the verge of falling properly in love for the first time and his thoughts were almost entirely focussed on the delightful possibilities that lay ahead. Beatrice was one of the most hotly pursued girls on the estate, and the idea that she had chosen him was as overwhelming as it was astonishing. Little did he realise that it was this naïve modesty, coupled with his height and broad shoulders, that had first caught her attention. And the fact that he was training to be a solicitor with a firm in Banbury had certainly not been a disadvantage. He also had no idea that the events at the fete had been planned in her mind for some time.

And so Ronnie strolled through the thick green foliage with an amiable grin on his face thinking the world was a perfect place to be, when three evenly spaced gunshots sounded ahead and to his right. A second later he was on the floor, face down, the smell of earth and grass in his nostrils. It was an instinctive reaction. He had served in the Oxfordshire Light Infantry in the closing stages of the war and knew the difference between a shotgun and a handgun.

And the three shots had come from a pistol. A German pistol. He was almost certain.

Rolling off the narrow path he rose cautiously to his feet, eased behind the trunk of a huge beech tree, and peered in the direction of the noise. Nothing stirred. He waited, just like they had waited for the Germans three years ago. But after five long minutes of inactivity, he stepped back onto the path and set off again.

Two hundred yards later as he turned into the undergrowth, heading for the site of the first snare, a figure appeared pushing through the bracken towards him. It was a woman in her sixties with grey hair, wearing a workmanlike dress. She was carrying a pair of binoculars and their leather case was slung on a strap that ran diagonally over her shoulder. A familiar figure.

'Hello, Ronnie, did you hear those shots?' she asked as she came up to him.

'I did,' he said, nodding.

Irritation showed in her face. 'I was watching a delightful charm of goldfinches feeding by the stream over there.' She waved vaguely behind her. 'Who was it?'

He shrugged. 'No idea. Not a shotgun though. Or a rifle.'

'Well, whatever it was, it certainly put the finches up, and every pigeon for a quarter of a mile, for that matter.'

They continued to talk for a while and then parted. Ronnie carried on through the pathless woods, walking unerringly towards the snares that he had laid close to the warren. After five minutes a gleam on the ground caught his eye. Something golden and shiny, tucked behind a tree root. He walked over and picked it up. It was a single cartridge case from a fired bullet. The word 'Mauser' was stamped on the base. German then, as he'd suspected. He studied it, then looked around, turning full circle. A steep bank lay in front of him, and the warren and the snares were just on the other side of it.

There was no one in sight. Mentally shrugging, he dropped the spent casing into his pocket and set off up the bank, pretty Beatrice Wray foremost in his thoughts.

Chapter Three

At nine o'clock in the morning, four days after the fete, the Reverend Tukes strode out along Dell Lane. Waking early, he'd completed the preparations for his sermon on Sunday and finding himself at a loose end until lunchtime, had decided to go for a walk. In so doing he hoped that a dose of vigorous exercise would help to shrug off the unease that had lurked in the back of his mind since his visit to the fortune teller. The man had made an oblique but undeniable reference to an error of judgement that he had believed he'd left well behind.

Not only was he uncomfortable with the idea that someone else in the village knew of the matter, he was also unable to fathom out how such knowledge had followed him from the east end of London.

Nevertheless, as he walked past the police station and the remaining buildings that led to the edge of the village, he felt his spirits rise. It promised to be a magnificent day. The sun was already full of mellow warmth and a fragrant combination of ripening hay and summer flowers teased his senses. As he approached the final cottage his cheerful whistling and pleasant speculation about where his feet would take him were interrupted by a voice from his left.

'That you, Reverend?'

He stopped and turned to see a middle-aged woman wearing a pinafore standing in the open front door. Her hair was tied back in a bun, and she looked tired.

'Palpably it is, Mrs Jenkins. And the best of the morning to you,' he replied cheerfully.

But her expression showed no joy in nature's benevolence. 'It's Herbert. I was hoping you'd come in for a minute.'

'Is he not well?' Although he already knew the answer to his question.

'More of the same.' She wrung her hands. 'I don't know what to do with him, Reverend, I'm at the end of my tether, I really am. The war isn't over for him, it's just the fighting's stopped. He's only twenty-two and it broke him.'

She nodded backwards down the hall and said quietly, 'Out there.'

A dark mood engulfed Tukes, like a mist moving upriver on the tide. *Cursed war.* He walked through the cottage into the garden. Her son was sitting on a bench, held upright as though on strings. The vicar went and sat next to him. Beyond a low wall the ground fell away until rich green treetops came into view, descending to the river at the valley bottom. The far side rose steeply, a jumble of fields, hedges and woods that mirrored a patchwork quilt in its rich, lush variety.

It was a sight to gladden the heart of any countryman. But when the parson glanced sideways at Herbert Jenkins he saw his cheeks were wet and his eyes were staring in desperation not fulfilment.

'Hello, Herbert,' Tukes said gently. 'A difficult morning, I'm guessing.' An instinct born of long years of service led him to reach out and take the man's hand and for a while they sat there in silence.

Then the young man said, 'I actually shite myself one time, you know. And I wasn't the only one. Imagine that, padre, soiling yourself through fear. And men died because of it. Because of my terror.'

Tukes had a moment of insight. The poor man was haunted, not by what he had done, but by what he had failed to do. He said quietly, 'I think fear is probably wisdom in the face of danger. It is not something to be ashamed of. There must have been many times when you were terrified.'

Herbert nodded. 'There was that.'

'But the war is over now, and you are, by the grace of God, home. Is that not something to be thankful for?'

'What about my mates who we left out there, padre? Or the blokes back here with no legs or arms or left blind. Where's God's grace for them?'

'I don't know. I cannot speak for Him and cannot conceive how the great war served His purpose. That is my honest answer.'

There was another silence then Herbert said, 'I won't be coming to church any more. I don't think I believe in God.'

In spite of the gravity of the moment Tukes felt a frisson of amusement and replied with heavy irony, 'You shouldn't let that stop you, you know. By my reckoning only about ten per cent of the congregation believe in my biblical god. The rest are firmly in Eve Dance's camp.'

'Are you and she enemies then?' The young man turned and made eye contact and Tukes sensed he was reaching out to him.

'Certainly not, and never mind that. Tell me how you feel. Sitting here now.'

The young man's eyes returned to the airy space between the garden and the distant ridgeline and after a moment said, 'I feel as though I've lost the right to live my life. To be the person I was before.'

'Why is that?'

'I went off Herbert Jenkins and I came home someone else. I don't know who.' He paused, then added in a tone of quiet

38

desperation that rent the vicar's heart, 'I don't know what's happened to me.'

Tukes said, 'It's not a failing on your part, you know. A lot of men who served feel the same way. I know that Innes Spense has met with some of them and helped them to understand how they're feeling.'

'But I can't control how I'm feeling, that's the thing, padre. It's like drowning on dry land.' He glanced at the churchman. 'D'you hear that John Rex killed himself in Leyland. Won a medal and all, he did. His mum found him hanging from an apple tree. I tell you, I can understand why he did it too.'

Tukes squeezed his hand. 'It would be desperately sad to survive the war and then die when you're back home and safe.'

The young man laughed briefly and bitterly. 'I didn't survive. At least the dead have got some peace.'

'Will you see Dr Spense? If I arrange for you to have a talk?'

'You think I'm ill then?'

'I think you are a brave man who has a right to feel better than you do. Will you do that for me?'

He nodded. 'Alright.'

The two men, one young and one old, sat and talked for another twenty minutes, staring out over the ancient landscape, then the vicar left. In spite of the rawness of the conversation, Tukes felt curiously uplifted. He'd helped and he knew it.

That is why I'm here, he thought.

*

The vicar wasn't alone in having been left uneasy after a visit to the fortune teller's tent. Other residents of Great Tew also had things on their minds. Worrying things. And one of them was George Wishaw.

Thinking that it would be a bit of fun to have his fortune told, he had paid his sixpence to Edna Williams and waited for the summons from within. On entering he saw the fortune teller

39

sitting behind a table, which was draped to the grass with a crimson cloth. A crystal ball lay in its exact centre. He was dressed in a richly coloured cloak and turban, wore what Mr Wishaw suspected was a false beard, and appeared to have stained his face with a brown preparation of some kind. In the dimly lit tent, the overall effect was surprisingly effective, and he sat down opposite the apparition with a thrill of amused excitement.

'Mr Wisham, a thousand welcomes.' The fortune teller raised his hands in salutation.

'Wishaw, it's George Wishaw.'

'Ah, just so.' The man appeared to glance down into his lap, before continuing, 'I will consult the all-seeing ball.'

Moving his hands around the glass orb, he muttered confusing foreign words which, had Mr Wishaw been an Arabic speaker, he would have realised meant 'bring me tea and some dates, and get a move on whilst you're about it'.

The man in the turban had not spent three years fighting the Turks in Palestine without learning something.

After a few moments he muttered, 'Ah yes, the glass is clearing, and I can see your past and your future, Mr Wisham.'

'Wishaw.'

More gentle hand movements around the glass followed, then the revelations started coming. 'I sense that you are not at peace in your mind. There are worries that pursue you, from the past. And that might not be all that is pursuing you. Am I right?' The bearded man met his eye.

Alarmed, Wishaw rocked back on the stool and said uneasily, 'Maybe.' Fifteen years earlier George had fled juvenile detention from a place called Borstal in Kent and settled in Great Tew. His name in Kent had been different, and up to that precise moment he had been confident that no one in the area knew his history.

There was a pause while the fortune teller manipulated his hands again, and repeatedly issued an instruction in Arabic to 'feed and water my horse', before he said, 'I sense that you are safe here, Mr Wisham.'

'They're not after me?' he blurted.

'They will always be looking, but they will not find you.'

The session continued along familiar lines, with promises of a 'surprise in love' and 'financial good fortune' to come. But as George Wishaw left the tent, the idea that someone in the village knew his secret was deeply worrying and he wondered what he should do about it.

The unfortunate Mr Wishaw was not alone.

Over the course of the long, hot summer's afternoon, many people left the tent in a very reflective mood, and some were downright horrified. Mrs Rosemary Kennedy emerged appalled that someone other than her husband seemed to know that she was half German, being under no illusions about the impact that news would have on her reputation in the village. Captain Grant Perry also had food for thought. In 1919 he had been quietly eased out of the army due to certain financial irregularities in the officers' mess. His family had influence and it had all been hushed up, so the idea that someone living locally was aware of his unfortunate difficulties was a considerable concern. And poor Lizzie Midding, who had paid one too many visits to the Promised Land when she was seventeen, emerged from the tent struggling to control her tears. She had fallen pregnant and had the baby while spending six months 'caring for an invalid aunt' in Dartmouth. Her new husband had no idea that she'd once had a baby and given it up for adoption.

And there were others. An elderly grey-haired lady pushed the flap aside and strode off grim-faced and even the Reverend Tukes wore an expression of bemused contemplation when responding to Mrs Williams' 'Alright then, parson?' as he stepped out of the dimly lit tent. 'He's very good they say,' she added with a cackle.

'Quite remarkable,' he replied, and walked off, his hands in his pockets.

Even then, it might have all been contained. The fortune teller, his face still bearing the effects of his make-up, dismissed the whole business as an enormous bit of fun as he relaxed with a decent measure of brandy that evening. And there was no way anyone with a vested interest in keeping their particular secret was going to say anything. So there was a strong chance that it all might have petered out.

But the violent death of Vaughan Pentire crushed any hope of that.

*

In the first few months of 1921 there had been significant changes to Constable Burrows' personal and professional life. With the demise of Constable Brown, fired for corruption the previous year, and the retirement of another officer west of Leyland, Colonel Dance had decided to reorganise the arrangements in north-west Oxfordshire. The borders of various beats had been altered and finding himself in need of a new sergeant to co-ordinate day-to-day policing in the area south of Banbury, the chief constable had bowed to the inevitable and promoted the promising and incorruptible Burrows.

The move was unusual for one so young, but the colonel was sure it was the right thing to do. Recognising that Burrows' trusty police bicycle would not be sufficient for his new remit, he had also authorised the purchase of a Matchless V-twin motorbike and sidecar which now resided in the shed at the back of three-bedroomed Lea House further along Dell Lane, into which the Burrows family had moved in April.

Although reluctant to leave his beloved police counter, the move had been forced on Burrows when his wife had told her husband that young Matilda Hermione would be having a new brother or sister at the end of the summer and what did he think of that, with only one bedroom in the police house?

In addition, his promotion to sergeant meant that the Great Tew beat itself required a new constable, who would need somewhere to live. He knew the colonel had been frustrated by the length of time it had taken to find someone, but after receiving a telephone call one morning three and a half weeks after the fete he set off for the police house.

'I'm going to meet the new constable,' he advised his wife, adding, 'I hope he's a decent fellow. He'll be an ex-soldier, I imagine.'

But when he entered the room with the counter he was confused, then stunned, then appalled.

'Ah, Burrows, meet your new officer for the Great Tew beat.' The chief constable gestured at the figure standing by the window. 'Constable, this is Sergeant Burrows.'

Burrows stood rigid, momentarily incapable of speech as the woman saluted briskly and said, 'Good morning, Sergeant. WPC Mabel Dixon.'

He swallowed audibly and turned to his commanding officer. 'A female?'

Jocelyn Dance chuckled, rather pleased with his sergeant's reaction. 'I can see I have promoted a man of rare insight and discernment,' he remarked.

At that rather loaded moment the door opened and a slim and tidy-looking man in his early thirties appeared. He was wearing a valet's house coat and black trousers with a thin grey stripe. Clearly sensing an atmosphere he stood and looked at the three police officers uneasily.

'Can we help you?' Burrows asked.

The man nodded and gathered himself. 'Yes, good morning, Sergeant. My name is Aiden Connors, from the Dower House. I'm unable to find my master this morning and am concerned.'

43

'Oh yes? That would be Mr Pentire?' Burrows looked at Connors, who nodded. 'When you say you can't find him, what do you mean exactly?'

'I took up his tea tray at half past seven this morning as usual, but his bedroom was empty and his bed hadn't been slept in. I've searched the house and there's no sign of him, but the study door is locked. I knocked and called but there was no reply. The curtains are drawn, so you can't see in from the garden.' He shrugged and added, 'I thought I'd better come down here.' His faint Welsh accent lingered in the room.

'There's just two of you in the house normally?'

'Yes.'

'And no note or letter? An unexpected telephone call summoning him away, perhaps?'

'Nothing.'

'Is the study door normally kept locked?'

'No.'

'So, your concern is that he might be in there having been taken ill last night?'

'Yes, unconscious maybe. Or even just still asleep.'

Or dead. The intuitive but unwelcome thought came strongly into Burrows' mind, and he reflected that a few years of experience in the police tended to make you expect the worst. He looked at Dixon who looked back, her face expressionless.

'When did you last see him?' he asked.

'Yesterday evening. I served him his supper and cleared up. Then I went out. Thursday's my night off and I normally go down to the King's Head for a game of darts.'

'And you didn't see him when you came back?' Burrows saw Dixon had her notebook out and realised she must have had the same premonition of trouble as he had had.

'No, the lights were off, so I just went on up to bed. That wasn't unusual, he isn't a night owl.'

'What time did you get back?'

44

'About half past eleven.' Connors eyed the notes the WPC was taking uneasily and added, 'Look, I'm not saying anything's wrong, I just didn't know who else to tell.'

'Just getting the essentials down, Mr Connors, nothing to worry about,' Burrows replied soothingly. 'Alright, we'll come back with you and have a look.'

The colonel stirred and said, 'Well, Dixon, it looks as though you've got something to get your teeth into straight away. I'll leave you two to get acquainted.' With a nod to the valet he left the building.

It took eight minutes to walk from the police station up the high street and along the drive between the common and the Glebe allotments that led to the Dower House. Connors opened the front door, walked into the elegant high-ceilinged hall and indicated an oak door on the right.

'Here we are.' He knocked again firmly and called, 'Mr Pentire, are you there, sir?'

There was no answer. The sergeant tried the door himself, then put his ear against the panelling and called out, with the same result. 'And this door isn't normally kept locked?' he reconfirmed with Connors.

The man shook his head. 'The house safe is in there and I believe Mr Pentire locks the door if he's got the safe open, but otherwise no. If he's in there when I bring his tea, it's always open.'

'Let's have a look outside,' Burrows said. They turned left out of the front door and walked the short distance to where a single large sash window comprising two panes of glass, one above the other, looked out over the front garden. As Connors had described earlier, the curtains were closed, and it was impossible to see into the room.

With his height the sergeant could see through the glass that the catch on the bottom of the upper frame was pointing into the room, meaning it was engaged under the neat brass locking bar on the lower frame.

Knowing it was useless, but curiously compelled to try anyway, he pushed the lower frame upwards, but it was securely locked. They returned inside and stared at the door.

'You didn't notice anything unusual or untoward in the rest of the house, Mr Connors? Nothing out of place, for example?' Dixon asked.

'No, everything seems normal as far as I can see.'

Burrows clicked his tongue in frustration and glanced at his watch. 'It's only quarter past eight. Constable Dixon, nip down to Nobby Griffin's and see if he's still at home. It's the cottage on the corner of the high street and Rivermead. Tell him we've a door needs opening and he's to bring his tools.'

'Right you are, Sergeant.' She departed with admirable economy.

Connors looked at the police officer. 'Cup of tea while we're waiting?'

Nobby and Dixon arrived back half an hour later, the WPC's procession down and back up through the village having caused an absolute sensation. At Burrows' direction the carpenter knelt down and set to work. Within ten minutes there was a distinct sound of the deadbolt clicking back and a corresponding grunt of satisfaction from Nobby. He stood up and put his hand on the handle.

'Thank you, Mr Griffin.' The sergeant laid a firm hand on his shoulder and pulled him back from the door. He didn't want Nobby telling everyone in the Black Horse that he'd been first into the room. Stepping forward he pushed the handle down, but to his surprise the door didn't move.

'Bolted. From the inside, I reckon.' Cheated of his moment of glory, the stand-in locksmith's voice carried a certain relish. The sergeant knelt down and peered through the keyhole but could see nothing. 'Key's still in the other side,' the voice added helpfully.

'Thank you, Mr Griffin,' he repeated and climbed to his feet, trying not to let his irritation show. After a moment's hesitation he made a decision. 'Right, I'll have to break the window.'

The little procession of Burrows, Dixon and Connors repeated its passage out of the front door and onto the lawn, with Nobby bringing up the rear. The sergeant withdrew his truncheon from the pocket sewn into the thigh of his uniform trousers.

'Stand back.' Then he broke the glass in the top of the bottom pane. It shattered noisily and a furious cawing sounded from the rookery high in a stand of beech trees to their left. In the still air the noise also carried to the Glebe allotments fifty yards away, and would have attracted the attention of old Mr Willett, had he not already been leaning on his spade watching events with interest.

Within moments Burrows had carefully reached into the jagged gap and pushed the catch back so it lay parallel to the frame. With the window released, he raised it and climbed in. Moving the curtains aside he stared into the room.

In the dim light he could see a large desk facing the window. Vaughan Pentire was sitting behind it, slumped forward, his face resting left side down on the blotter.

He walked into the room, his eyes on what was clearly a corpse. Behind him he vaguely registered the sound of Dixon climbing in. He slowly completed a full circle of the desk. Pentire's right arm was slack to his side, pointing downwards. A pistol lay on the floor beneath it. There was a small hole in his right temple and the left-hand side of the blotter was stained with a considerable quantity of blood, a result, he assumed, of the bullet exiting the other side of his head. A note and a pen lay on the desk to the right of the body.

'Wait there, please.' Dixon's firm voice interrupted his thoughts. He turned to the window. Connors had followed the WPC in and Nobby, his face wreathed with excitement, had one leg over the sill.

Pleased that the WPC had acted, Burrows said, 'No. Stay there, Mr Griffin.' He held out his hand like a policeman directing traffic on Piccadilly, then crossed to his WPC and said quietly, 'It's a suicide. Go up to Langford Hall and try and find Dr Innes Spense, will you. She lives there. It's official business so use the front door. And on the way out put the fear of God into Nobby Griffin about gossiping or we'll have the whole village peering through the window in half an hour.'

She nodded and turned to where the carpenter was frozen abeam of the frame, peering at the desk. 'Outside, you.'

As they left Burrows eased the curtains back to let in more light and was amused to see Dixon in the middle of the lawn, leaning over the diminutive villager, poking him in the chest to emphasise every word. He looked terrified. Then he turned to the manservant.

'Was your master right-handed?'

'He was.' The man was grey with shock and kept glancing at the bloodstained blotter.

'Come and have a look at this note, will you, Mr Connors.' He walked over to the desk and picked up the piece of paper. It read:

I'm sorry for the upset I've caused.
Vaughan Pentire

He showed it to the valet and asked, 'Is this his handwriting?'

Connors craned his head. 'Yes, it looks like it.'

'Then, at the risk of stating the obvious, I'm sorry to tell you that your master has committed suicide.'

48

But instead of acknowledging this, the valet mirrored Burrows in doing a slow circumnavigation of the desk. He stood behind the body and studied the hand with the gun below it, and the bloody wound on its temple.

Then he walked round to the policeman and met his eye.

'Oh no he hasn't,' he said.

Chapter Four

Later in the afternoon Sergeant Burrows, WPC Dixon and the chief constable held a council of war in the study at Marston House.

'Right then, bring me up to date, Sergeant,' Colonel Dance said as they took their seats. 'From your telephone call earlier I understand the situation up at the Dower House is indicative of suicide. A fact confirmed by Innes Spense.'

Burrows frowned. 'Dr Spense confirmed that the cause of death was a gunshot wound to the right side of the head. She does not have a medical view on who fired the bullet.'

'When did he die?'

'That's a tricky one, sir. Apparently, this hot weather plays havoc with the temperature tables the medical people use, and the study was sealed up tight and very warm. Given the general condition of the body her best guess is sometime between eight o'clock last night and two o'clock this morning.'

'But your initial assumption from the available evidence was that Pentire had shot himself?'

'Correct. He left a note in his own handwriting. It read, *I'm sorry for the upset I've caused*, and he'd signed it.'

Jocelyn Dance grunted then said, 'But his man Connors disagrees?'

'More than that, sir. He insists it is murder.'

'How so?'

'Vaughan Pentire served in the war. He was badly injured in his right arm by an exploding shell early in 1918. They did a decent job of fixing him up under the circumstances, but he was invalided out and sent home. Connors' point is that the main damage was to his elbow. Although he concealed it very well, he simply couldn't bend the joint much more than forty-five degrees. If you'll permit me, sir…'

The sergeant leaned forward and laid his right arm flat along the desk then raised his hand to forty-five degrees. 'This is the maximum flex the man could manage according to Connors.' He sat back in his chair, keeping his arm locked at the same angle.

'Wait a minute.' The colonel opened a desk drawer and drew out a revolver. 'Try the real thing.'

Burrows took it dubiously. 'Is it unloaded, sir?'

'Of course it is. Carry on.'

The sergeant raised his hand and manoeuvred his shoulder. 'You can see it would have been very difficult for Mr Pentire to bring the weapon to bear on his temple with the injury he had.'

'But not impossible, I'd say. He could just about get a bead on it.' The chief constable stood up and manipulated the arm, then squinted over the sights. 'How about like that?'

Fearing imminent dislocation of his wrist and shoulder Burrows opted for a non-committal, 'Er…'

WPC Dixon coughed gently. 'Beg pardon, sir, I was just going to mention that the doctor was certain the gun had been fired from close range. "Less than six inches" was the phrase she used.'

'Ah. That is a different matter. A shame you didn't tell me that, Burrows. I do need the full facts, you know. Well now, if we place the gun here…' he dragged the sergeant's arm into a position close to his right temple, 'we can clearly see that the elbow is bent well beyond ninety degrees.'

He looked at his two police officers and added, 'So it appears Connors may have a point.'

'Yes, sir, thank you, that is the conclusion we had reached as well.' Burrows placed the gun gently on the desk and rubbed his wrist as Jocelyn Dance resumed his seat.

'Talk me through exactly what happened when you went up to the Dower House.' He pulled a notepad towards him and picked up a pen.

'When we arrived the study door was securely locked. It's a stout door and close-fitting, so faced with the option of smashing it in or breaking a window I chose the latter. The study overlooks the front garden, and the lawn runs all the way up to the base of the wall. It's a large sash window and was locked tight. I broke the pane at the top of the lower one and released the catch.'

'Right. So, pushing the curtains aside you climb in and discover Mr Pentire at his desk, a pistol fallen from his hand and a suicide note on the table. Given that scene, and barring his man's reaction, the assumption anyone would make is that Pentire took his own life having first drawn the curtains and locked the door.'

'I'd say so, yes. The door was bolted on the inside too,' Burrows observed.

'A bolt as well as a lock?'

'I gather the house safe is in that room, one assumes it was there to provide additional security.' He gave a little shrug. 'It would be more convenient to quickly slip the bolt if one intended opening the safe perhaps.'

'And the key was on the inside of the door?' Burrows nodded. The colonel drummed his fingers lightly on the desk. 'What about the rest of the room? Describe it for me.'

Burrows thought for a moment, picturing the scene. 'The study leads directly off the hallway. It's the first door on the right from the front door, the next one leads into the dining room.'

'Is there a connecting door between the two rooms?'

'No, sir. There is only one door into the study. If you were standing with your back to the window, the door is halfway down the left-hand wall and the fireplace is in the middle of the right-hand wall. The desk is in the centre of the room facing the windows. There's a drinks table to the left of the fireplace and a sideboard along the wall that's common with the dining room. It's about twenty feet square, I'd say, with pictures on the walls and a large rug with polished floorboards showing along each wall. A nice room, sir.' Burrows concluded his description with a brief nod.

His superior eyed him. 'You have a pleasingly suspicious mind, Sergeant. What's your take on this? Did he kill himself, do you think?'

'I can't see any other explanation as things stand. The note is evidence of remorse, although for what I cannot imagine. And it's clearly impossible for anyone to have killed him and left the room secured as it was. But Connors will not be moved, sir.'

'What do you intend to do next?'

'I think we need to be clear about his arm. I'll ask Dr Spense to re-examine him to see if she can establish the range of movement he could manage.'

'Very well, report back after that. But you'd better be quick, remember she and Edward delayed their honeymoon but they're leaving imminently, I think. And, Burrows...'

'Sir?'

'Let's not forget that the safe is in that room. Make sure it hasn't been tampered with. Finally, I'd have a good look at this man Connors. He might have been in the pub during the evening, but he was the only one who was in the Dower House with Pentire during the night.'

The sergeant nodded. 'Point taken, sir.'

When the sergeant returned home for tea, he related events to his wife, including the astonishing news about WPC Dixon. If truth be told, Laura Burrows was far more interested in this intelligence than the demise of Vaughan Pentire. So much so, in fact, that she made it her business to call in to the police house later that evening to 'say hello and make sure you have everything you need'.

Invited in for a cup of tea she gently grilled the woman for fifteen minutes and extracted the essential details. She was aged twenty-eight and widowed, her husband having been on board HMS *Queen Mary*, which had been blown up at the battle of Jutland, killing all but seven of her twelve-hundred-man crew. He had been a Cumberland man, but she was a native of Oxford, still had family in the city and having served as a female police auxiliary during the hostilities, had seized upon the chance to assume a permanent position as the first female police officer in the county force. She seemed a bright and very pleasant person but, in truth, the entire tête-à-tête between the two of them was coloured by the relief that Laura Burrows had felt when she first set eyes on her.

Whatever her policing abilities, the new constable was unlikely to be a distraction to her husband. As well as being six feet tall and powerfully built, Mabel Dixon was as plain as plain could be.

*

The following morning Dr Innes Spense, née Knox, and her husband Edward joined his mother in the small dining room at Langford Hall for breakfast. They had their own suite of rooms in one wing and normally started the day together up there, and Claire Spense habitually had breakfast in bed, but today was notable. Innes had finally completed her psychology course and in an hour they were finally leaving for their honeymoon. Fenn was driving them to Oxford, for the London train. They were travelling first to Paris and then on to Capri. A locum doctor was arriving later that day to provide cover during their absence.

Jaikie, Innes's four-year-old son, who the village believed was her dead sister's child, was not going. It had been discussed but wiser heads, namely Edward's mother, had insisted that the

54

two of them went alone. The wean was now attending the nursery class at school in the mornings and would be looked after by Lady Claire and the Langford staff, with enthusiastic support from Ellie the maid at Marston House for the rest of the time.

'I'm sorry Piers isn't around to see you off this morning, he dashed off to town yesterday on some emergency or other,' Lady Langford remarked in her base voice.

'That's quite alright,' Innes answered, 'he came to find me and said cheerio, and he did seem a bit preoccupied.'

'Are you all packed?' Lady Claire enquired.

'Crikey, I hope so, surely there's not more,' Edward said with a pained grin.

His wife raised her chin and gave him a cool look. 'As the bulk of my packing and preparations are for your own personal delectation, I suggest you refrain from such pointed observations. I will look gorgeous, and you will locate porters. That is the natural order of things.'

'Welcome to married life, dear boy.' His mother met her daughter-in-law's eye and gave her a warm smile, then changed the subject. 'Did you manage to complete your examination of poor Mr Pentire yesterday?'

'I did. I've not had time to do a formal report, but I've jotted down the essential findings. Sergeant Burrows told me explicitly what he was looking for.'

'And did you find it?'

'I believe so.' There was a pointed silence, but as Innes said nothing further and just smiled pleasantly back at her mother-in-law, Lady Langford had to make do with that.

Edward snorted in amusement. 'Nothing doing, Mother.'

She cleared her throat, dabbed her lips with her napkin and rose. 'The idea that I might be interested in confidential medical information is unworthy of you, Edward. I will merely remind you that, as owners of the estate, it is generally a good idea to know what's going on before everyone else. Especially when the information is already known within the family.'

She gave Innes a guileless smile and added, 'I'll see you off at ten. Don't forget your bathing costume.' And with that she sauntered slowly but with tremendous style out of the door, pausing only to gently knock a small figurine on a side table over with her finger.

*

Down at the police house Burrows and Dixon were poring over the report that had been delivered by a Langford footman at eight that morning. It was handwritten on the doctor's surgery notepaper and read as follows:

> *I conducted a further examination of Mr Vaughan Pentire late of the Dower House, Great Tew, at 6 p.m. on the 16th of July 1921 in response to a specific request from the Great Tew police. The question that required an answer was this: Was Mr Pentire physically capable of shooting himself in the right temple with his right arm? The contention being that a war wound restricted the movement in his elbow to such a degree that he would not have been capable of such an action.*
>
> *After an external and internal examination my view is that Mr Pentire could not have inflicted such a wound on himself. Put simply, he couldn't bend his arm into the required position, given that powder burns suggest the weapon was probably no more than six inches from his head when it was discharged, and the line of the bullet is perpendicular to his skull.*
>
> *There is a proviso, however. Examining a dead and live body are very different and my opinion should be viewed as highly probable, but not definitive.*
>
> *Yours, Dr Innes Spense*

'She's hedging her bets,' Burrows said as he put the letter down on the counter.

Dixon nodded. 'It's understandable. Unless Mr Pentire was screaming in pain when she manipulated his arm, she can't say

56

with absolute certainly what he would and would not have been capable of.'

He nodded. 'Connors says he needed help dressing. Reaching buttons and so on. I'm inclined to believe him.'

'Which leaves us with a number of questions.'

'Doesn't it just, Constable Dixon. Namely, who murdered him? Why? And, above all, how did they get out of the study?'

Twenty minutes later the two police officers were sitting with the valet in the kitchen of the Dower House.

'I'll start by asking you not to leave the village, Mr Connors,' Burrows said. 'You're not a suspect at this moment, but I do want you to be available to help with our enquiries, if you please.'

The servant looked unhappy. 'That's alright, for a day or two maybe, but I'm not earning now, you know. Mr Pentire paid my wages at the weekend so I'm four days down already. I'll have to get another post as soon as I can.'

Burrows didn't react to this and proceeded with his first question. 'Take me through the detail of events on Thursday night, please. From your perspective. Dixon will get it down and you can sign it, so we have an official witness statement from you. Let's start from the point you served supper.'

The picture that emerged was clear enough. Connors had cooked and served his master's meal at seven o'clock, then cleared away and confirmed with Pentire that it was alright to go out. He had set off for the King's Head about ten to eight.

'You prefer it to the Black Horse?' Burrows asked.

'As I said, I play darts. There's a good Thursday night match on normally.'

'That's your regular night off then?'

Connors nodded. 'Mr Pentire was very generous like that. He was a decent master and I'm sorry to see him gone.'

'Did you leave the pub at any time before you departed to come home?'

He thought for a moment. 'No.'

'What time did you leave the public house?'

'About quarter past eleven. The house was in darkness. I let myself in by the back door, locked up and went to bed.' He shrugged. 'That's it.'

'How had Mr Pentire been that day. Did he seem normal?' Burrows asked.

'Yes, completely so.'

'So, you went to bed. Did you get up at all in the night?'

'Once, but only to use the lavatory.' He smiled apologetically and glanced at Dixon. 'The beer…'

'It was all quiet?'

'Yes. I heard St Mary's chime four, but that's all.'

'Where is your room in the house?'

'On the top floor. I've got a bedroom and a little sitting room up there. With a nice view over the common, as it happens.'

Burrows pictured the dormer windows above the roof line. 'Alright. And in the morning?'

'I took his tea up at the normal time and found he wasn't in bed. I searched the rest of the house but couldn't gain entry to the study and after knocking and calling for some time, came down to the police station.'

'How did you obtain your position with him?' he asked.

Connors smiled. 'Oh, there's a bit of a story to that. It goes all the way back to the war.'

Burrows perked up. 'Oh really? Carry on, I'm all ears.'

The valet shifted in his chair as though getting comfortable, then started talking. 'I was in the South Wales Borderers and volunteered before conscription, as it happens.' He gave the policeman a quick glance, as though seeking merit for this decision. 'Things went alright for me until summer 1915 when I got a bullet through the calf while doing sentry duty. A German sniper out in no man's land. They were terrible those snipers, you just couldn't see them at all, and they'd fire right through the

58

observation slit. Lucky it wasn't my forehead, that's where most of our boys got it. We were issued with periscopes in the end.'

He paused and cleared his throat, then carried on. 'They reckoned mine was a ricochet that bounced around in the trench before it found my leg. The following day I was in a field hospital near Ypres, but then the wound got infected, and I became very ill. I was shipped home, and it was two months before they finally got on top of it. Thankfully I've still got my leg. A lot of blokes weren't so lucky.'

He tapped his right thigh and smiled. Burrows nodded silently.

Connors continued, 'Anyway, the point is, I was sent to a hospital in Tunbridge Wells that specialised in infections. I shared a room with a private from the Oxfords whose name was Terry Craig. He'd been blinded and couldn't read his mum's letters, so I used to do it for him. He was from Great Tew and told me what a nice place it was, and it stuck in my mind. We were together for about two months and became good pals.'

'What happened to him?'

Connors' face clouded over. 'He didn't make it.' He stared at the window. 'I forgot the rules. Out there you soon learned not to get too close to people. One minute they were joking and having a laugh with you, the next their guts were spread all over the trench, like jam on a crumpet.'

There was a silence, then Burrows said, 'So, you recovered and were let out of hospital. What then?'

'I wasn't fit for combat, so they gave me an office job in Antwerp. Helping with the shipping. It was okay and then finally the war ended, and I was discharged and came back to Blighty in 1919. I kicked around for a couple of years. I'd been a footman before the war, and I went back into service in London but couldn't settle. Then one day I saw an advert that mentioned Great Tew. A gentleman looking for a manservant. You'll understand why it caught my eye. I met Mr Pentire in a hotel on the Strand, and he said he had taken the Dower House and was looking for a man. We found we suited each other, and here I am.'

The sergeant stood up. 'I'd like to see Mr Pentire's bedroom now, please. And your own.'

'As you wish.' Connors led the two police officers up the main staircase and onto the landing where a corridor ran the width of the building. Green trees and lush foliage showed through windows at either end, and four doors were evenly spaced along its length. 'These are all bedrooms which look over the front lawn. Mr Pentire has the far one in the corner with a double aspect.' He turned left and walked to the last door, opened it and stepped back.

The room was simply decorated and furnished and had none of the opulence that Burrows had seen on his occasional visits to Langford Hall. A double bed lay to his left, a dressing table was placed before the window at the front of the house and a pair of wardrobes ran along the wall that was common with the bedroom next door. A small rug lay on the wooden floorboards and a bedside table with a lamp and a pile of books completed the furnishings. The feeling was of an uncomplicated man with simple tastes.

'Does anything in here look out of place?' Burrows asked.

Connors shook his head and gestured vaguely at the interior of the room. 'No. As you can guess, my master wasn't one for fuss or bother.'

'How did he occupy his time?' Dixon asked, curious.

'He was a bit of a scholar. Medieval history and so on. He used to go into Oxford regularly and the library is full of his books. Quite valuable some of them, he said. He told me all about it once, but I'm afraid it went right over my head.'

They completed their examination of the room, which yielded nothing whatsoever of interest and moved upstairs to Connors' quarters. These were comfortable enough but, again, provided nothing in the way of intelligence.

Although, Burrows reflected as they descended the stairs, *it would be better if we had the slightest idea what we're looking for.*

In the hall he turned to Connors and said, 'You told us it was murder. If you are correct, how did the perpetrator get out of the study while leaving the doors and windows locked?'

The man shook his head. 'I have no idea.'

The sergeant frowned, then remarked, 'You're also the only one who knows what really happened here between the time you got back from the King's Head, and Mr Pentire's discovery in the morning. Frankly, Mr Connors, we only have your word for it.' He met the man's eye and added, 'Is there anything else that you are aware of, that we need to know?'

'No, I don't think so.' The lie came fluently to the valet.

Burrows nodded at Dixon and made for the door. He opened it, turned, looked back down the hall and said firmly, 'Don't leave the village, Mr Connors.'

As they walked back down the high street Burrows asked, 'What did you make of all that then, Constable?'

'It had the ring of truth about it to me.'

'Any misgivings?'

She hesitated. 'When he was talking about what happened that night it felt like he'd rehearsed what he was going to say.'

'I agree. He knew he'd be questioned and had it all off pat and ready. But I'm wondering if he's told us everything.'

'Yes, that's it.' She snapped her fingers in satisfaction. 'What he said was true, but he didn't tell us all of it.'

'You may well be right.'

Up at the Dower House Aiden Connors sat thoughtfully in the kitchen. He sensed that the sergeant suspected he knew more than he was saying. And he was right. There were things that he knew that they didn't.

And his life would be much easier if it stayed that way.

Chapter Five

In the Black Horse the arrival of WPC Dixon and the demise of Mr Pentire had been discussed at length and, in the case of the female police constable, with sheer astonishment.

'A woman. And a strong one at that,' Nobby Griffin observed to the Reverend Tukes. 'I reckon she'd get the better of me, although I'd go down fighting,' he added with a certain amount of relish.

'She'd snap you in half, soon as look at you.' Beatrice Wray paused in the act of pulling a pint and added, 'Sometimes things need a woman's touch and it's a sign things are changing for the better. Women did men's work during the war, and I don't see why that all has to stop now the soldiers are back.'

Tukes nodded. 'You make a fair point, but surely no one thinks the men who served their country should be done out of jobs. They should be able to come back to the places they had before they were called up.'

The barmaid nodded. 'Of course that's true. I'm just saying women have proved they can do more than people think and Mabel Dixon is a sign of that. Things are changing, vicar. Most women over thirty have got the vote now and I reckon it'll be all women before too long.'

The expression on Nobby's face gave a clear indication of his opinion on the suffrage of women and he opened his mouth to give Beatrice the benefit of his views but Tukes, who had had a trying day and did not wish to referee an argument, intervened.

'What's the latest regarding poor Mr Pentire,' he enquired innocently, well aware that the occupants of the Black Horse had, with no disrespect intended, discussed the death with enormous enjoyment. The small number of real facts available had been quickly exhausted and within an hour of the news breaking, the regulars had started engaging in that most satisfying of substitutes – wild speculation.

Theories abounded about why he might have taken his own life and the prevailing feeling was that he was the victim of a frustrated romance and had killed himself in an agony of unrequited love.

Swiftly abandoning the issue of women's rights, Beatrice Wray became round-eyed and nearly tearful at the thought. As she finished pulling the pint and placed it on the counter, she remarked, 'It's such a tragedy, the poor man. I mean he was quite handsome in his way, and not very old.'

'Fancied a wriggle yourself did you, Trixie?' Bert Williams enquired with a smile as he slid some coins over and lifted the glass.

She glared at him, her voice rising above the general hubbub in the crowded bar. 'Certainly not. I'm just saying, he must have had a few choices. He had money after all, to be living up there.'

Betty Shaddock, a plump and comely farmer's wife in her fifties grinned. 'Good looking, single and rich. I can't think what you'd see in him, Beatrice.'

'She's right,' Bert observed. 'You sure it wasn't you he was in love with, Trixie?' Then as an afterthought he eyed her corkscrew blonde curls and added with a sly grin, 'We all are.'

Well aware that this was how rumours started, she snapped back at him, 'Just you get this straight, Bert Williams, I had nothing to do with him. And as for you being in love with me, I'd have thought your wife and your wife's sister were enough to keep you going.'

Mrs Shaddock glanced over at her ageing husband slumped fast asleep in the far corner of the bar and then back at the lean, masculine countryman standing next to her. She let her hand brush his, smiled up at him, and said quietly, 'Oh, I don't know. Always room for one more, eh, Bert.'

It was at this loaded moment that the weight of the knowledge Nobby Griffin was carrying finally proved to be unbearable and he cracked. In spite of the fearful warning WPC Dixon had given him, the urge to gossip was so embedded in the villagers that it was only a matter of time. And that time was now.

'I was there,' he said. 'I was in the room.' This revelation produced a pleasingly astonished reaction from those in earshot.

'Eh?' said Bert, tearing himself away from Mrs Shaddock's warm brown eyes.

'What?' said Beatrice.

'I beg your pardon?' said the Reverend Tukes, who had frozen in the act of biting into a pickled walnut, leaving a trickle of inky juice on his chin.

'What did you see?' Bert asked, feeling it was his turn again.

'They asked me to unlock the study door and I did, but it was bolted from the inside, so Sergeant Burrows broke a window and climbed in. WPC Dixon followed and then Mr Connors. I was after them. He was bent over his desk and there was blood everywhere. Now what I saw was…'

Nobby told his tale to a spellbound audience, concluding definitively with, 'So there you are, Vaughan Pentire killed himself at his desk. There was a note and everything. Shot himself in the

64

head. I saw the gun.' The drama of the moment clearly justified a slight embellishment, he felt.

But his moment of glory was crushed when a thin and rather reedy voice piped up from his right-hand side. Turning he saw an old and skeletally thin man standing there. He had clearly been listening.

'What's that, Mr Willett?' he asked.

'He didn't kill himself.'

'Oh yes he did. I've just been telling you. I saw it.'

'And I'm telling you that I saw Sergeant Burrows break the window and you all climb in. Then, after you and Mabel Dixon left, I walked across the lawn and had a listen by the side of the broken window. Well you do, don't you,' he added with a slight gesture of embarrassment.

A fulsome murmur of understanding and approval passed around his riveted audience.

'And?' asked Stanley Tirrold, who had joined Beatrice behind the bar.

'Sergeant Burrows says to Mr Connors, "Your master's committed suicide."'

'Exactly,' said Nobby.

'But Mr Connors replies, "Oh no he hasn't." Then he tells Burrows that he's been murdered.'

The gasp of astonishment at this piece of intelligence was enough to silence the whole pub.

'Blimey,' said Bert. 'What happened next?'

Mr Willett coughed. 'You know all this talking is making my throat dry.' He paused meaningfully.

'A pint of cider for Mr Willett, Stanley,' Tukes called. 'On my tab.'

'Thank you kindly, parson. And perhaps a brandy to keep the cold out.'

'It's eighty degrees outside,' the vicar observed dryly, but nevertheless signalled his acceptance to the landlord.

Once the old man had fortified himself, he took up the tale. 'There's not much else to say. I had to move away as Dixon was coming up the drive with Dr Spense, but I heard Connors say something about his arm. Anyway, the point is, he didn't top himself, someone did it for him.' He glanced around the silent pub and remarked, 'Someone in the village, I reckon.'

There was a moment's silence then a roar of excited voices erupted, primary amongst them being Nobby's. 'Alright then, if someone was in there and killed him, how did they get out again? The door was locked and bolted from the inside and the windows closed tight. I saw the sergeant undo them. So, I say to you, Mr Willett, how did they get out?'

Silence fell again. The old man raised his pint and drank deeply, then wiped his mouth with a practised backhand stroke and looked at Nobby, a grim expression in his eyes.

'Maybe you want to ask Eve Dance that question. I don't know what was in that study that night, but it seems to me whatever it was, it weren't human.'

*

'Back again, Sergeant?' As he opened the front door of the Dower House, Connors' greeting carried a note of judgemental surprise which Burrows found rather irritating.

'I hope I'm not inconveniencing you,' he replied with some irony, 'but as you are the one insisting your master did not kill himself, I am obliged to make further enquiries.' He eased past the manservant and Dixon followed. 'You can carry on with your duties,' he added, 'we wish to inspect the study again.'

As Connors disappeared into his lair at the back of the house the police officers entered the study and shut the door. Dixon looked around. The window glass had been replaced, the bloody blotter removed, and the top of the desk wiped clean. Beyond that, at the police's insistence, nothing else had been touched, indeed she had been sent to observe the clean-up to ensure this was the case.

'You'd never know anything happened here now, would you, Sergeant,' she remarked.

He nodded. 'True enough. But we know, and it's our job to find out how and why.'

'They know in the village it was murder. Mrs Dale asked me directly this morning.'

Burrows nodded. 'It was only a matter of time.'

'They also know about the sealed room. She said there's a strong rumour going around that the death was caused by an evil spirit of some sort.'

'That's Great Tew for you,' he muttered. 'Mind you, it's also widely believed that when young Jaikie Knox was kidnapped last year, his life was saved by a spectral black dog, conjured up by Eve Dance.'

Dixon raised her eyebrows. 'The chief constable's wife?'

'The very same. Didn't know he was married to a witch, did you?'

She swallowed. 'Anything in it, Sergeant?'

He looked at her. 'We are the police. We deal in facts not speculation.' And with this oblique answer, the young WPC had to be satisfied.

The pair of them conducted a search of the study, carefully examining the door and windows, the chimney and the base of the walls. There were no clues whatsoever, although they found the spent bullet in the wood panelling above the fireplace and noted the word 'Mauser' etched into its base.

'It's in the right place more or less, I suppose,' Dixon observed. 'He was sitting at his desk and the bullet passed through from the far side of his head and up into here. It was probably deflected a bit.'

Burrows also examined the outside of the safe and visited Connors in the kitchen to enquire about the whereabouts of the key. The servant said he thought Mr Pentire had kept it on his key ring and Dixon was despatched back to the police station to sift through his personal effects, which they had kept in Great Tew when the body had been moved to the undertakers. The gun had also been retained. It had been identified as a Mauser C96 semi-automatic pistol and an officer at county headquarters had reported that such weapons had been standard issue to German officers during the war. Many British serving men had brough home souvenir weapons and the assumption was that Pentire had done the same.

The only fingerprints on the gun were Vaughan Pentire's but at the colonel's suggestion they had checked the bullets as well. There were plenty of half prints and smudges on those, all seemingly from the same hands, but none of which matched the dead man's. The conclusion was that the gun had been loaded by the murderer who had then wiped it clean and wrapped it in Pentire's hand, having forgotten about the bullets. Burrows' tentative suggestion that they take the fingerprints of everyone on the estate had been flatly refused by the chief constable.

'Have you any idea of the chaos that would cause, Sergeant? Would you like to take Lady Langford's, for example? Or the Reverend Tukes'. Or your own wife's?'

'Er no, sir, I see your point.'

'I'm glad to hear it.'

So the discrepancy in the fingerprints had been noted on the file but no further action was planned.

Dixon returned half an hour later with a key and the safe was opened. It contained a quantity of cash and some legal papers including a will, which Burrows read there and then. It left his estate in its entirety to his parents in the event he predeceased them. When he told Dixon she asked a question which he wondered about later.

'The poor things. Do you think it's better for a son to have killed himself, or been murdered, Sergeant?'

Whatever the answer to that vexing question, after an hour of detailed investigation their only trophy was an inch-long single thread of blue fabric that lay on the floor under a corner of the desk. 'From a dress, I'd say, Sergeant. Probably a visitor at some time,' Dixon remarked as she peered at it. 'It must have caught on something.'

Burrows bowed to her superior knowledge, his mind preoccupied by the simple and frustrating truth. There was absolutely nothing to indicate how the murderer's exit had been achieved.

'Do you think Connors did it, Sergeant?' Dixon asked as they walked back down the high street.

Burrows sighed. He wasn't in a good mood. Lying in bed that morning he had convinced himself that a detailed search of the study would reveal the method by which the murderer had escaped. He had failed, and it irked him.

'Use your noddle, Constable. I told Connors that his master had committed suicide and his reaction was to tell me that he hadn't. He'd hardly do that if he'd killed him, would he? He was all set to get away with it. To my mind that puts him in the clear.'

Dixon wasn't entirely sure about this. If Connors had killed Pentire and, for reasons unknown, been obliged to do so by shooting him in the right temple, then he might be worried about the verdict being contested by his parents who must know about his disability. If so, announcing it was murder was a very clever way to put himself in the clear, while dealing with that potential issue.

However, her superior's tetchy tone of voice didn't invite contradiction, so instead she filed the thought away for future consideration and said, 'Yes, fair enough, Sergeant. What do you think we should do next?'

'I'd like you to look into Mr Pentire's background, particularly his actions over the last few weeks. Someone in the village had a reason to kill him and if we can't find the way the murderer got out of that bally study, we might as well look for a

69

motive. It can't be robbery. We can assume he had his keys, including the one to the safe, on him at the time of death, and the safe contained quite a sum of money which the killer left untouched.'

The WPC approached this task with her usual diligence and the result was that three days later a review meeting between the pair of them took place under the oak tree in the garden of the Black Horse. It was early evening, and they were both in civvies. For Burrows this meant taking his uniform jacket off, rolling up his sleeves, and leaving his helmet behind the counter at the police station. The villagers understood that on such occasions he could be approached informally and matters of interest could be discussed off the record.

Dixon however had changed completely, replacing her blue serge jacket and skirt with a flamboyant summer dress which was cut with a considerable décolletage. This had been noticed by the steady stream of weary labourers who came in to quench their thirst and there was general agreement amongst them that, while the statuesque Mrs Dixon might not have the face of an angel, there were certainly compensations.

Which was exactly what she intended.

Burrows, however, sitting across the table from what he subsequently named 'the valley of death', found himself hoping fervently that his wife was busy at home and concentrating so hard on his notes that his face assumed a furious scowl, leading WPC Dixon to enquire if she was in trouble.

'No, no, not at all, Constable,' he replied. He glanced up as a man sauntering past with a pint of cider muttered 'Bloody hell' under his breath and knocked his knee against another table. 'Now then, let's get on. Tell me about Vaughan Pentire.'

She cleared her throat and started speaking, referring to her notes as she did so. The details were straightforward. He was thirty-five years old and hailed from Shrewsbury. There was enough family money for him not to require gainful employment and this, in turn, had allowed him to pursue his interest in medieval history.

'He had a visitor's reading ticket at the Bodleian and drove himself in two or three times a week,' Dixon remarked, 'so he must have been keen.'

Burrows nodded. 'Unmarried?'

'So it seems. Perhaps he just hadn't met the right girl. I understand his parents have been down to Banbury to collect the body. He'll be buried where they live.'

He nodded. 'The colonel spoke to them. Your observation the other day about the question of suicide or murder was a good one. In the end I believe he told them there was some doubt about the circumstances and we were investigating.'

'Connors has offered to pack up his things. Should we agree to that?'

'No, not for the moment. We'll make sure they find their way back to his mum and dad in the end, but I'd prefer the house left as it was the night he was killed for the time being. What about Pentire's war record? Was he out in France?'

'I'm not sure. I asked for a copy of his file, but nothing's turned up yet.'

'It might be quicker to ask his parents. What about the last few weeks here in Great Tew? Anything of note? Any rows or disagreements?'

'To be honest I've not picked up on anything. I spoke to the Reverend Tukes who confirmed he was a regular churchgoer. Stanley Tirrold had barely seen him, and the same down at the King's Head. He seems to have been one for a quiet life.'

At that moment a shadow appeared over them. It was Bert Williams, clearly struggling to maintain his focus. 'Can we help you?' the sergeant enquired.

'Maybe I can help you, actually,' he replied, dragging his attention away from the policewoman. 'I wasn't going to mention anything, but they're saying it's murder with Mr Pentire so I'm

71

coming forward. Thirsty day, ain't it,' he added, glancing hopefully at their half-full glasses.

'We'll see about that. Go on.'

'As it happens, I was out having an evening stroll the night he was killed. Just to stretch my legs, and I was on the common beyond the allotments. You can see the front of the Dower House from there, and I saw something. As I say, thirsty work this.' He glanced meaningfully at the glasses again.

Burrows lost his temper. 'Bert, if you've got something to say then say it. I'm not being bally well held to ransom by the local poacher. Cough up or I'll put you in the cell, I swear it.'

'Alright, alright.' He held up his hands. 'I saw a flash of light. Like a torch, just for two or three seconds, by the study window.'

'Inside or outside?' Dixon was leaning forward, her notebook in her hand.

'I'm goin' to say outside, but I'm not one hundred per cent sure. The light flashed against the pane, and I thought I saw a figure, but it was only a quarter moon. And the flash lost me my night vision.'

'What time was this?' Burrows asked.

'About half twelve.'

'Right. Anything else to add? Like what you were doing up there, prowling about after midnight.'

'Nope.'

'You sure?'

'Yep.'

'You didn't hear a shot?'

'No, but there was a stiff breeze from the south-east and there was a deal of noise coming from the trees. And any gunshot would have been blown away from the village anyway.'

Burrows gave a brief nod. Bert's opinion tallied with the other replies he'd had to that question. It had become obvious they would not be able to tie down the time of death by that method.

'Well, you can go then. But on your way, stop by the bar and buy me and the constable another pint.'

Bert frowned and stood up. 'That's a bit harsh, Sergeant. I'm doing my best to help you.'

'And I'm not arresting you for attempting to extort alcohol from an officer of the law in exchange for information in a murder enquiry. Consider yourself lucky.'

'Blimey.' He disappeared muttering into the rear of the pub.

When their drinks had been delivered, and Bert had departed with a final poorly concealed and admiring glance at Dixon's magnificence, Burrows looked at her and asked, 'What do you think of that then?'

'The light? I'd say it's the first firm indication we've had that someone was near the Dower House during the period Mr Pentire was killed. In fact, I'd go beyond that and suggest that person was involved somehow. They may even be the murderer.'

'I agree, but what would they be doing showing a light?'

'A signal maybe?' She shook her head. 'To be honest, I'm afraid I've no idea, Sergeant.'

Chapter Six

On Skye it had been three uneasy months since Cameron Breck's great-grandmother had told him he was a father. Both his grandmother and mother had clearly been curious about what the cailleach had said to him during their private discussion, and in the days following her funeral his mother had asked him directly. He had dissembled, muttering about 'some advice for life', but the older woman had looked at him in a penetrating way that he found alarming. He wondered if she had guessed the truth.

Since then their curiosity had apparently faded into the background, but Cameron was not fooled and knew his mother would return to the subject when it suited her. So one morning, when she invited him to sit down for a cup of tea and a chat, while his grandmother lurked by the fireplace, he hurriedly announced he was 'just away out for a stroll' and fled through the kitchen.

Emerging from the back door of the manse he walked through the outskirts of Elgol and took the coastal footpath along Loch Scavaig. It was a brisk morning with a rising breeze from the north-west that sent foot-high wavelets onto the rocky beach, and he sniffed the salty air, glad to be out of the house.

Since his great-grandmother's astonishing news, he had thought of little else. He knew that the child couldn't be local as he had been careful not to get tangled up with one of the village girls, whose ambitions were limited to inheriting a croft of their own. So the boy must be a product of one of his liaisons when he had been away from the island. Which begged a question.

Who was the mother?

He walked along the loch shore, across the wide beach below the stone farm at Camasunary and on round the headland, mulling it over in his mind. Cameron Breck was an ambitious young man, but he was also lazy. The point at issue was how the child could be an asset to him. If at all. He had no interest whatsoever in a clinging wife with a bairn on her hip and if that was what was on offer he would decline.

And that, surely, would be what was on offer. What other possibilities were there? And yet the old woman had clearly said the child would affect his life. With a frown he paused and looked ahead.

The faint path had reached a great slab of rock that guarded the entrance to Loch Coruisk. There was a sheer drop on his left where waves driven by the rising wind crashed noisily onto the granite ten feet below, and the way led up and across the steep diagonal plate. It was known locally as 'The Bad Step', and to a man from Edinburgh it would have been a terrifying prospect, but Cameron didn't hesitate, clambering smoothly with hands and feet above the surging water, the foot and handholds as familiar as the stairs in the manse.

He walked on to the waterfall where the fresh water of Loch Coruisk reached the sea then turned and climbed the Peak of Pity to the summit. There he sat and rested, looking up towards the speck of the distant black house. It was empty now and would probably remain so, he thought. A tiny dwelling cupped in the palm of the vast, soaring glen.

There had been three girls in all. The first two had been brief flings in Glasgow during his ill-fated time as a trainee life insurance salesman. After two months at head office, he had been despatched to Dundee to work under a senior man, selling policies door-to-door for the Medical Insurance Union. There he had met

75

another girl and for a while had rather liked her. She was pretty and obliging and her parents were comfortably off, and he had fleetingly wondered if life with her would be agreeable. She was an only child too, and in time would inherit the house where she lived. But the management of the Medical Insurance Union had become suspicious about the discrepancies between his cash collections and deposits. With the threat of further enquiries hanging over him he had simply not gone in one morning and, the same day, climbed onto a train bound for Oban with an illegally gained ten pounds seven and six in his pocket.

He hadn't bothered to say goodbye to the girl, confident that he would never see her again. And he had barely thought about her since.

But now she was back in his head. If she had found herself pregnant then she certainly hadn't come looking for him, he mused, although he had been deliberately vague about where he was from. He hugged his knees and stared down at the restless surface of Loch Coruisk. The vertical rock produced strong downdraughts that bounced on the water, creating ripples that made complicated patterns in the steel-blue reflection of the crags.

He had enough of his great-grandmother's soul to appreciate the extraordinary beauty of the scene in front of him, but he also knew full well that a life on Skye was a hard life. For little reward. He wanted more, and he wanted it easy.

Thoughts floated through his mind. Both the Glasgow girls were forgettable. In fact, he couldn't remember their names. If either of them had a child of his they could keep it and good luck to them. But the girl in Dundee, pretty Nancy Brown, might be worth a visit. If she was living at home with his bairn, he didn't doubt he could wheedle his way back into their lives. And it would be nice to see her again and share her bed.

And so, high on the Peak of Pity, in that wild and desolate place, he made a decision. He would travel to the brown stone city of Dundee to see his old lover.

Every sense told him it was she who had the baby.

*

Two weeks later Breck dismounted from the bus at the end of Ridge Street and paused for a moment to observe a large housing complex being built across the road. A sign proclaimed it was the Logie Estate, offering 'New homes for deserving veterans and their families'. He guessed there were more than a hundred semis under construction and the sight confirmed the impression he had had since arriving in Dundee. The war had been good for the jute trade on which the city's prosperity was based and there was money in the community.

After a ten-minute walk through the suburbs he came to a halt and eyed the house across the road where Nancy Brown lived with her parents. Standing back under the shadow of a tree he lit a cigarette and loitered. Twenty minutes later a neatly dressed brunette in her mid-thirties appeared, pushing a pram along the opposite pavement. Breck watched with surprise as she turned into the gate. Seeing she was alone, and stirred to action by some instinct, he quickly crossed the road and hailed her as she fiddled for the key in her bag.

'Excuse me, madam.'

She turned and saw a pleasant-looking slim fellow in his mid-twenties wearing grey flannels and a tweed jacket. Even on a dull day his hair glowed like the embers of a campfire. He was smiling and his accent was from the islands. 'May I help you?' she enquired, pausing in her search.

'I was told this is the Brown residence. Would that be correct?' He made a show of squinting at the number by the side of the door and added, 'Ninety-six Ridge Street?'

Her face cleared. 'Until recently it was, but they moved four weeks ago to a house on the edge of town. Mr Brown had a promotion. He's the managing director at Anglo-Eastern Jute these days.' She smiled and the transformation in her tired face was noticeable. 'Quite the go-getter, they say.'

77

'Things seem to be going well for everyone just now. The place is buzzing.' Breck made a vague gesture back down the road towards the new estate.

'I suppose so. The city had a good war regarding money. Although there's far too many widows and orphans around, I'm afraid. Most of the lads round here joined highland regiments and they took a terrible pasting. A quarter of them never came back and many that did have dreadful wounds. Everyone lost someone they know. We're to have a new memorial built in the town centre to remember them and every name will be on there.'

He nodded. Scottish regiments were highly regarded and had seen a great deal of heavy fighting. 'I was in the navy. Coastal command out of Campbeltown. Chasing Hun submarines.'

She nodded in approval. 'You did your bit then. And came home unscathed. Lucky you.'

They continued to chat for another five minutes during which Cameron Breck elicited the Browns' new address then, with a friendly farewell on both sides, they parted. As she opened the front door he saw a man sitting in a wheelchair in the hall, waiting for her.

Another bus ride and ten-minute walk brought him to a pleasant suburb where the town gave way to undulating countryside. The road was lined with plane trees and stretched away downhill around a left-hand bend. Large houses stood in generous plots and the front gardens were well tended. He walked on cautiously, not wanting to run into Nancy or her parents by accident.

The Ferns was similar to its neighbours, a stone-built detached residence with bay windows, a little mock turret and a grey slate roof. A tall cedar tree rose behind it. The brunette had been right, he thought. Mr Brown had gone up in the world. He walked slowly past and saw a maid moving in the window to the right of the porch. So someone was home.

A hundred yards down the street a narrow path ran between two fences, and he ducked along it, happy to be out of sight. Then he stopped and lit a cigarette. It was time for a proper think. Up to this point he had imagined he would simply walk up, knock on the door and spin some tale about being called away by a family emergency. But the sight of the big square house had made him pause. It was a long way from Skye here and his instincts told him he needed a better plan.

He ran through the dates again in his mind. He'd arrived in Dundee in March last year and had quickly become close to Nancy. Then there had been the trouble with the money, and he'd fled in May. If she'd fallen pregnant early that month she might have only realised after he'd left.

Supposing she'd given birth around the turn of the year, by his reckoning the child would be around seven months old now and while Nancy would surely be delighted to see him back, her parents might be more sceptical. The prospect of living in comfort in the fine detached house with a maid and Nancy to share his bed wasn't a bad one. And a nice cushy job at the jute factory would surely follow. But he would have to be careful. There were no flies on Mr Brown, and he knew he could expect some searching questions before he was allowed into their lives again, no matter what the neighbours thought about an unmarried mother in the house next door.

Thoughtfully he stubbed his cigarette out on the brick wall and walked back to the end of the path. An elderly couple were coming towards him along the pavement but there was no one else in sight. He nodded to himself, his mind made up.

He needed to arrange to meet Nancy on her own and have a quiet word, with her parents well out of the way.

*

As Cameron Breck pondered his next move, in continuing fine weather Eve Dance was climbing towards the summit of Green Hill on the Langford estate.

79

During the war a friend of hers had worked as a scientist down on the south coast developing devices known as 'listening wells'. They were wide, shallow, circular depressions in the ground with a skilled listener posted in the centre and were designed to detect the sound of Zeppelin engines as they passed overhead, beyond the range of normal human hearing. As the technology had advanced, the human had been replaced by a microphone, but the idea of listening devices buried in the landscape had struck a chord with Eve.

Because she had one as well. And it had heard something.

That night in April, when she had stirred then suddenly jerked awake, she had believed that it was the imminent passing of a fellow adept of the natural that had woken her, as though a distant spiritual drum had sounded with a single great beat. But now she was not so sure, because some days ago she had sensed a second pulse, and her instincts told her it was connected to the first.

Breathing heavily she reached the ridgeline and turned left, walking slowly and alone along the old high-level track, the distant echoes of past travellers resonant in her head. Lost voices, quiet conversations, the jingle of harnesses and the creak of wheels. At the great standing stone on the summit of Green Hill she stopped and reached out to them and was rewarded with a gentle thrill of pins and needles that washed over her.

Hello again.

Smiling, she knelt down, arms to her sides, feeling her skin prickle as the latent energy stirred and flowed around her. Then, raising her head to the sky, she freed her mind and let go of her body, rising higher and higher until she was drifting like a goshawk riding a thermal high above the ancient landscape.

Far below, the ground shimmered in the summer heat and in her enlightened state she could see the earth's energy rolling over the fields and hills like the swell on a wide ocean. It was a familiar sight; the great engine at work and the source of the

80

paganism that was the backdrop to life on the estate. The villagers sensed the natural power embedded in the land and instinctively responded to it, as their ancestors had done for thousands of years. It was the heartbeat of their world. It anchored their lives, it drove the seasons, it was the essence of life itself. And it was why, five thousand years earlier, they had placed the stones of Creech Hill Ring and its great outer circle of monoliths in the exact place where two of the energy lines crossed, creating a crucible of power that pulsed across the landscape like a lighthouse beam in the night sky.

What was it? What happened? she asked.

And a picture slowly formed. Of high mountains, remoteness. A wild place. And as she pursued the image, she had a sense of another adept. Passed and distant now, but a message that was still alive. A young life. A young man, in fact.

Why me. Why here? The picture was fading. She tried one more time.

Is he coming here? A brown stone city swam into her mind. A grey sea. Further north. *No, he's not coming here.*

And then she was back on Green Hill, the hot sun on her face and the breeze stirring her hair. She leaned back against the stone and stared across the valley to Great Tew where the tall tower of St Mary's rose above the dense foliage.

Whatever it was, it's a long way away. Nothing to worry about.

*

Cameron Breck sat on the bed in his cheap hotel room in Dundee and reflected on the events of the day. He had been in the city for a week and for the last four days he had discreetly watched Nancy Brown arriving for work at the jute factory then followed her to the bus that took her home at the end of the working day. He guessed there must be a staff canteen because she had not appeared at lunchtime. Understandably there had been no sign of the baby and he assumed it was at home under the care of a nursemaid while she was at work. And he had to admit the sight

81

of her strutting along the pavement, hat at a jaunty angle, had reminded him of why she had first caught his eye.

It's time. I'll speak to her tomorrow.

The following afternoon Nancy had completed her typing and was tidying up when the hooter blew. Five minutes later she joined the throng flowing out of the factory gates and headed towards her bus stop. The crowd rapidly thinned as not many of her fellow workers lived in the neighbourhood of The Ferns, and within a few minutes she was walking alone. As she turned the corner, she saw a young man standing by the stop, his hat pulled down low over his head. Something about him was familiar and as he looked up at her, she stopped in astonishment.

'Cameron Breck. As I live and breathe. What happened to you?'

He gave her a little lop-sided grin. 'Hello, Nancy. Sorry it's been a while.'

She walked forward, eyes fixed on his, confusion showing on her face. 'What are you doing here?'

'I've come to see you. There was a family emergency on the island, but I came back as soon as I could. I've been thinking about you, Nancy. An awful lot.' Again, the grin, she noted. He'd always thought he was a charmer.

'I'd given up on you. Disappearing with no trace and no note. Why didn't you write from home? You could have explained what was going on.'

He moved his hands vaguely. 'Aye, I should have done. I know that and I'm sorry. I was embarrassed to leave you like that. Especially after we were so close.'

His words hung in the air between them, and for a moment he thought that she would forgive him there and then. But she was made of sterner stuff.

'You've got some nerve, running away and then turning up again out of the blue.' She glanced around and whispered fiercely, 'And you're right, especially after what we got up to.'

82

He reached for her hand and took it. 'I just can't get you out of my mind, Nancy. I know I've behaved badly, but it couldn't be helped. I'm here to make amends and see if we can make a go of it.'

'Have you got a job?'

'Not just now, but there's work in the city. Maybe even in the factory, eh?' He smiled.

She breathed out and stared down the street, thinking hard, the shock slowly subsiding. A group of children were hunched over something on the pavement. After a moment a faint cheer reached her, and she realised they were playing marbles.

'What do you say, Nancy? Will you give it a go?' He had both her hands now and was clearly getting ready to kiss her.

'Wait.' She stepped back and held up her hand. 'Just wait a moment, Cameron Breck. I'm going to need a better explanation than that. And a bit more time.' She looked at him, anger stirring. 'Surely you can see that. You can't just run off then reappear and expect me to welcome you back with open arms.'

'I thought you liked me,' he said in a plaintive tone which added to her irritation.

'I thought the same. But then you buggered off without so much as a cheerio. After you'd had your fun.'

There was a silence as a girl walked past and gave them an arch glance, clearly sensing an interesting conversation. Shouts and a kerfuffle drifted up from the marble players where a disagreement of some sort was being addressed in the traditional way.

He could see indecision on her pretty face and played his trump card. 'I've been thinking about the baby.'

Her eyes opened wide, and she rocked back, startled. 'The baby?'

'Aye. The baby.' He nodded meaningfully.

'What baby? Was that the emergency, back on the island?'

'Eh? No. No way, Nancy. I'm talking about your baby. Our baby. I want to help look after it.'

She barely managed to stifle a burst of laughter. 'Our baby? I don't have a baby, you ignoramus. You might not have taken precautions, but I did. It's all about the timing. I haven't had a baby. What on earth gave you that idea?'

Then before he could say anything else her face hardened, and she put her hands on her hips. 'Oh, wait a minute. I see now. You thought I was pregnant and scooted off. That was it then.'

But the young man barely heard her. He was astonished. Nancy Brown was not the mother of his child. He stared at her slack-faced and said, 'Definitely? You definitely haven't got a child?'

But even as he said it, he realised how ridiculous it sounded, and the girl duly obliged.

'Do you think I wouldn't know?' she responded witheringly. 'What on earth are you thinking? Turning up here after a year away and accusing me of having a child out of wedlock. Are you out of your mind?'

He was vaguely aware of a bus approaching from behind and seconds later it drew up. The girl got onto it, and he made to follow her, but as he reached for the handle she spun round and hissed, 'Oh no, Cameron Breck, this is where we part company. For good.' She glanced at the conductor and added briskly, 'This man is bothering me, would you prevent him boarding, please.'

'Is that a fact, miss?' Cameron found himself confronted by the generously proportioned conductor who continued, 'That's you on the next one then, son. Don't worry, only half an hour to wait.' With that he pressed the bell and the bus accelerated away.

Chapter Seven

Cameron Breck sat moodily on the train as it pulled slowly out of Dundee station and crossed the Tay rail bridge heading for Glasgow, where he'd change for Oban and the ferry to Skye. It was an ignominious retreat. He'd waited for a day or two after his disastrous meeting with Nancy before making a final decision, even to the point of wondering if she was lying about the child. But there was little doubt that she'd told him the truth. Her anger and astonishment had been genuine, and it was clear all his boats had been burned.

Whatever the future held for him, it would not involve a cosy berth at The Ferns with a new young bairn, a pretty wife and decent prospects.

But as well as anger and frustration at the turn of events, a genuine confusion underpinned his mood. His great-grandmother had been unequivocal. He was a father, and the son would be important to him. But if the mother wasn't Nancy Brown, then it must be one of the two girls from Glasgow. Girls whose names and faces he could barely remember and who would surely be impossible to trace.

He sighed and lit a cigarette, staring out at the swirling waters below. Maybe he'd go to sea again. With his naval experience he'd get a ticket as an able seaman no problem. There were any number of blue water shipping lines running out of Glasgow and he could see a bit of the empire, perhaps even make a fresh start in Canada or Australia. Plenty of men had done it. He puffed and let his mind wander, remembering his first day in the navy. There had been about fifty of them, all lined up in an office in Oban to take the medical and sign on the dotted line, then he'd been sent off to basic training at Greenock on the Clyde. They'd been a decent bunch of lads and one had even ended up on the same vessel, HMS *Clarion*.

He'd got his call-up papers at the manse in May 1916 and travelled to the enlisting office in Oban, arriving on the afternoon ferry the day before. His mother had been upset of course but his father put on a good show, shaking his hand and saying, 'You stay out of trouble, especially tonight in Oban, Cam. They'll be a few lads out to celebrate their last night of freedom before the navy gets their hands on you. Just take it steady.'

He smiled, remembering an epic pub crawl with some young men he barely knew. A drunken session that had ended up back in the bar of the hotel where he was staying.

And the girl. The beautiful and willing girl.

Stunned he sat bolt upright in his seat, startling the woman opposite. How could he have forgotten? Easily enough actually, he reasoned. It had been a fleeting encounter, she had left quickly afterwards, and in the morning as he struggled into his clothes and made his way, still drunk, to the recruiting office, the thought of his impending naval service had been uppermost in his mind.

And active service had been exactly that. There hadn't been any time for romantic reflections in the fierce battle with the U-boats that lurked along the convoy routes in the western approaches. Put simply, he had forgotten her. A drunken one-night stand, of no significance.

And yet. He concentrated hard, trying to remember details of the evening. She'd been with a party of youngsters his age. They weren't islanders. They'd been a jolly, noisy bunch. And clever. Before she'd joined him, he'd heard snatches of their conversation. Not the sort of thing locals talked about. Highbrow stuff. He grimaced. *What was her name?*

'You okay, pal?'

The middle-aged man with the woman opposite was staring at him, a faint frown of concern on his face.

He grinned back. 'Oh aye, just trying to remember a girl's name.'

The man nodded. 'Those were the days,' he said, which elicited an elbow in the ribs from his wife and a roll of her eyes.

'You were keen enough to settle down, as I recall, Jerry McKenzie,' she remarked dryly.

Breck smiled with her. 'Are you heading for Glasgow?'

'Aye,' she replied, 'our boy's training to be a doctor down there, we're going to see him.'

'At the university,' her husband added, the pride in his voice obvious.

And somewhere in the young man's head a memory chimed. It was a snatch of conversation that had drifted to him as he stood at the bar. Just before the girl had walked up and said, 'Hello.'

Actually, it was just one word, but understanding came in a tumbling rush as he realised its implications. 'Vertebrae'.

No one used that word in conversation. They might say backbone. Or spine. But vertebrae was a medical term. *The group of young people had been medical students.*

He looked at the couple. 'There's a medical school there then? In Glasgow?'

'The best in the country. Where the brightest go.' Like her husband, the mother bristled with pride. 'Five years it takes them to train, then they go off to work in a hospital or as a doctor in the community.'

'Well that's a fine thing, I'm sure you're very proud of him.'

87

Later he fell asleep and as the train rattled southwards, he found himself dreaming of that night. He remembered her calm, blue-grey eyes. In his dream he tried to remember the conversation. He'd nodded and said, 'Can I buy you a drink,' and when she'd agreed he'd extended his hand and said, 'Cameron Breck.'

But her reply remained frustratingly, tantalisingly, out of reach. He drifted round the scene and finally, more in hope than expectation, he pictured his great-grandmother's face as she looked at him outside the black house and said, 'You have a son.'

What was her name?

And suddenly, incredibly, the mist cleared, and he could see her in all her beauty facing him at the bar. She was smiling and shaking his hand.

'Innes Knox,' she said.

And at that moment six hundred miles south a witch living in an ancient village suddenly stopped and stared distractedly at the rose bush she was deadheading.

Because the great drum had sounded again.

*

Glasgow university occupied several buildings built in a gothic style in the Gilmorehill area of the city and Cameron Breck decided that the main entrance would probably be in the largest of these, which was crowned by an enormous clock tower. He entered the reception area at ten o'clock in the morning as the chimes echoed high above him and the first rush of students had disappeared to their lectures.

The hall was high and ornate stonework decorated the pillars that supported the arched roof. A single desk lay thirty feet away across a black and white tiled floor and, as he approached, the dark-haired male attendant looked up from some paperwork. He was in his forties and wearing a pair of wire-framed spectacles.

'Good morning, may I help you?'

Breck realised the man thought he was a student. 'Good morning to you. I wonder if you can. I've travelled from Oban where I work as a solicitor's clerk. My boss has sent me to enquire about a student who studied here. We believe she must have completed her studies in 1917 or 1918.'

'Oh yes? And what is your interest, may I ask?'

Breck glanced around and leaned forward confidentially. 'It is a matter of an inheritance.'

'I see. And do you not have a home address?'

'No, that's the point. Her parents are deceased and there is no forwarding address for her at her former family home. We do know she was studying to be a doctor here during the war though.'

'Can I ask why the solicitor has not enquired by letter? So there is a formal record of the request?'

'I was in Glasgow on other business, and he asked me to call in.'

He doesn't believe me.

'A female student, you say?' The man was looking at him in an old-fashioned way.

'Aye, that's right.'

'Do you have any identification?'

'I do, but it's in my other coat in the hotel.' Breck realised that the exchange was not going well.

'I'm afraid that without identification and a written letter of request on headed notepaper the university would not be able to release information about any student.' The man behind the counter paused and added the *coup de grâce* with a malign smile, 'No matter how much you love her. Good morning.' He bent his head back to his work.

Thus dismissed, Breck retreated across the tiled floor and emerged onto the street, relieved to be released from the ordeal but angry at having been so comprehensively bested. He found a coffee house and sat thinking about the exchange. As the hazy memories of that night with Innes Knox had become clearer, he had become increasingly convinced that she was the woman he was looking for. It was also obvious that the trail from the university was the one to follow. Especially as he had no other means of finding her whatsoever.

He glanced up as pair of girls came into the café and took a table in the far corner. The prettier of the two glanced over and met his eye. He smiled instinctively and she gave him a quick and careful smile in return before bending her head to her friend.

Any moment now…

Sure enough, twenty seconds later her friend casually turned her head and looked over at him. He pretended not to notice, letting them play their game. Looking around he realised that the café must be affiliated to the university in some way. At the far end of the room a large wooden board mounted on the wall had a double column of names inscribed in gold lettering, with a year after each one. Above them a title proclaimed 'Presidents of the Glasgow University Debating Society'.

He stared at the names which read like a roll-call of the clans. And as he did so, something occurred to him. The degrees granted by the university would be a matter of public record. Each year the award ceremonies for each faculty took place before an invited audience. Surely the library would have a record and at the very least he should be able to establish the year Innes Knox had qualified. He sipped his coffee in some satisfaction. That would be a step forward.

He looked back at the girls. *Where is she now?* he wondered. One thing was certain. Whatever happened, when he found her, he would be a damn sight more circumspect than he had been with Nancy Brown. His humiliation at her hands still burned and he would not make the same mistake twice. In the meantime, there was the question of money. He was running short of cash and would have to find work to tide him over as he continued his research.

Two days later Cameron Breck had a job working shifts as a deckhand on the Greenock ferry and on Saturday morning he visited the central library and searched through the back copies of the *Glasgow Evening News* for the lists of graduating students from the School of Medicine. He was sure he had overheard one of the students in Oban toasting his friends and saying, 'Here's to one more year before we're let loose on the public.' There had been a general cheer in support of this sentiment and from this he had deduced, not unreasonably, that the beautiful girl with the clear blue-grey eyes would have qualified the following year, 1917.

But the School of Medicine award lists did not reveal a Dr Innes Knox that year. Surprised, he consulted the records for the following year with the same result. Stumped and frustrated he paused at this point and stared thoughtfully up at a dirty stained-glass window.

If she had realised that she was pregnant in the summer of 1916, then she would hardly have continued with her studies. Nine months to have the baby, then another nine to look after it as a wee infant. She would have been absent for getting on two years by the time terms and holidays were considered. And then she would have had to study for her final year. He was looking in the wrong place.

With a gleam in his eye, he returned the newspapers to the desk and asked for the equivalent copies for 1919.

And there she was. Dr Innes Knox, Dumfries, Galloway.

She had taken a sudden and unexplained two-year sabbatical, when in 1916 she was all set to complete her final year and qualify. The timing fitted perfectly, he thought, with a surge of triumph.

Innes Knox had had his baby.

*

Nearly four weeks after the death of Vaughan Pentire, Sergeant Burrows received a message from the Misses Rudge, two elderly spinsters who lived in a house on the outskirts of Little Tew. Would he call in on a matter that required the utmost discretion?

With his constable folded into the sidecar Burrows negotiated the track over Tan Hill and descended towards the hamlet. He drove through it and stopped outside a small house that stood alone surrounded by fields about four hundred yards along the road that led towards Dell Lane and, ultimately, Banbury.

'I don't know them very well,' he told Dixon as they surveyed the property. 'They're sisters and have been here for years. They own the draper's shop in Great Tew. I don't know if either of them ever married.'

'They keep a tidy garden, sir,' the constable observed. And she was right, the front garden was attractive and well tended.

He nodded, then climbed off the bike. 'Well let's see what they want.'

The door was opened by a tall grey-haired lady in her early sixties. She carried herself well, although Dixon noticed that her dress was an old-fashioned cut and been washed many times. 'Good afternoon, officers.' She nodded approvingly at the constable, adding, 'Yes, we heard they'd recruited a woman, good for you. I'm Geraldine Rudge.' She turned and indicated another shorter figure who had appeared behind her. 'My younger sister, Xanthe.'

'Sergeant Burrows and Constable Dixon, attending as requested, Miss Rudge,' came the reply.

'You'd better come in.' Dixon couldn't help noticing that the woman appeared to glance furtively in both directions along the empty lane before closing the door behind them.

Five minutes later they were sitting in a pleasant enough parlour to the rear of the property, although it was apparent from the slightly frayed furniture covers that this was not a house where money was abundant.

'How can we help you, ladies?' Burrows asked, once tea had been served.

There was an uneasy moment of silence as their two hostesses looked at each other. Xanthe was a little plumper than her sister and her face was kind but there was clear indecision in her eyes. Geraldine, on the other hand, just looked angry. Burrows felt the older sister was the senior partner in most things.

The silence lengthened. To her sergeant's approval, Constable Dixon let it. In the distance a shotgun fired twice. *A miss and a hit*, Burrows thought. *Or maybe two misses. Rather like the ladies in front of me.* Hiding a smile he waited, then Geraldine said, 'We have received an unpleasant communication in the post.'

'A letter?'

'Yes, I believe the term is a poison pen letter. Its contents are not nice.'

'I see. When did it arrive?'

'To be honest it was some weeks ago. Before the fete in June. It has taken us time to pluck up the courage to tell you.'

'Can you show it to us?'

Again, the long pause and indecision, then finally Xanthe rose and walked to a chest of drawers, opened the top one and removed a single sheet of paper. She handed it to Burrows. He held it so Dixon could read it too. It was typed, with no salutation and no signature. There was a brown stain running along the bottom of the page.

What a pretty pair of sisters. But one of you has a secret, don't you? A nasty little secret that folk would be very interested to know. I might tell them. Or maybe you'll pay for my silence. I'll write again.

He stirred and made to speak but was so surprised to feel Dixon's leg pressing against his own that he momentarily lost concentration. She leapt into the silence.

'That's a horrible thing to receive. I'm very sorry it's happened to you.'

Burrows registered vague surprise at her offering such an opinion, completely missed their genuine expressions of gratitude, and concentrated on the police aspects of the matter.

'What's this stain?' he asked.

'We threw it away, but then thought we'd better keep it. That happened when it was in the bin, I'm afraid. It's tea.'

He nodded. 'And the envelope?'

'We didn't retrieve that.'

'Pity. But it arrived in the normal post, you say? Not slipped through the door.' The sisters nodded.

To his astonishment, the pressure on his leg recurred and Dixon said, 'Do you mind if I ask you a question?'

'No, I suppose you must make enquiries.' It was Xanthe who answered.

'To whom is the letter refer—?'

'Me,' Xanthe interrupted. 'Me. Many years ago I made a stupid mistake that I had thought was well behind me. It appears not.'

'And are you sure it is that to which your correspondent refers?'

'If you are suggesting our lives are peppered with incidents about which we may be blackmailed, you are very much mistaken,' Geraldine replied waspishly. 'My dear sister was a silly girl. It was dealt with at the time and there matters rested until this letter arrived.'

'What was the nature of the incident? Did it involve a man?'

Xanthe stirred uncomfortably in her seat. 'No, it did not. The whole thing was dealt with quietly within a small group.'

Burrows said, 'And you have received no further letters?'

'Not so far, no, but as you can read, one may be expected at some point. One assumes it will be a demand for money.'

94

Dixon asked, 'You mentioned a small group, Miss Rudge. Is it possible one of those in the know at the time would have written this letter?'

The sisters exchanged glances. 'No, I'm sure they would not. We've lost contact with them and I'm not sure they are even aware of our address.'

'But they might have told someone else?' Burrows tapped his foot. 'Otherwise, how does anyone else know?'

A single tear appeared on Xanthe's gentle face. 'I'm sorry, I have no idea.'

*

Dixon was bristling with rage as they arrived back at the police station. And, as it happened, so was her sergeant.

'It just makes me absolutely furious that some malicious individual feels he can write such horrible things. Those poor women being blackmailed. It's obvious there's no spare money in the household. It's just awful, isn't it, Sergeant.'

But Burrows had other things on his mind. 'Did you press your leg against mine to stop me speaking?' he demanded. Her agonised grimace was answer enough. Tight-faced he stared at her. 'I'll thank you to remember who is in charge here, Constable. Whatever gave you the idea that you can speak over me?'

'I'm very sorry, Sergeant.' If Burrows was expecting any further explanation, he was disappointed as nothing else was forthcoming.

'Stand to attention when you're addressing me,' he snapped. 'Well? Explain yourself.'

Eyes fixed on a point over his left shoulder, she said, 'I just felt it was very difficult for those two sisters to come clean about the letter and acknowledging that fact might help them to talk about it.' She paused and added, 'A bit of sympathy for their predicament. Rather than rushing in straight away.'

'Rushing in?' Burrows' eyes bulged and his mind boggled at the judgement being laid upon him. 'Did you say rushing in?'

Distress showed on her face. She gestured hopelessly and replied, 'No, really, I am not criticising you. Not in any way. You know much more about these things than I do. It was just an instinctive thought. I'm terribly sorry, Sergeant.'

He stared at her. 'I mean, apart from anything else, you pressed yourself against my leg. That is definitely not in the Oxfordshire County Police Manual.'

A faint whimper sounded from the straining, Amazonian young woman in front of him. In their short time together, she had formed an excellent impression of her sergeant's abilities as a police officer but knew he was inclined to bluntness and on occasions missed the bigger picture. Those were not faults of hers.

After a moment she said, 'Perhaps we could have a sign. Just in case it crops up again.'

'What on earth do you mean?'

WPC Dixon swallowed and pressed tentatively on. 'Just once or twice I've thought of something that could be useful to ask, especially if we are interviewing a suspect. If I want to say something when you're busy doing important questioning, I could cough and scratch my nose. So you know I want to speak.'

Irritated though he was, this remark gave Burrows pause for thought. He knew from bitter experience of working alone that speaking to people and trying to think of the next question while trying to read everything into what they were saying wasn't always easy. Things could be missed. And there was nothing wrong with WPC Dixon's wits, he knew that.

He looked at her. 'You know, that isn't a bad idea. Alright, we'll try that. Now, what do you suggest we do about the Misses Rudge?'

Chapter Eight

Frustrated with their lack of progress in the murder of Vaughan Pentire, Burrows had assembled his troops on the front lawn of the Dower House. Alongside WPC Dixon were Constable Riley from the new Leyland beat and Constable Bull from the south Banbury beat. Present at a distance was the stick thin Mr Willett, who was yet again leaning on his spade in the Glebe allotments and wondering if this new intelligence would be worth another free pint.

'I want a thorough search of the entire house with the aim of turning up anything of interest to our enquiries. If you're not sure, come and find me.' Having completed this simple summary of the task, Burrows rang the bell and waited. Connors appeared and the policeman informed him that they intended to search the house.

'Don't you need a warrant for that?' he asked.

The sergeant pushed past him saying, 'You're the one who told us this was a crime scene, so no, we don't.' Having set Riley and Bull to work in the downstairs rooms, he led Dixon up the main staircase to the landing. 'I'll do this floor myself.' He pointed to the door that opened onto the back stairs and said, 'Go up to the servants' floor and search there. Start with Connors' room. Have a good rummage and report anything suspicious.'

And with that they fell to work.

Burrows searched Vaughan Pentire's room thoroughly and found the remnants of a dressing-up costume in a box under the bed. There was also a large quantity of stage make-up, which prompted him to go in search of Connors.

'I found this.' He lifted up a tin. 'Was Mr Pentire involved in the stage?'

'He was a very artistic gentleman and made reference to amateur dramatic performances on more than one occasion, sir. I think that was why he wanted to play the fortune teller.'

'What! He was the fortune teller? Why didn't you tell me that before?' Burrows demanded.

The valet looked nonplussed. 'You didn't ask.'

With a muttered curse, he returned to the bedroom, wondering what the implications of this news might be. He searched for another ten minutes, found nothing more, and emerged onto the landing just as Dixon appeared, carrying a bag.

They met at the head of the stairs. 'I found this tucked under a wardrobe in an empty bedroom up there,' she said. 'I've only had a quick look, but they make interesting reading.' She dipped into the bag and handed him an envelope. Burrows took it, removed the letter and studied it as they stood next to the rail on the landing.

24th September 1915
Willow Cottage

My dear Terry,

How are you getting on? All well here although it's hard for everyone with so many of you lads being away. At least you're not at the front anyway. Your dad's alright and sends his love. He'll be going down to the King's Head in a little while I think – it's Friday evening here. I miss not getting your letters but if you can't see at the moment, I forgive you for not writing!

98

Anyway, I promised to keep you in the know with any gossip from the estate so here's a tasty little titbit for you to think about while you're lying in bed. No names, no pack drill, because I suppose you'll have a nurse read this to you, but do you remember that schoolteacher who likes to give herself airs and graces? Sets herself above us because she went to university and all that. Well guess what? It turns out she's got a brother in the loony bin. It's not shellshock, he's been locked up in an asylum for years. Since before the war.

It's a bit much, isn't it? Her in charge of educating all the children round here while madness runs in the family. No wonder she kept that quiet, there'd be a riot if folk found out!

Anyway, your dad's just called cheerio so he's off out and I'm going to settle down with a book. I'll write again next week. You keep safe now.

Much love,

Mum

Burrows stared at Dixon as Connors' tale of meeting Terry Craig in hospital came back to him. 'How many?' he asked.

'Fifteen.'

'All like this?'

'I've only read two but yes, I imagine so.'

'Connors shared a room in hospital with Terry Craig. Craig was blind and he used to read out the letters his mum sent him. When Craig died Connors must have pinched them.'

In the silence that followed a voice said, 'Actually, I didn't steal them. Not purposefully.'

They spun round. The valet was standing on the half-landing looking up at them. Sunlight from the large window bathed his body and cast his shadow onto the wall. 'Come here, please.' Burrows beckoned him up the stairs. He climbed towards them and came to a halt as the sergeant said, 'These are letters that Agnes Craig wrote to her son Terry when you were in hospital together in Tunbridge Wells. Am I right?'

When the valet nodded, he continued, 'Why didn't you hand them back to him?'

Connors shrugged. 'He couldn't read them, could he? And I wasn't walking so well in those days, so they just stayed over on my side of the room, in my bedside locker. Then Terry took a turn for the worse. I was away one morning having treatment on my leg and when I came back his bed was empty and freshly made up. The nurse said he'd died.' His face took on a distant look. 'I told you. I was quite upset, as it happens. We'd become mates.'

He shrugged and carried on speaking. 'The letters just got left behind and I kept them. When I came to Great Tew I thought I'd look up his mum and call in. Have a chat and tell her about how I'd known him. I planned to return the letters to her then. But it turned out she'd died, and his dad had moved away.'

'So why conceal them? They were hidden in another room.'

Connors said nothing and, in the silence, Burrows made some deductions, the meeting with the Misses Rudge foremost in his mind. 'I think you saw an opportunity to make a bit of money,' he said. 'You realised that people would pay to keep the information in these letters quiet. You've been blackmailing people, haven't you. My word, you must have been delighted when you saw that advert for a position in Great Tew. It put you right on the spot.'

Looking alarmed, the valet said, 'I don't know anything about any blackmail. I don't know what you're talking about.'

But Burrows' brain was galloping ahead. 'It was you who told Mr Pentire what to say when he was fortune-telling at the fete, wasn't it? You used the information in these letters to brief him, so he'd look like the real thing.'

Dixon looked at the sergeant in surprise. 'Vaughan Pentire was the fortune teller?'

Burrows nodded grimly. 'Yes. Mr Connors has only just seen fit to mention it.'

The WPC looked at Connors like a hungry dog eyeing a bone. 'Well that certainly explains why he was so good. Spookily accurate, they said in the pub. There are rumours he knew stuff that he shouldn't. Especially for someone who'd only been in the village a few months.'

Connors glanced at her, his expression uneasy. 'It was just a bit of fun. The morning of the fete I wrote notes about people on a piece of paper and gave it to him. He never saw the original letters, I just said I'd been in hospital with a fellow from the village who told me loads of gossip.' He smiled. 'He was delighted and said it would put the finishing touch to his performance.'

There was a silence and as Riley and Bull arrived on the stairs the sergeant put two and two together. 'It ended up putting the finishing touch to his life, Mr Connors,' he said. 'I'd heard rumours about the fortune teller too. Everyone thought he'd arrived with the fete and left afterwards, but now we hear it was Mr Pentire. I'd say someone in the village guessed who he was. And he was murdered because that someone was so worried by what he told them, they chose to kill him rather than risk him telling anyone else. Are these all the letters?'

'They're all the ones I've got.'

Certain that he had located the source of the poison pen letter the Misses Rudge had received, Burrows put a large and heavy hand on the valet's shoulder. 'Aiden Connors, I am arresting you on suspicion of blackmail. You'll come down to the police station with me now and we will interview you formally.'

As they moved towards the stairs he paused. 'Wait a moment. That piece of paper with the secrets on it. The one you gave to your master. It wasn't on his body or in his study. What happened to it?'

Connors met his eye and gave a knowing smile. 'I've been wondering that.'

101

When they got back to the police house, faced with the fact of his arrest and clearly upset, the valet made a further statement.

'I didn't tell you everything about Mr Pentire's death. There's something that doesn't show me in a good light, and I don't want to be sucked into a murder enquiry. I've got to earn a living and if my name's in the papers, it wouldn't go so well with new employers, would it?'

Stony-faced, Burrows simply raised his eyebrows so with a deep breath Connors pressed on. 'It was the whisky glasses. The morning we found him I noticed that two of the tumblers were not quite where I'd normally put them. I realised that someone other than me had washed them and put them away.'

'I see. And your conclusion was that Mr Pentire had received a visitor that Thursday night, after you'd gone out?'

'Yes. Normally he'd just leave his glasses in the study or library for me to tidy up. It was almost like he was trying to conceal the fact that someone had come round and then slipped away before I got back.'

'You're sure? About the position of the glasses?'

He nodded firmly. 'I am.'

'Had that happened before?'

'No.'

'And Mr Pentire was not in the habit of entertaining guests?'

'No, he wasn't. Not when I was there anyway.'

'So presumably there would normally just be one glass to clear up the mornings after you'd been to the pub?'

Connors shrugged. 'Not necessarily, if he'd had a drink in the library and another in the study. Or just wanted a fresh glass. That happened.'

'So, it's the washing up that is unusual? That's what you're saying.'

'You don't employ a man then do your own dishes, do you?'

'Do you know who the visitor was?'

'No.' The reply was unequivocal.

Dixon coughed and scratched her nose. Burrows gave her a brief nod. 'Do you suspect you know who it was?' she asked, giving the question a wider perspective.

'Honestly, I don't. He never had visitors. Well, apart from the parson who called in a couple of times soon after we'd moved in. Drumming up business, I suppose.'

'You mentioned something about not showing you in a good light? How do you reach that conclusion? It seems to me you failed to notice a minor detail about the glassware. It's hardly a hanging offence,' Burrows pointed out.

Connors grimaced. 'There's something else. When I go out to the pub, I do have a couple of drinks. They're a pally lot down at the King's Head and I'm sometimes a bit tiddly when I get back.'

'Drunk.' Dixon made a note in her book.

He looked at her. 'I'm just saying I'd had a few.'

'Never mind, carry on.'

'Alright. Well, I got in and it was all exactly as I told you, and I'm sure I locked the back door and checked the front was locked too. But when I went down the following morning the back door was unlocked.'

'Oh really?' Burrows sat up.

'Unlocked,' Dixon repeated, bending over her notebook.

Connors glanced at her uneasily and carried on. 'My immediate thought was that I'd forgotten to lock it. But the thing is, I can remember doing it and then walking down the hall to check the front door. When I went to bed that back door was locked, I'm sure of it. And when I came down at seven o'clock it wasn't.'

He sat back and folded his arms.

103

Dixon looked at him then said, 'And you kept quiet about this because a servant who forgets to lock the back door might not be what a potential new employer is looking for?'

This suggestion elicited a brief nod from the valet. 'If it was ever mentioned in court and reported.' He shrugged meaningfully.

'And the key was in the lock on the kitchen side?' As Connors nodded again, Burrows continued, 'So, what is your explanation?' Although he was fairly sure how matters were looking.

'I reckon someone unlocked it and left the house during the night.'

'I agree, it does look like that. In fact, I'd go further. I'd suggest that when you went to bed, you were sharing the house with a dead body and a live murderer.'

'Blimey.' Connors swallowed.

The sergeant warmed enthusiastically to his theme. 'If what I'm thinking is correct, when you got back from the public house, the perpetrator was locked in the study with the body. He may well have washed the glasses you mentioned, after killing Pentire. Either way, he hears you return, waits for you to lock up and retire then, when he's sure you are asleep, he exits the house by the back door. A door which he cannot relock because the key is on the kitchen side.'

'Why wouldn't he leave earlier? Why wait for me to get back?'

'I don't know.' Burrows scratched his chin. 'Maybe he was worried about meeting you coming in.'

'And how do you reckon he got out of the study and left it all locked up?'

'We don't know that either,' Dixon observed, eliciting a look from her sergeant.

'It's a tough one, that. There's talk in the pub that whatever did it wasn't human.'

104

'Have you ever known a ghost to fire a gun, Mr Connors?' The glare that accompanied this question was not conducive to further conversation, and the sergeant followed up with, 'Lock him in the cell, Constable.'

When Dixon returned, he said to her in an agony of frustration, 'I don't mind telling you, Dixon, this bally locked room mystery is getting my goat. We've no idea how the murderer got out of the study.'

'Well we've got a motive for the killing now, and three clues, Sergeant. There was a light shown late that night by the study window. It appears Mr Pentire had a visitor earlier in the evening, and someone left the house by the back door during the night.'

Burrows looked at her. 'True, but I'm damned if I can join those up in a way that makes any sense at the moment. I'll tell you one thing though.' He gestured at the bag containing the Craig letters. 'I bet the person who killed Vaughan Pentire is one of the people mentioned in there.'

*

Later that day, he called in to Marston House and brought the colonel up to date on the search of the Dower House, Agnes and Terry Craig and the fact that Vaughan Pentire had been the fortune teller.

'It was Pentire? That's a development.' The colonel bristled with excitement, like a terrier spotting a rat. 'So if he was using Connors' crib sheet and someone guessed who he was… well there's your motive, Burrows. Who is mentioned in the letters?'

Burrows handed over a list and the colonel looked down it, his expression becoming more and more gloomy with every second.

'This is damned awkward, Sergeant. Some of these names are people of considerable standing and substance.'

'I understand that, sir. For the moment I'm going to ask Dixon to establish if they had their fortune told at the fete and if they have an alibi for the night of Pentire's death. Once we know that I'll report back. In the meantime I've arrested the valet for blackmailing and he's in the cell, but I don't think he's the murderer. There simply isn't a motive. He was happy with his master and was onto a scheme that was going to make him a tidy sum of money. Why upset the apple cart by killing him?'

The chief constable nodded. 'Agreed.' He looked back down at the list. 'There are people from all over the estate on here. I'll leave you to work out the best way to do it, but if Dixon is going to do most of the leg work, I suggest you teach her how to ride the Matchless. It'll be a lot quicker.'

He paused and then picked up his pen and struck out four names. 'These people are personal friends of mine, it's inconceivable that they are murderers. Tell Dixon to leave them alone.' He handed the piece of paper back and stood up. 'Carry on.'

*

A heavy late-afternoon heat lay over the village as Burrows returned to the police station and addressed his constable.

'We have a task before us, Dixon. Each of the people mentioned in the Craig letters must be visited to see if they had their fortunes told, and if they have an alibi for the night Pentire died. I've made a list and put addresses on it.' He passed it over.

Dixon took the list, quickly scanned down it and hesitated. Coming back from Little Tew she'd realised something obvious and Burrows' list confirmed it. She said tentatively, 'When I read the Craig letters, I noticed the same thing I imagine you did. You know, about the Rudges not being among the people mentioned.'

'Eh?' Burrows looked at her in surprise.

'I'm just wondering why the Rudges received a poison pen letter when there's no letter about them in the ones we found

106

at the Dower House. You'd think there would be one. I'm sorry I didn't notice it earlier.'

Burrows eyed her and after a brief pause said, 'Wait here, would you.' He rose and went downstairs to the cell where the valet currently resided. Five minutes later he reappeared.

'He's sticking to his line about knowing nothing about the poison pen letters. My guess is that once he'd blackmailed the Rudges he burnt that letter so there was no evidence against him. That makes sense, doesn't it, Dixon?'

'It certainly does, Sergeant.'

'Well spotted though. I wondered how long it would take you to notice. You'll also notice that the names of Lord Langford, Giles Stafford, the Reverend Tukes and Captain Perry have been struck through. At the chief constable's instruction. Do not visit them.'

'Right.' She met Burrows' eye and at that moment they heard the front door open, and footsteps enter the room with the counter.

'Hello?' a male voice said hesitantly.

Burrows was nearest the door and stood up, but Dixon sped past, beating him to the counter by a second or two. A man in his Sunday best stood there. A large, plain-looking fellow with tightly curled hair and a pleasant if rather nervous expression.

'Hello, Hector,' said the WPC in a voice that Burrows had not heard emanating from her before. Although he recognised the tone. When his wife used it, it generally meant he was in for a pleasant evening.

'Evening, Mabel.' Hector eyed Burrows nervously and twisted his cap. 'You did say six o'clock.'

'Mr Dean,' the sergeant said. 'What can we do for you?'

Dixon turned to him. 'I was planning on having a walk with Mr Dean, if that's alright, Sergeant. And maybe a drink at the Black Horse?'

107

She put the question to Hector with her eyes and he nodded enthusiastically. 'Oh aye, it's certainly warm enough for a pint or two.'

Feeling oddly protective of his WPC, Burrows did a quick mental assessment of Hector Dean. He was the foreman at one of the larger farms on the Langford estate and had a good reputation as far as he knew. And had served in the Oxfords and been mentioned in despatches. A sound man. 'I see, well I'm sure what we were discussing will wait, but please get straight to it in the morning.'

She grinned her thanks and, from what Burrows could see, gave her beau a look of considerable encouragement before saying to him, 'I'll be ten minutes,' and disappearing upstairs.

The sergeant indicated the bench and said, 'Wait there then, Mr Dean,' and retired to the office where he stared at an article about a new design of handcuffs in the *Police Gazette* with a singular lack of concentration.

WPC Dixon, walking out? What was he to make of that?

Finally, a clattering on the stairs indicated the re-arrival of the lady in question and she poked her head around the door to call out, 'Just off then, Sergeant. I'll start first thing.'

Burrows glanced up, swallowed and nodded, his eyes firmly back on the *Police Gazette*. But there was no escaping the truth. The valley of death was putting in another appearance and for a forbidden moment his imagination dwelled on the image of her hurrying down the stairs. But as the door slammed, he turned with firm resolve to the Mafeking Mark Three Wrist Restraint and its many qualities.

*

Later on at Lea House a conversation took place as the sergeant and his wife retired to bed.

'I believe WPC Dixon is walking out,' he remarked.

'What!' Laura's eyes gleamed with interest. Even though she had inspected her husband's new colleague, and concluded that she presented no threat, the chatter circulating around the village about *that dress* had given her pause for thought. To the extent that she had instructed Beatrice Wray in the Black Horse to telephone her if it put in another appearance, so she could have a discreet look and reassess matters.

Therefore, the news that the garment had worked was noteworthy. And if she was honest, something of a relief.

'And who is the lucky fellow, may I ask?' she continued.

'Hector Dean. Foreman at Heys Farm.'

'Do you approve?'

This tricky and rather laden question gave her husband pause for thought. 'He's alright, I think. You have to be careful though, as a police officer. About that sort of thing.'

'About that sort of thing?' A merry laugh sounded in the bedroom. 'You certainly do. As I recall you were in danger of being a lifelong bachelor until I intervened.'

'Yes, well I trod pretty carefully until I was sure.'

Smiling, she slid her arms around his neck and said quietly, 'Oh really, Sergeant? As I recall, you were a quick and rather enthusiastic convert. Once you realised the finer points of what was involved.'

It was the second time he'd heard that tone of voice that day and his previous inference was subsequently proved correct.

As for WPC Dixon, she returned to the police house at about half past eleven, gently kissed Hector Dean goodbye on the cheek at the door and made herself a cup of tea. She'd been married before and now her grief had passed, she realised that she had been given a chance to make a more informed choice about a new life partner.

Aware that she was no siren, eighteen-year-old Mabel Dixon had jumped at the first man who'd shown an interest and had gradually realised that her husband wasn't quite what she had been led to believe. Although he had died a patriotic death, his life had been dogged by petty crime and gambling. The marriage had not been dreadful, just disappointing, and in her more honest moments, she acknowledged that she was happier now than she would have been if her husband had returned from the war.

Sometimes she wondered if she was alone in that sentiment. Many, many wives had been heartbroken to receive the dreaded brown envelope. But a good few, she suspected, had not.

She carried her tea through to the parlour and sat down to review the evening. Hector Dean had a bit of pluck, she had to acknowledge that. He had come up to her while she was standing in uniform by the market cross and introduced himself, then started talking.

It had taken her a moment to realise that he was not addressing her as a policewoman.

'… so anyway, I'm on my own in my cottage and I've got a good job with prospects, and I noticed you, Mrs Dixon. I noticed you and thought, "she looks nice". So, I've come here now, to ask you if you'd like to have a walk out with me one time to see if we might be suited. To see if we like each other.'

And she had looked at his big frame and his friendly and rather anxious brown eyes, and agreed that, 'Yes, I think that could be arranged, Mr Dean'.

They had walked up the track to the top of Tan Hill and told each other a bit about their lives. She had explained about her husband's death and asked about his own war service. He had joined the Oxfords when conscription was introduced and arrived at the front just in time for the slaughter at Delville Wood. Emerging unscathed, he had managed to survive the war and returned to his job in 1920.

'Eighteen months they kept us in uniform, after the ceasefire. Stuck in France. There was a lot of ill-feeling about that,' he remarked.

'They were worried about so many men used to extreme violence arriving back at the same time, I think, Hector.' In fact, she knew that to be the case. There had been briefings about it in the Oxford police.

After their walk they'd repaired to the Black Horse and sat in a corner of the snug bar away from too many prying eyes. And it had been nice. Very nice. She sipped her tea thoughtfully and decided that Hector Dean would be given further opportunities to present his credentials. And the fact that she was living alone in the police house would be a considerable help in that regard.

Chapter Nine

As Mabel Dixon was reflecting on her evening, Beatrice Wray and Ronnie Back were lying entwined on a mossy bank deep in the Promised Land. It was midnight, still warm, and the moon's glow gave every leaf a spellbinding silver gilding. To Ronnie, as he stared upwards through the trees with the girl of his dreams in his arms, it put the final flourish on an exceptional evening.

He had already decided to marry Trixie, if she'd have him. It was just a question of when to pop the question and, as a sudden wild exhilaration engulfed him, he realised the moment was now. *On this magical night.*

Without hesitating he said, 'I love you, Beatrice Wray. I really do. Will you marry me?'

He felt her jump in his arms, and she wriggled to her knees and looked down at him, a wide smile on her face. 'Are you sure, Ronnie? It's for life, you know.'

In the preceding half hour Trixie had folded her dress down to her waist and as she leaned over him, her pale skin bathed in moonlight, he was never so sure of anything in his life. He rolled onto his knees and faced her. 'I want to be with you for the rest of my life. I swear it.'

Eyes warm, she took his hand and said, 'And you'll look after me and provide for our family, in the future?'

'That I will, I'll be a solicitor in three years. We'll be alright then.'

'Then yes, Mr Ronnie Back, I will be your wife.' Eyes wide with invitation she lay back down on the bank and then her face clouded. 'Ouch!' She felt underneath her hip and grasped a stone. But when she held it up the moonlight caught it and she saw it was glistening.

'What's this then?' she asked.

He peered at her hand. 'It's an empty bullet casing. I found it ages ago. It must have been in my pocket.' He indicated his discarded trousers.

'It says Mauser on the bottom. Where did you find it?'

'Oh, somewhere over towards Little Tew. Never mind that.' Grinning, he leaned over her, but she put her hand on his chest.

'Just a minute, Ronnie. They said that Mr Pentire had been killed by a Mauser. That's the gun they found.'

He looked at her. 'Really?'

'Yes, they were talking about it in the pub. A German officer's gun, they said.'

He nodded. 'I heard some shots before I found the bullet. A bit too familiar, they were.'

'You better tell Sergeant Burrows. Just in case.'

'Yes, yes alright. Come on now, Trixie.'

But she maintained the pressure on his chest. 'Promise me you will, alright?'

'I promise.' He took the casing and tossed it over to his trousers, then turned back to her. 'Now then, what about this?'

She looked down and giggled. 'Alright, Ronnie. As he's asking so nicely.'

*

The ardent young man was in the office in Banbury all the following day, but when the bus dropped him off at the market cross, he strolled up Dell Lane, entered the police station and rang

113

the bell on the counter. WPC Dixon appeared in her uniform blouse and chewing. The smell of fried bacon drifted through from the back.

'Yes?' she enquired.

'Sorry to catch you at your tea,' said Ronnie, 'I've got something for you.' He placed the casing on the counter with something of a flourish.

She picked it up and turned it over in her hand. 'A Mauser bullet casing?'

'That's it. A German officer's gun.'

'And you came by it how, exactly?'

'I found it in Lye Cross woods a couple of days after the fete.'

She looked at him thoughtfully. 'Why are you bringing it in now?'

'Someone told me that Mr Pentire had been shot with a Mauser. They're unusual round here. British officers had Webleys, so I just thought…' He tailed off and shrugged.

'Where exactly did you find it?'

'It's off the path. I'd have to show you.'

'What were you doing over there?'

'Let's not get into all that. Do you want it or not?' As a trainee solicitor Ronnie was not at all keen to have his rabbit snares exposed to the law. In fact, as he stood there, he made a mental note to ask Bert Williams to look after them from now on.

'Yes, it may be of interest. Can you come back in the morning, and we'll go over to the woods, and you can show me exactly where it was?'

Ronnie nodded. 'Yes, if you like.' And with that he set off for the Williams' cottage. Bert was at home and in a few short sentences he offered him the snares.

Bert looked interested. It was a good spot, by the warren, and had been handed down to Ronnie by his dad. 'Why are you letting them go?' he asked, curious.

'I'm training to be a solicitor. I can't be involved in that sort of thing any more.'

'What sort of thing?'

'It is illegal, you know. They're Lord Langford's rabbits.'

Bert scratched his chest vigorously and remarked, 'Really? I had no idea.'

'Well do you want them or not? Because if you do, you'll have to have them moved by half past ten tomorrow morning because I'll be over there with the police.'

The poacher looked even more interested. 'Why's that then?'

'I found something over there. A bullet casing, they want to have a look.'

'Oh yes?'

Within a few short minutes Bert had extracted the tale from Ronnie, agreed to take over the snares for a fee of one good rabbit a fortnight, and promised to move them before the inspection the following day.

*

The heavily laden Matchless drew to a halt as indicated by Ronnie and he climbed off the back as Dixon squeezed out of the sidecar and Burrows swung his leg over the saddle. They were parked on a sloping grassy track overhung by green branches. On the right, a steep bank topped by a high hedge of hawthorn and blackthorn rose like a leafy wall, leaving a narrow sky-blue ribbon below the trees. Dense woodland lay to their left, with a narrow path twisting into it.

It was a remote spot and when a sudden breeze moved the branches it seemed to Ronnie as if their arrival had disturbed the scene in some way. *As though something had been happening.* With a slight shiver he pointed to the path. 'Along there.'

Ten minutes later he stopped and looked around. 'It was about here that I heard the shots.'

'What!' Both police officers were staring at him. 'You heard gunfire?' Burrows said.

'Not half. Three of them. Brought it all back, I can tell you. I had my face in the ground before you could say basket case.'

'Was someone shooting at you?'

'No, I soon realised it was far off. Where I found the casing, I presume.'

'Did you see anyone?'

'No. Oh, hang on, Xanthe Rudge was out bird-spotting. I met her and she had a good sounding off about whoever it was. She'd been watching goldfinches.'

'What were you doing here, Mr Back?' Dixon asked.

'Just having a walk. Shall we press on.' He strode off and shortly afterwards led them off the path and through the undergrowth. Finally, he stopped and had a surreptitious glance around. There were no snares in sight.

'Just here, I reckon it was.' He smiled disarmingly and gestured in a half circle with his hand.

'Where exactly? Show us, please.'

He walked over to the tree and pointed downwards. 'Just here, by the root.'

'Alright, wait there, will you?'

He watched as the two police officers conducted a thorough search of the ground for a twenty-foot radius. Finally, with a grunt of satisfaction, Burrows held up another casing, like a prospector finding a nugget of gold. 'That's two.'

'There are no footprints, Sergeant,' Dixon said. 'It's too dry.'

'No. And there were definitely three shots, Mr Back?'

'Yes.'

'So, what were they shooting at?' he wondered aloud.

'There's a rabbit warren over here,' Dixon called from the top of the bank. 'Perhaps they were having a pot shot or two.'

116

He nodded. 'That must be it. Alright, we'll head back.'

But as they trooped back through the undergrowth, Ronnie Back had his doubts. Any countryman would know you didn't hunt coneys with a heavy pistol. They'd be blown apart. Which only meant one thing.

Whoever had been in Lye Cross woods that afternoon hadn't been shooting at rabbits.

After Ronnie had been thanked and sent on his way, Dixon asked, 'Could it have been Mr Pentire himself, in the woods with the gun?'

Burrows thought for a moment. 'It's possible, but I'm more inclined to believe it was the murderer. I'm pretty convinced that whoever fired those shots used the same gun to put a bullet into Pentire's head, then left it there staged to look like a suicide. We'll ask the police armourer to compare the bullets to see if they came from the same gun.'

*

Late on Saturday, Eve kissed her husband goodnight and told him to turn the light out when he was ready, then got out of bed and climbed the stairs towards the attic at Marston House. As she reached the door, a soft voice called up from the landing.

'Are you alright?' She turned to see Jocelyn standing in the light from the front window. He looked anxious. 'You just seem a bit preoccupied. I've noticed it over the last day or two,' he added quietly.

She smiled. He knew her so well. 'I am a little, if truth be told. But it's nothing to worry about.'

If he had hoped for more, he was to be disappointed and after a short silence he nodded. 'Very well, but be careful, Eve.' He held her gaze and could see the tension on her face. 'You're sure?'

'I've been having a rather odd dream and it needs further examination.' She shrugged and smiled down at him. 'It'll be fine. Go to bed, my darling, I won't be long.' With that she turned, unlocked the door with the only key in the house and let herself in.

The room was tucked under the eaves, with two dormer windows that cast pale squares of moonlight onto the Turkish rug and threw shadows into the corners. In the gloom a chaise-longue was just visible against one wall. After a few minutes preparation she was ready. In the middle of the room a large and very beautiful shallow bowl was filled with water and surrounded by four candles. An embroidered cushion lay before it, next to another smaller bowl filled with the ashes of some herbs she had burned.

With the heady smell of rosemary and sage drifting in the semi-darkness Eve sat down on the cushion and gathered her thoughts. Because her husband was right. She was uneasy. Over recent weeks she had had the same disturbing dream three times. In it she was surrounded by flames that crackled and roared. She knew she should run away but for some reason she couldn't. It was frightening and she needed to know what it meant.

Concentrating, she cleared her mind, closed her eyes and began to chant the familiar words. Words in an ancient language that few in England recognised, except for Eve and her kind – adepts whose natural abilities and knowledge enabled them to use the power they held.

After five minutes of rhythmic chanting she stopped, opened her eyes and leaned over the still water in the bowl. The light from the nearest candles showed like two suns floating on the surface and her face became slack as she fixed her gaze between them and let her mind drift.

Show me the burning. What is it?

Slowly she became aware of a flickering light. It started twenty feet away to her right then crept inexorably towards her, building all the time. A combination of flames and thick black smoke which caught in her throat. She tried to move away but

118

found her feet were rooted to the floor. Moments later she was surrounded by a wall of flame that closed in from all angles.

And then the pain started. A terrible burning, first in her feet, then her legs. Intense, agonising. She felt her hair singe and frantically tried to retreat back to the reality of the attic but as panic consumed her, the words wouldn't come. Just a terrible choking in the smoke and heat. She struggled and realised to her horror she was tied to a post. And she was going to die.

In the distance she heard a voice. A familiar voice.

'Eve, Eve, come back. You're alright, you're safe.' The words broke through and with a brutal emotional tearing, she was ripped away from the conflagration and found herself back in Marston House, gripped firmly in the arms of her beloved husband.

'You were screaming,' he said, his mouth close to her ear. 'Really screaming.' Dimly she registered footsteps thumping on the wooden stairs and Ellie and Mrs Franks appeared simultaneously at the doorway. Both were wearing dressing gowns.

'Are you alright, madam?' Ellie cried, real concern in her voice. 'We heard you from downstairs.'

'Yes. Yes, I'm fine, thank you.' She reached up and laid her hand over her husband's as he held her protectively in an embrace.

'Are you sure?' he murmured.

She nodded. Then said more firmly, her confidence returning, 'It was a bad experience. I was caught in some kind of fire and couldn't get away. Thank you, you can go back to bed.' She smiled her appreciation at the servants, and they disappeared.

'Back to bed for you too, Eve,' Jocelyn said. 'But perhaps a nightcap first.'

She descended the steps unsteadily and he helped her under the sheets before going downstairs and returning with two generous measures of brandy. They sat together and she explained

119

what had happened. He listened in silence, concern on his face. When she'd finished, she took his hand and added, 'Don't worry. I'm not sure what it means but not everything in the places that I go to is relevant to me or our lives. It's like walking through an unknown land and it can be very easy to take a wrong turning. I'm quite recovered now, and we'll put it behind us.'

He grunted and said, 'Well if you're sure, but do be careful, Eve.'

She leaned over and kissed him. 'Of course. Goodnight, sweet man. And don't worry.'

But as he switched off the light and she turned away from him, her face wore a grave expression and she lay awake and unmoving for a long time.

Chapter Ten

Outside Langford Hall, Lord Langford and his mother descended the main steps to greet the returning honeymooners. Jaikie simply ran down them and flung himself into Innes's arms as Fenn opened the back door and she climbed out.

Lady Langford gave her a quick assessing look and was delighted. Suntanned, clear-eyed and bursting with health and joy, her new daughter-in-law was clearly a very happy woman. And if she was any judge, her grinning husband was in the same fine fettle. She relaxed, the postcards hadn't lied, the honeymoon had been a success.

Amid much noisy chatter and laughter, the little crowd ascended the steps, crossed the hall and came to rest in the drawing room.

'Now you must tell us all about it,' Piers said, 'and perhaps we'll have a bottle of champagne to celebrate the happy return of the travellers.' He nodded to Dereham who smiled and disappeared.

'You must bring us up to date as well.' Innes laughed as her beloved son wriggled ecstatically in her arms. 'At least you had a postcard or two, we've heard nothing from you at all.'

As one bottle of champagne turned into two and the homecoming celebrations stretched into dinner and beyond, it was past eight o'clock before Innes returned from putting Jaikie to bed and sat down in the drawing room again.

'Tell me, what was the outcome of the death of Mr Pentire, Piers?' she asked as her husband and Claire chatted away.

He shrugged. 'It remains unresolved. The police believe it was murder but cannot work out how the perpetrator escaped from the study. Burrows is looking more and more lugubrious but is getting nowhere.

'Golly, you'd think it would have all been sorted out by now.'

Lord Langford nodded thoughtfully, his eyes curiously distant. 'One would indeed,' he replied.

*

Two days later news on Ronnie's bullet casing came through. It had been fired by the same Mauser that had killed Vaughan Pentire and they'd found half a fingerprint that matched those on the bullets in the gun.

So, there was no doubt in the sergeant's mind that the murderer had been in Lye Cross woods that day, and he privately thought Ronnie Back and Xanthe Rudge might have had a very narrow escape.

The following Sunday brought further developments. Acting on a hunch Burrows had despatched Dixon back to the Rudges to enquire if they had been fully truthful about paying the blackmailer. He was not surprised when she returned with the news that they had indeed paid up, depositing twenty pounds in a tin in an old barn near the summit of Tan Hill. Discussing this they had both realised that if Connors had then burned the letter from Mrs Craig about the Rudges, then he may well have burned other letters too.

'It follows that our suspect list may not be definitive, Dixon,' Burrows had observed. 'There may be other people who have been blackmailed and are therefore suspects that we don't know about.'

'How are we going to find them?' his constable had asked.

The net result of this tricky problem was that at the conclusion of the Sunday service the Reverend Tukes made an announcement.

'Before you go, I'd just like to mention one other thing,' he said. 'And it is a difficult matter, concerning sin.' As sin was an area of considerable interest and expertise in the village, this captured the attention of everyone. 'We are all God's children and as we know, temptation is part of our make-up. We are given the ability to make choices for ourselves and sometimes we choose well and sometimes we do not.'

The pained expression on the parson's face was so noticeable that Bert Williams nudged his wife and whispered, 'What's he been up to then?'

'He's talking about you, I reckon,' she retorted. 'Shut up and listen.'

Up in the pulpit Tukes pressed on. 'After all, who can say they have led an entirely blameless life? And the question is, if we have sinned, should we be punished for it? Should another man sit in judgement on us? Is that really fair?'

'Why don't you ask His Lordship?' a voice came from the back. 'He had no problem judging me.'

Tukes fixed him with a beady eye. 'I'm talking in a philosophical sense, Alan Farthing, and, as I understand it, you were carrying a bag full of trout at two o'clock in the morning. Bang to rights is the phrase, I believe.' He gathered his thoughts as a ripple of laughter sounded in the ancient church.

'In a recent conversation with the chief constable I was made aware of the fact that some unfortunate souls who live locally have received what I believe are termed, poison pen letters.' This statement had an electrifying effect on the people below him.

123

They literally all sat up as though a strong current had been passed along the pews.

'What?' someone called.

'I understand your shock, and it is a matter of great sadness that an individual appears to have chosen to profit from others' mistakes in this way. Money has been demanded in exchange for silence.' At this point he had to pause, as a burst of speculative conversation engulfed the pulpit like a raging sea.

Letting it run for thirty seconds, he then held up his hand and called, 'Ladies and gentlemen, your attention, please.' Slowly the hubbub faded and in the silence he continued, 'As the recipients of these letters are understandably reluctant to discuss the matter with anyone, it is difficult for the police to get a measure of the scale of the problem. So, my reason for mentioning this is to say that if you have received such a letter, or do so in the future, please either tell myself or report it to the police station.'

'Fat chance,' Nobby Griffin's wife whispered to her neighbour. 'Who's goin' to admit they've got a nasty secret?' This opinion was supported by a firm nod from the woman next to her.

'Plenty do though, Bridget,' she replied with a sideways glance.

'I can assure you neither myself nor the authorities are interested in the contents of the letters, we simply want to know if you have received one,' Tukes concluded.

This final remark was received with a hefty dose of scepticism by the assembled congregation and in an increasingly febrile atmosphere, they trooped out of St Mary's and spread out in the warm sunlight, forming little groups amongst the gravestones. For once no one approached Tukes for a chat and with a heavy heart he realised that his announcement might have caused more trouble than it was designed to solve.

'What have I done?' he enquired quietly of the colonel, who had ambled over wearing a wry smile.

'That's certainly put the cat amongst the pigeons,' he observed, glancing round. 'I'm afraid you've terrified them.'

'Terrified them? How so?'

'Oh, they've all got secrets. And you've just told them that someone else on the estate might know what they are.'

As the import of this struck him, the usually mild parson muttered, 'For heaven's sake, Jocelyn, I said what I said at your request. I was trying to help the police.'

'Oh, you may well have done that, padre. I wouldn't be surprised if someone sidles up to you in a quiet moment and admits they've had one.' He ran his eye across the churchyard. 'But I must admit I wasn't expecting quite so much of a reaction. I shudder to think what they're all worried about, I really do. We're better off not knowing in most cases.'

On the far side of the churchyard Innes noticed Eve trying to catch her eye as she and Edward stood chatting to a couple from one of the farms up the valley. Excuse me,' she said with a smile and walked over.

'Well? How was it?' The older woman asked with a smile.

'Rather wonderful, actually,' she replied. Then she frowned. 'Is everything all right, Eve? You look rather tired, if you don't mind me saying.'

Silently Eve took her arm and they moved away from the crowd before coming to a halt at the low wall above the steep slope that ran down to the River Cherwell. The view across the valley was glorious and it was a special place for Innes. The exact spot where, over two years earlier, she and Edward had had their first private conversation after a disastrous dinner party the night before.

'I've got a slightly tricky favour to ask you,' Eve said.

'Yes? Well I'll always help if I can, you know that.'

Eve glanced down at Innes's left hand where the famous Langford Ring sparkled in the sunlight, a great diamond surrounded by five rubies set in ancient copper-coloured gold. It was known to be a thousand years old and may well have been much older.

'I need to borrow your ring.' Eve said it simply, but Innes could feel the tension behind the request.

'Really? Do you mind me asking why? Only it's in my charge now and if I lost it the consequences would be beyond awful.'

Eve nodded. 'I know. It would be in my care and would not leave the estate. As to why I need it…' She hesitated, and her friend saw real turmoil in the eyes. She put her hand on the older woman's arm. 'Is something wrong?'

'I've been having a rather unpleasant premonition. I need the ring to find out why. I'm sorry to ask and I do understand its importance, but to people like me it's not just historic. It has other qualities.'

And it used to be mine. Three hundred years ago. Now I need it again.

'Would it be for long? Only Edward would probably notice, and Claire certainly would. Within minutes.'

Silently Eve nodded, seeing the anxiety in the young woman's face. She glanced over to where the crowd was starting to disperse. Edward was now on his own and looking round for his wife. She leaned towards her friend and said quietly, 'At the next full moon. I'll come to the study door at the hall at half past eleven at night and collect you. We will go to a certain place, and I will use the ring to do a certain thing. You can be there. Then, when I've finished you can take the ring back and we'll return to the hall together. It will never be out of your sight. Is that alright?'

Surprised and a little alarmed at the intensity of her friend's delivery, Innes nodded. 'Yes, very well. The study door at half past eleven. And you're sure the ring will be safe?'

126

'I guarantee it.'

*

'Morning, Dixon. How are you getting on?' said the colonel as he arrived at the police house the following Wednesday.

'Very well, sir, thank you.'

'And you've got yourself a young man, I believe? Well that didn't take long, but I'm pleased to hear it. As I recall telling the sergeant here, the villagers like their police officers to be settled and Hector Dean is a solid fellow.' He gave her an encouraging smile.

Dixon flushed with embarrassment. 'I'm not sure we're at that stage yet. It's very early days.'

The colonel seemed surprised. 'Really? They've almost got you married off in the Black Horse, but I'm sure you know better than them.' Sitting down on the most comfortable chair he addressed Burrows. 'Anyone come in and report a poison pen letter?'

'Not so far, sir, no.'

'Well Tukes has had one. He came round last night and told me. Got it a week after the murder apparently.'

'Golly,' Burrows replied.

'Quite. He paid up as well. Twenty pounds into a tin in the old barn on Tan Hill. I thought he looked a bit peaky when he was addressing the congregation on the same matter last Sunday. How are your enquiries going with the suspect list, Dixon?'

'I'm making progress, sir, but it's taking time because people are out working in the fields and so on.'

'Right, well as quickly as you can, please. Burrows, sum up where you've got to, will you. Start from the beginning.'

'Well, as you know, sir, Vaughan Pentire was killed on the fifteenth of July, roughly three and a half weeks after the fete at which he played a starring role as a remarkably good fortune teller. We believe that one of the people who visited him became so

127

alarmed at his knowledge of their secrets that they decided to kill him.'

'The three-week gap, presumably being the period during which they came to a decision and worked their courage up?'

'One assumes so, yes. Although there must have been quite a lot of planning and preparation involved too. The scene in the study was carefully designed to look as though Pentire had taken his own life – right down to a remorseful note in his own handwriting.'

The colonel stroked his chin. 'How did the perpetrator get him to write that?'

'As of now, we have no idea, sir. I'm sorry. The truth is we also have no idea how he then managed to spirit himself out of the study. Although it does appear someone used the back door to leave the house as that became mysteriously unlocked during the night, according to Connors.'

A cough and nose scratch from the WPC produced a brief nod from Burrows. 'Bert Williams reported seeing the flash of a torch on the study window late that night. We think it's very likely it was the murderer, but we haven't worked out what they were up to.'

'Was it inside the study, or out on the lawn?'

'On the lawn, Bert thinks, but he's not certain.'

Her superior eyed Dixon unencouragingly. Burrows hastened on.

'Pentire's man, Connors, is convinced that his master received a visitor that night, and that the pair of them tried to conceal the visit by washing the glasses they used.'

'So you have a mysterious light at the window, an unknown visitor, and a back door that unlocks itself in the middle of the night. But you still have no idea how the murderer got out of the study?'

A pained look crossed Burrows' face, but he chose not to answer, instead saying, 'There's something else. Two days after the

128

fete Ronnie Back found a bullet casing in Lye Cross woods after he heard someone shooting. It was from the same gun that killed Mr Pentire.'

'The Mauser? What were they firing at?'

'At this precise moment we're not sure, sir.'

The colonel looked distinctly unimpressed. 'So four clues in total, but no way to connect them. What about the crib sheet that Connors wrote for Pentire to use when he was fortune-telling. Has that been found?'

'No, it's completely disappeared. It wasn't on the body and is not in the Dower House. We believe the murderer stole it and is now using its contents to send the poison pen letters.'

The chief constable frowned and said, 'I thought Connors was the blackmailer?'

Dixon said, 'For the first letter, to the Misses Rudge, yes, sir. That arrived some time before the fete and we're sure it was sent by Connors in an attempt to extort money from them. But the remainder of the letters have been received since Mr Pentire's murder and coincide with the disappearance of the crib sheet. The valet has been under investigation since the murder, he'd hardly be sending out blackmail letters at the moment. Hence our conclusion.'

'So whoever killed Pentire is now writing the poison pen letters.' The chief constable nodded to himself, then said, 'Realistically, what are the chances of convicting Connors for writing that first poison pen letter to the Misses Rudge?'

Burrows slowly shook his head. 'It's all conjecture really, sir. He flatly refuses to admit anything at all and there's no proof. The letter was typed but we didn't find a typewriter in the Dower House, although he could have got rid of that easily enough. And any other fingerprints on the letter have been overlaid by the Rudges themselves when they handled it. There's simply no real evidence.'

'No other fingerprints at all?'

129

'Nothing. I imagine they've looked at it many times.'

The colonel nodded. 'Yes, I'll bet they have, the poor women. Look, I think we have bigger fish to fry here, Sergeant. Let Connors out and tell him to stay in the village for the moment, but otherwise focus on finding the murderer. Agreed?'

'Very well, sir.'

Chapter Eleven

After four weeks working on the Greenock ferry Cameron Breck had enough money in his pocket to continue his research and caught the train to Dumfries. Once there, he visited the town library and consulted the electoral role. There were seven addresses in the town that had the surname Knox attached to them. None had the prefix 'Doctor', so he assumed that wherever she was practising, it wasn't in Dumfries, but there was reasonable chance that one of the addresses contained her parents.

Writing them down, he decided that the simplest thing would be to visit each one. With no danger of meeting their daughter he felt he could concoct a reasonable story that might elicit a location and address for her. Accordingly, having secured cheap digs, the following morning he set off armed with directions to the first house from his landlady.

And he struck gold at the third address.

Cambridge Close was a tidy cul-de-sac of brown stone bungalows on the southern side of the town. He guessed the gardens must have a view of the River Nith from the rear and imagined it was a nice place to spend a retirement. Arriving at

131

number twenty he walked up the short, paved path and knocked on the door.

There was a sound of movement inside and then a woman in her early sixties appeared. One look at her luminous blue-grey eyes was all it took for the memories to flood back. Suddenly Breck was sure he was in the right place.

'May I help you?' she enquired pleasantly.

'Mrs Knox, is it?'

'Aye.' She nodded.

'My name's Cameron Breck, I'm an old friend of Innes's, from the university. I was hoping to catch up with her. Does she stay here?'

'From the university?' The woman was staring at his red hair, a curious expression on her face. 'Were you studying to be a doctor too?'

'Aye, that's right, I'm working out on the islands now.'

There was a pause, then she said, 'On the islands? So what brings you to Dumfries, Mr Breck?'

'Well as I say, I'm hoping to reconnect with Innes.'

'You've made a special trip?' A note of surprise infused the woman's voice.

'I was in town for other reasons and remembered she said she was born here. I asked around and here I am.' He gave her a warm smile, but inside Breck was cursing quietly; why was everyone so infernally curious?

'Born here? Is that so.'

A man appeared behind her and gave him a nod. 'Morning.'

'Good morning, sir,' Breck replied.

'Rory, this is Mr Breck, a friend of Innes's from the university. He's just in town and looked in to try and catch up with her. She explained she was born here in Dumfries.'

'Oh yes?' The man nodded slowly. 'Well, she's working down south in England, Mr Breck. We're expecting a letter soon

132

from her with her new address, but we can't let you have one just now, I'm afraid.'

'Ach, I was hoping to drop her a line, you know.'

'Of course, well why don't you come in and write her a note. We'll be happy to forward it to her once we know where she is staying. Give her your address so she can reply direct.'

Presented with this inarguable logic, Breck had no option but to allow himself to be ushered into a study where a desk and writing paper stood waiting. Five minutes later he emerged and handed Mr Knox a sealed envelope with *Innes* on the front and underlined.

'There you go.' The older man took the letter. 'This should be in her hands by early next week and I'm sure she'll write back straight away.'

With a further exchange of pleasantries, he passed down the hallway, said his goodbyes and left.

As he turned out onto the road Mr Knox shut the front door firmly and looked at his wife. The blood had drained from her face.

'It was him, wasn't it?' She stared at her husband. 'The red hair, the face. Just like Jaikie.' She raised her hand to her mouth. 'My God, Rory, will it never end?'

Looking ashen himself, Mr Knox held up the note. 'Should I open it? Or burn it?'

She hesitated, indecision clear on her face. 'No. I'll write a note and send it on as we said. He clearly doesn't know where she is, and we won't be the ones to tell him. But she must know. We must warn her.'

'What does he want, do you think? And how could he know about the boy? He must be guessing, surely.'

His wife looked at him. 'Who knows? But he has no idea how close to hitting the jackpot he is. He simply mustn't find her, it'll be disastrous.'

Mr Knox nodded. 'There was something about him, wasn't there? Not a good feeling.'

She stared through the front door as though watching him depart. 'No, Rory, I don't think he's a very nice man at all.'

Consumed with anger and frustration, the young man in question walked slowly down Cambridge Close to the corner where a post box was embedded in the wall. Once out of sight he stood and wondered what to do.

Innes's parents had lied. He was sure of that. There was something about her that they wished to hide, and he was determined to get to the truth. The letter he had given them contained a blank sheet of paper. He had nothing to say to the girl until he met her and could see no reason to forewarn her.

Would they send it on?

On balance he thought they probably would. They were fundamentally honest people even if they had clearly been dissembling as he stood on the front doorstep. What would they do now? He imagined they would discuss his visit over a cup of tea. And stare at the envelope he had left. Perhaps even speculate about its contents. Then one of them would sit down and write a note to Innes and enclose it.

He looked at the post box. It was the one at the end of their road. The one they would inevitably use. He stared at the label on the front, then glanced at his watch. The next collection was at seven o'clock the following morning. He was willing to bet that by then, the letter to Innes would be lying in there.

And that letter would have her address on it.

A chilling coolness ran through his body. There was no doubt in his mind about what he had to do.

*

Don Lang was sixty-five years old and, with a long career in the Dumfries postal service behind him, was looking forward to retirement. Five years earlier, recognising that his best days on foot and bicycle were behind him, the manager at the sorting

134

office had put him in charge of one of the vans that they used for collections and deliveries, and at seven o'clock in the morning it pulled up at the end of Cambridge Close, the first stop of his round.

He dismounted from the van carrying an empty sack and, jingling his keyring cheerfully, approached the post box. Then he paused and frowned. A low groan had sounded close by. He looked around but could see no one.

But the noise sounded again, and he walked ten feet to the end of the wall and peered round the corner into a little copse that lay behind it. A second later he started in surprise then said, 'Are you alright there, son?'

A young man was sitting propped up against a tree, his legs stretched out. He peered blurrily at the postman and said, 'Can you help me, I've been robbed.'

'Robbed!' The postman hurried forward and dropped the sack onto the ground, throwing the keyring onto it. He knelt next to the man, concern clear in his eyes. 'What happened? Were you attacked?'

'Aye, rather like this.'

He swung his left hand, which had been lying concealed along his body, and hit the postman on the head with a half-brick. It was a vicious blow, and the older man uttered a hollow moan then dropped to the ground. As crimson blood welled up from his temple, his cap tumbled off and rolled across the grass.

Ignoring him, Cameron Breck leapt to his feet and ran to the corner of the wall. It was still early and the only people in sight were a couple approaching on the other side of the road, a hundred yards away. He eyed them for a second then made up his mind and ran back to his unconscious victim. He grabbed the keys and the sack and, after a moment's hesitation, the cap, which he jammed on his head.

Ten seconds later he was inserting the key into the post box. About twenty letters lay in the bottom of the wire container and he quickly loaded them into the sack then straightened up and shut the box. He walked quickly back into the trees. The old man was stirring and Breck didn't hesitate. Picking up the half-brick he hit him again and the postman subsided without a sound. Satisfied, he knelt down and emptied the sack onto the ground. Quickly he sorted through the letters, looking for one addressed to Innes Knox, but to his intense frustration none of them matched what he was looking for.

A man's voice suddenly sounded from the road.

'Where's Don got to then? Here's his van and, see there, the box isn't shut properly.'

Breck cursed silently, realising that the two people he had seen probably often met the postie in the morning. He could imagine they would stop for a brief chat. He glanced down. The man had a stillness about him that he recognised from the war. He'd seen dead men lying on the deck of HMS *Clarion* and wondered if he'd killed him.

Frantically he stuffed the letters back into the sack as a woman said, 'Have a look behind the wall, Jim.'

'I'll no' interrupt the poor man if he's having a riddle, woman,' the male voice retorted.

But his companion was persistent and with a grumble, the man conceded and Breck sensed him walking towards the corner. He looked around, the trees did not offer enough cover and he would be spotted. He crept to the corner and, as the man appeared, swung his fist straight into his face. Blood spurted from his nose, and he reeled backwards with a cry. Breck turned and sprinted away, the woman's panicked voice calling, 'Jim, what's happened!' following him through the trees.

Half an hour later in the privacy of a deserted alley behind a warehouse he was able to have another look at the contents of the post box. He was certain that Mr and Mrs Knox would have written to their daughter but, as he carefully studied each name and address, it became very obvious that hers was absent.

Frustrated, he put the sack down and stared at the River Nith flowing past the end of the alley. And something occurred to him. Innes Knox was a qualified doctor and her parents, of all people, would be proud enough to use her correct title on the envelope. He rummaged in the sack, pulled out the one he remembered and stared at the address with a hiss of satisfaction.

Dr I Spense,
Langford Hall,
Great Tew,
Oxon

Innes Knox was married and living in a hall. His heart leapt. Now he had something to go on.

By mid-morning there was considerable police activity in the area around Cambridge Close. Don Lang was clinging to life and lay in a private room in Dumfries hospital. Jim and his wife were also there, in another room, where Jim's fractured nose and broken teeth were being attended to.

He couldn't remember anything, but his wife had been quite clear. 'I saw a red-haired young man running away through the trees,' she said firmly to the inspector who had assumed command.

Acting on this intelligence the police commenced house-to-house enquiries in the area and in due course a constable named Weston knocked on the door of number twenty Cambridge Close.

A well-preserved woman in her sixties with attractive blue eyes answered the door.

'Good morning, madam, there's been an incident in the area and we're just asking local residents a couple of questions, if you don't mind.'

'Oh yes?' She nodded.

'In particular, we're asking people if they remember seeing a young man with red hair yesterday or early today. Maybe walking around, or loitering?'

It was Constable Weston's thirtieth visit that morning and as heavy rain had set in two hours earlier, he was not at his best, which meant that he missed the fractional hesitation and flash of shock that passed over the face of the woman he was addressing.

'What's this?' A man joined her in the hall.

'The constable here is just wondering if we've seen a red-haired man.' His wife looked at him.

Her husband laughed shortly. 'There's plenty of those in Scotland. A bit like asking if you've seen a blonde in Sweden.'

The woman turned back to the policeman, smiling. 'He's got a point, but nobody springs to mind, I'm afraid. What's happened exactly?'

'I'm not at liberty to say at present, madam.'

'Aye, well, sorry we can't help you,' the man replied. 'And sorry about the weather too, they've not given you much of a job this morning, have they?' He reached for the edge of the door.

Taking his cue, the policeman stepped back from the porch and glanced up at the sky. 'It looks set in for the day too. Ah well,' he nodded gloomily to them, 'thanks anyway.'

He turned and plodded back to the road.

For the second time in twenty-four hours the Knoxes shut their front door and stared at each other in shock.

'I wonder what he's done?' she said quietly.

'Steady now, we don't know it's him, whatever it is. I wasn't joking, Elizabeth, every fifth man around here has red hair. Don't worry about it. He got nothing from us, and my guess is he's long gone from here. There's no way he can find out where Innes is, especially now she's changed her name.'

*

At quarter past eleven on the first night of the full moon Eve Dance walked quietly up the high street and turned into the gates

138

of Langford Hall. For most of the day she had been quietly preparing for what was going to happen next. She was carrying a bag with certain items in it, and two days earlier had written a number of letters.

She ghosted through the grounds, sometimes visible, sometimes blending into the shadows cast by the moon, as though already halfway to another world. At the French windows that gave access to the study she knocked quietly and was relieved to see Innes appear.

'Where are we going?' the younger woman asked in a low voice as they stood together.

'Creech Hill Ring,' Eve answered. 'Shall we…' Without further conversation she struck out across the lawn, heading for the long tree-lined ride that led to the stones.

Sensing her preoccupation, Innes followed, watching the long dark cloak that the older woman wore swirling gently about her body. Beyond the gardens the moon lit the open parkland with a cool grey glow, throwing midnight blue shadows under the trees and hedges and, as they moved silently through a landscape heavy with scents and secrets, she felt a rising excitement.

After twenty minutes of walking they reached the beginning of the ride. Far ahead the two sentinel stones that marked the entrance to Creech Hill Ring showed faintly. Innes frowned and squinted between the rows of trees. *Is something moving down there?*

Not long afterwards she had her answer. As they passed into the ring four figures appeared. Two men and two women. They were dressed in cloaks too.

'These are my friends,' Eve said quietly. 'They will help and protect me tonight. May I have the ring now?'

Innes slipped it off her finger and watched Eve slide it onto her own. 'We're going to light a fire and then do something that will, hopefully, enable me to understand the nature of the premonitions I'm having. Will you wait over by the yew tree. Go out of the circle and don't come back in whatever you see and hear. Do you promise?'

The young woman looked at her friend. 'If you're sure.' Then unable to resist her curiosity she asked, 'What is it you're doing?'

'I'm going to cross over to another place. Where the gods and spirits reside.'

'And your friends are going to help you get there?'

Eve smiled in the moonlight. 'No, Innes, they're going to help me get back.'

She nodded towards the tree. 'Off you go then. Keep under the branches.' Then Eve led her friends into the middle of the ring where a small bonfire had been built. The wood must have been soaked in some kind of flammable oil, as it caught immediately a flame was applied and, sure enough, moments later the sweet smell of lavender drifted across the circle towards Innes.

Afterwards, when she was back in bed, Innes struggled to remember the exact details of the rite the five witches had enacted. The image of the bonfire was clear, and the moment when, to her astonishment, they all cast off their cloaks to reveal their pale, naked bodies in the glow of the flames. And the daggers in their hands. But beyond that the picture was blurry; a mesmeric kaleidoscope of figures moving with purpose in the firelight, and Eve kneeling, head back, her arms outstretched to the sky.

But she remembered the chanting. Low and rhythmic, in a language she didn't understand. The words had a hypnotic, resonating power that seeped into her head and induced a trance that left her motionless and unblinking as she watched the figures silhouetted by the flames.

Suddenly she heard Eve scream in pain. A dreadful, raw cry. As she watched, the four adepts stood around her and all placed their hands on her head. And the chanting changed from a background pulse to something more urgent. One voice was leading, and the others were responding. They knelt down and the

140

pace of the words quickened as Eve screamed again, then fell to one side.

Alarmed, Innes took a step forward. But as though she had sensed the movement, one of the women by the bonfire looked over, held up her hand and shook her head. To her astonishment, Innes felt herself being physically stopped from moving forward. It was a moment she would remember for the rest of her life. Proof of something she could never explain.

What happened next was unclear. She remembered walking with them back down the ride, the Langford Ring safely on her finger, and Eve with a helper on each arm. She peeled off at the entrance to the garden and said, 'You'll see her safe home?'

'We will.' It was the taller of the two men who answered. He was wearing glasses which, for some reason, she found strange. 'She'll be alright. Don't worry. We saw some of it and we know how to protect her.'

It was only some weeks later that the full significance of this final remark became clear to Innes. Nevertheless, the following afternoon she made it her business to call in at Marston House and see her friend.

They sat outside on the bench with the apricot-coloured rose behind and after the necessary enquiries about how she was feeling, Innes simply said, 'What happened?'

The petite blonde with tired eyes looked at her. 'Do you really want to know?'

'Yes, I do. Very much.'

With that Eve started to speak.

Chapter Twelve

Great Tew, September 1654

It had been raining all day when, in the fading light of early evening, two figures on horseback appeared from Dell Lane and drew their horses to a halt by the market cross. Both wore the wide-brimmed hats and black coats that signified their puritan loyalties and in the royalist village of Great Tew this was noticed immediately.

'Where is Langford Hall?' the younger of the two men called to a thin grey-haired woman watching them from a doorway. She did not look welcoming.

'Who wants to know?' she replied.

'My name is Matthew Pritchard. And my business is the Lord Protector's business. Where is the hall, crone?'

If this calculated insult struck home, the woman showed no sign of it. Pausing long enough to show the men that an answer remained her prerogative and not theirs, she finally gestured up the high street towards the big church that dominated the village.

'The gate's on the right.'

With no acknowledgement, Pritchard and his companion steered their horses towards the church. 'We're a long way from London here, Matthew,' the second man muttered. In contrast to his fresh-faced companion, he was heavily bearded and wore a sword. His demeanour suggested that he knew how to use it.

'Who's that?' The woman's husband joined her at the door.

'Puritans,' she replied, watching their progress up the rain-lashed street. 'Heading for the hall.'

'What do they want?'

She kept her gaze on them until they disappeared, then said, 'They've come to kill someone.'

Twenty minutes later Colonel Richard Wrington, owner of the Langford estate, was disturbed at his rest by a servant who came to tell him about the visitors. He hurried downstairs and found the two men being assisted out of their coats at the foot of the great oak staircase.

'Gentlemen, welcome. I am Colonel Wrington. To what do I owe the pleasure?'

The younger of his two guests removed his dripping hat and passed it without looking to the servant, then stared directly at Wrington. His face was pale, as though he lived only in the shadows, and he had curiously expressionless eyes.

A man whose blood was forged in winter. The thought came unbidden to his host.

A thin smile appeared on the visitor's face. 'We've come about the witch,' he said.

*

Jane Meadenham was fifty-five years old and lived in a one-room cottage about half an hour's walk from Great Tew. But, as the colonel and his visitors ate supper in the dining room of Langford Hall, she was languishing in a locked storeroom in the stable block. There were no windows and she had been sitting in the dark for two weeks, only emerging once a day for half an hour, a courtesy offered by a sympathetic ostler who was a distant relative. Although he was careful not to let that become public knowledge.

For the last thirty years Jane had lived a quiet life with her husband, working in the fields at the estate's command and providing basic medical services to the village through her comprehensive knowledge of herbs and flowers. She had helped many more people than she might have done harm to, and there were women and children alive in the village who would not be so without her presence at the birthing chair.

She was also given to roaming the countryside at night and, it was whispered, capable of much more. It was said that if you asked the wise woman for help with a particular problem, for a fee she would provide it. By and large the residents of Great Tew and the Langford estate turned a blind eye to these rumours, not least because it was well known that she had the patronage of Lady Olivia up at Langford Hall, a woman who, it was rumoured, was even more capable in certain matters.

But nevertheless she had enemies, chief amongst whom was the Reverend Mayton, vicar of St Mary's, who considered her to be a witch. So when her husband suddenly collapsed in a field and died, six months after the hall had fallen to the puritans, he had seen his chance, asked for an audience with Colonel Wrington and accused Jane Meadenham of murdering her husband by witchcraft. A crime by any statute.

According to the churchman, husband and wife had been observed arguing half an hour before his death and the woman had subsequently been seen with a black cat on her lap. This damming evidence was accepted without question by the squire of Langford Hall, a man who owed his position to the puritan cause, having been granted the estate and lands by Oliver Cromwell himself. Eager to reinforce his credentials as a man of God, he had despatched a messenger to Oxford, stating that he had a witch confined at Langford Hall and needed an experienced man to deal with her.

That man was twenty-eight-year-old Matthew Pritchard who had an unquenchable passion for hunting down ungodly,

144

Satan-worshippers like the accused. To date he had personally been responsible for the deaths of thirteen women (and no men) and was keen to move on from this unlucky total as soon as possible.

As he sat and broke bread with the colonel, he felt a deep satisfaction that this ambition was about to be fulfilled in the best of ways. 'The murder of a husband by witchcraft is punishable by death,' he intoned.

The relish in his voice was barely concealed and his host sensed a darker motive than mere justice in the man's words, but replied evenly, 'Very well, will there be a trial?'

'She will appear before me in the morning. You and the reverend will be witnesses and Baxter my companion will scribe a fair record of the session. Nothing more will be needed.'

In this god-forsaken place, he added mentally.

Wrington nodded. 'There's a tree that's used for hangings on the far side of the common. We can do it tomorrow afternoon.'

But Pritchard held up a finger in admonition. 'Oh no, Colonel. There will be no hanging. Murder of your husband by witchcraft is Petty Treason…' He raised his eyebrows meaningfully.

His host moved in his chair. 'You have the advantage of me there, I'm afraid. What does that mean?'

'It means we burn her.'

Pritchard laughed, eyes bright. It was like a corpse getting up to dance a jig, and the colonel made a mental note to get him out of the village as soon as humanly possible.

Up to this point, Eve had been staring sightlessly towards the old brick wall on the far side of the lawn as she spoke, but now she paused and looked at Innes who was shocked to see tears running freely down her cheeks.

Reaching out Innes took her hand but said nothing. Her friend returned her gaze to the red bricks and resumed the story.

'They took her to the common, tied her to a pole and then piled wood and straw faggots around her. Colonel Wrington made his men do it because no one in the village would. The vicar and the puritans watched. Then they lit it.'

Seeing her distress Innes said gently, 'I'm very sorry to hear that and it's a terrible thing, but it was a long time ago. People were different then. Surely there's no need to upset yourself so greatly now.'

But Eve shook her head violently. 'You don't understand. The past is never far away in Great Tew. It's bound to us, like the seasons. And I felt her terror. Tied there. Then heat and smoke all around me, and finally the pain. Dreadful, unbearable pain. They told me I was screaming last night.'

Innes nodded. 'You were.'

Eve looked at her, raw anguish in her eyes. 'I went through it all with her. Every moment. Can't you see it now? The dreaming, the premonitions. It's so obvious. Jane Meadenham died of burning and I will too.'

*

In direct contrast to Eve Dance, half a mile away Burrows was rather enjoying himself. He was in the rick yard at Home Farm watching Samson, one of the estate's two steam traction engines, at work. The estate had recently purchased a corn threshing machine and Samson provided the motive power to drive it.

Mr Givell the engine's driver and chief engineer was high above him. As the sergeant watched he hauled back one of the levers and Samson's great drive wheel started to rotate, turning a long leather belt that stretched across a twenty-foot gap to the threshing machine. Burrows couldn't help grinning as the belt turned a smaller drive wheel on the thresher and it sprang into life, as though woken from a sleep.

The engineer called out 'Ready?' to the men on the thresher and received a wave in return. Reaching to his side he pulled a lever attached to a cable that stretched across the gap and twenty feet away a handle was pulled through ninety degrees. With a *clunk* the threshing machinery engaged and two farmhands, moving with the economy of men used to physical labour, started to fork bundles of corn into the inlet from the huge hay wain drawn up next to it.

Burrows found the noise and drama of it all rather exciting and moved round to the rear of the thresher where another man was standing waiting for the grain sack to fill up. When it was full, he pushed a lever and closed the pipe briefly, then smoothly unpegged the sack, hooked another in place and reopened the pipe. To his side a further farmhand was raking up the corn stalks which were emerging from a chute. Little was said as the men worked in complete harmony with the machinery.

And Samson's smoothly rotating drive wheel brought it all to life. It was a marvellous thing, Burrows thought.

'Enjoying yourself, Sergeant?' A voice caused him to turn. Piers Spense was standing there. He gestured at the machinery and added, 'Quite something, eh?'

'It really is. I enjoyed watching the steam engine driving the roundabout at the fete as well. There's something about them, isn't there.'

'Action at a distance, if I remember my science master correctly,' the noble lord observed. 'It means something happening in one place which causes an effect elsewhere. Like the drive belt is doing.' As Burrows nodded, he took his arm and drew him away from the noise before asking, 'How are you getting on with that business at the Dower House?'

'I'll be honest with you, sir, we're still unsure how Mr Pentire's murderer managed to leave the study after killing him.'

'Yes, it's a tricky one. You've checked for secret passages, I assume?' A wry smile accompanied this remark, before he added, 'You're certain it's murder then?'

'There's strong medical evidence to suggest that.'

'Any suspects?'

'We're pursuing enquiries,' Burrows replied rather woodenly. There was a silence, and the policeman got the impression that Lord Langford would have liked to ask for further details but wasn't sure how to, without appearing obvious.

'So no one particularly of interest at this stage then?' he observed finally.

'As I say, sir, we're exploring different possibilities.'

'And now these poison pen letters too. Who is sending those, do you think?' Burrows was an astute man in his way and did not miss the shadow of apprehension that passed across Lord Langford's eyes. *He's had one.* The thought was suddenly clear in his mind.

'We're investigating various leads, sir, and are asking anyone who has received such a letter to report the fact to us.'

'Have there been many?'

The sergeant hesitated. That was reserved information. However, the question was coming from the most powerful man for many miles around and one who could make or break his career with a few words. 'With great respect, sir, I'm not at liberty to say. People have told us in confidence.' Then before he could stop himself, added quietly, 'Shall I add you to the list?'

Burrows couldn't tell if it was the impertinence of this question or its accuracy that produced the look of shock on Lord Langford's face.

'Certainly not, Sergeant. Whatever gave you that idea?'

'Absolutely nothing, sir. I really cannot think why I asked.'

'Neither can I. Going round accusing a Lord of the Realm of having nasty secrets is hardly an astute career move, wouldn't you say?'

'Yes, my lord. I mean no, my lord.' To his horror he found himself standing to attention and out of the corner of his eye he could see Mr Givell looking across to them, clearly curious.

Piers Spense leaned into him and hissed, 'For the avoidance of doubt, Sergeant Burrows, I do not lead the kind of life that leaves me open to blackmail. Are we clear on that?'

'We absolutely are, sir, yes.'

'Then I'll wish you good day.' With a long stare Lord Langford turned and headed back to the hall.

*

The following morning Burrows was standing by the window in the study at the Dower House, hoping for inspiration and reflecting sorrowfully on the implications of falling foul of Lord Langford. He hadn't told Laura, knowing she would be appalled at his stupidity.

Turning, he looked back at the desk. The sun's rays were slanting in at an angle and lighting up the thin Turkish rug that lay in the middle of the floor. And he noticed something. A foot in front of the desk two faint square depressions showed in the pile. He walked forward, knelt down and inspected them, and then peered at the leg of the desk. He opened his hand and put his thumb and finger along one side of its base, then moved his hand to the mark in the rug. It was a match.

He stood up and scratched his chin. The desk had been moved. It had stood in one place for long enough to leave slight indentations in the rug and the sunlight had allowed him to see them. But now it was in a different position, further away from the window. He sat down in the chair and looked around hopefully. The rear of the desk was level with the fireplace to his left and the centre of the door to his right.

Then a further thought occurred to him, and he stood up and pulled the chair back. Kneeling down he put his head into the footwell and examined the rug. Some of the bloodstains were well under the table. Too far under. The desk had been moved after Pentire had been shot. And it hadn't been by the people who'd cleaned up the desktop, Dixon had made sure nothing else had been touched.

149

Why would you move a desk? There was no obvious advantage to its new position that he could see.

He was still pondering this when he heard the crunch of car tyres on the gravel outside. Shortly afterwards a door slammed, and the front door knocker sounded. As Connors had gone out, he rose and answered the door himself. A tall, well-dressed man in his forties was standing there and was, perhaps understandably, taken aback to see a police sergeant in the hall.

'Ah. Police. Good morning. My name's Archie Deville, Mr Pentire was a friend of mine and I've come to take back possession of a couple of books he'd borrowed from me. Medieval history and quite valuable.' He hesitated and then said, 'It'll be a difficult time of course, but I didn't want them getting mixed up with his estate. Sorry and all that.'

To Burrows the man seemed plausible. He ascertained the names of the two books, jotted them down in his notebook and then led the way into the library. One book was sitting on a side table, the other was on the shelves. Deville showed the sergeant his name plate in each of them.

Burrows checked and then nodded. 'That's fine, sir. I'll take a note of your address. Just in case.'

He did so and then the man casually dropped his bombshell. 'Dreadful news of course, how's Lord Langford taking it?'

'Mr Pentire's death, sir? I'm not sure he's directly concerned, other than as a landlord.'

Deville smiled. 'Oh no, they knew each other in London. Good pals in fact, I'm sure of it. Although I don't know Langford very well myself and Pentire was more of an academic contact than a friend of mine.'

Burrows stared at him. 'Sorry, sir, just to be clear, you're of the opinion that Mr Pentire and Lord Langford knew each other before he moved into the Dower House?'

150

'Yes, they were thick as thieves. Up in town.' He glanced at his wristwatch. 'Anyway, must dash, I'm dining in this evening.' And with that he tucked the books under his arm and a minute later the whine of a self-starter sounded from down the hall.

Left alone Burrows struggled to assimilate this new information. No enquiries had been made at the hall about the death and Piers Spense certainly hadn't come forward to say the victim had been a friend. Was that simply because no one had asked him? Or had he deliberately concealed their relationship and, if so, what were the implications?

Sensing deep waters and with his difficult conversation from the previous day uppermost in his mind, he shut and locked the front door and set off for the police station.

Chapter Thirteen

As though pleased with its achievements so far that morning, the twelve thirty from London arrived at Oxford station with a satisfied hiss, as a plaintive cry of 'Oxford, Oxford' echoed down the platform like the distant call of a marshland bird.

Amongst the crowd descending from the opening doors was a red-headed young man in a tweed jacket and flannels, bearing a single suitcase and a sense of purpose. He headed for the exit, pausing only to enquire about the best method of onward travel to a village called Great Tew. Noting his accent, the porter suggested that his two choices would be to hire a car and driver or take the bus.

'How long does the bus take?' the young man enquired.

'Well over an hour. It's the Banbury route but it meanders all over the place. It will get you there in the end though,' he observed with an encouraging smile, adding, 'on holiday, sir?'

'I've someone to see.'

'Well, I'm afraid you've a wait now. One's just gone and the next, and final for the day, I might add, is not until five o'clock.'

'What's it like? The village.'

'It's a very quiet place, sir. Not much happens up there.' The porter chose not to mention the two violent deaths which had occurred since the end of the war, or the persistent rumours of witchcraft for which Great Tew was renowned locally.

The man glanced around. 'Maybe I'll stay overnight here and travel up in the morning. Can you recommend a hotel?'

The porter had already noted the quality of the clothes his interlocutor was wearing. 'If you turn right out of the station forecourt, two hundred yards down on the left you'll see the Royal. That might well suit you, sir.'

Thanking him, the man turned and was soon out of sight.

*

At lunchtime the following day the bus from Oxford wheezed along Dell Lane and came to a grateful stop next to the market cross, where a small queue of villagers waited to board for the onward journey to Banbury. Three people descended the step; an elderly couple and the red-headed young man carrying his suitcase.

Five minutes later the bus had departed and the couple had disappeared, leaving the young man standing alone and staring thoughtfully up the high street to where St Mary's church presided over day-to-day events in the village. There were a few people about but, absorbed as he was, he failed to notice a slightly built and rather dishevelled man in his mid-forties staring at him with an expression that combined alarm and astonishment to a nicety.

If anything, the anxiety on Nobby Griffin's face deepened as the new arrival politely stopped a pair of elderly grey-haired ladies and asked for directions to Langford Hall, as he was 'planning on paying a visit later'.

The Misses Rudge were most helpful. 'You'll find the gates up the high street to the right,' said Geraldine. And her sister Xanthe added, 'There's no lodge, you can just walk up the drive to the house. It's about a quarter of a mile.'

153

Thanking them, he enquired where he might obtain a bite of lunch.

'I understand the Black Horse will do a sandwich,' Xanthe continued. She pointed up the slight incline. 'It's past the hall gates, just before the church.'

'I'm sure that will do fine,' the visitor replied and with a cheerful salute set off in the direction indicated. Moving with some stealth, Nobby Griffin followed. But instead of trailing the man into the pub, he lingered outside until he saw him take a seat in the garden and set about getting around the outside of a pint of cider.

Satisfied that he would be there for at least half an hour Nobby went in search of Bert Williams, to whom he passed on the news that a red-haired stranger had arrived in the village and was enquiring about Langford Hall.

Forty minutes later, replete with two pints and an excellent beef and mustard sandwich, the red-headed young man was surprised to receive a summons from the other side of the thick hedge which ran along the rear of the garden.

'Pssst.'

He looked in the direction of the luxuriant foliage and then glanced around. The lunchtime crowd had left, and he was alone.

'Pssst.' There it was again. Curious, he cocked his head on one side and awaited developments. These arrived in the form of a hand and then an arm with the sleeve rolled up, which appeared around the end of the hedge and beckoned him.

Sensing no threat, which was a grave mistake on his part, he rose and walked over.

He hadn't noticed Nobby Griffin when he got off the bus, so he didn't recognise him now. He was standing by the trunk of another huge oak tree at the end of a narrow alley which appeared to lead down to some farm buildings.

'Hello? What can I do for you?' the young man enquired courteously.

'Have a look at this.' The older man held out his hand, which seemed to be clutching something wrapped in a cloth. 'I tell you, I ain't seen nothin' like it before. I reckon it's worth a bob or two. What do you think?'

The young man leaned forward and at that precise moment a strange darkness descended on him as the bright sunlight of a perfect summer's day changed to an opaque brown cloud, as though he had fallen into a tidal estuary.

'Hey!' he cried. 'What's going on?' But before he could react or struggle at all, a rope was quickly bound around his waist securing his arms and another around his ankles. This was tightened and pulled hard, flicking his feet sideways and causing him to crash heavily to the ground.

'Goddam it, what are you up to!' The young man's red hair was a fine indicator of the shortness of his temper and, encased in the large flour sack which had been dragged down to his waist, he cursed and thrashed on the ground, looking not unlike a seal that had discovered an unexpected live wire on a beach.

Nobby and Bert watched dispassionately for a moment then sat down on him, causing a temporary cessation in the noise.

'Now you calm down and listen quietly. If you kick up rough, we'll just hit you on the head and leave you here. If you want to behave yourself, we'll walk you down to a barn and have a little bit of a chat.'

'I've not got much money on me, if that's what you want,' the muffled voice from within the sack said.

'It's not money we're after. Just a talk. Now are you going to behave?'

There was a pause as the captive considered his options. It didn't take long. 'Okay.'

155

Ten uncomfortable minutes later he was pushed over onto a pile of hay and one of the two voices said, 'Right then, we've got some questions for you.'

'I've got a few for you too,' came the spirited reply. Young men do not take kindly to being bested in combat, especially after a surprise attack, and the tone of voice indicated a burning belligerence had taken up residence inside the flour sack.

'Who are you and why are you here?'

'None of your goddam business.'

A further session of violent thrashing followed and slowly subsided. In the silence that followed, the man who had lured him to his fate said, 'I don't think we'd better untie him, Bert.'

'We said no names,' came the fierce reply.

'Right. Sorry.'

'Bert, huh? Well, I've got your number now, pal. Just you wait until we can have a set-to, fair and square.' The dust inside the sack caused him to growl this out in a rather alarming way.

Bert and Nobby glanced at each other. There was no denying the transatlantic accent. 'Where are you from?' Bert asked.

'Winnipeg, Manitoba.'

'Where's that?'

'Canada, you goddam hicks. My name is Dougal McCredie.' Silence greeted this remark, so he added, 'Of the Winnipeg McCredies,' in case further clarification was needed.

'Canada?' Bert and Nobby exchanged another look, this time of surprise. 'Why are you here then?'

'I've business up at the big house, if you must know.'

'Right. And what would that be? You're taking trouble to someone, I reckon.'

'I'm doing no such thing.' A prolonged and floury coughing fit interrupted his discourse at this point, but he finally managed to add, 'My family are related to the Spenses. I'm Lady Langford's great nephew twice removed and I'm in England to

156

study at Cambridge university. At my mother's request I am visiting to say hello from the folks in Canada.'

'A likely tale. We were told to beware of a red-headed stranger arriving in the village.'

'What? By whom?'

'It was predicted on the talking board,' Nobby blurted before Bert could shut him up.

There was a silence as the young man in the sack considered the implications of this unwelcome news. Finally, he said doubtfully, 'You mean, a Ouija board? Like talking to the spirits?'

This time the two men didn't reply, so he continued, 'In my pocket I have a letter from Lady Langford inviting me to dine and stay the night at the hall this evening. It's got my Cambridge address on it. Why don't you take a look if you don't believe me?'

Bert and Nobby retired out of earshot to discuss matters.

The upshot of this was that five minutes later, Dougal McCredie heard stealthy footsteps approaching and the cord that was tightly binding his legs was cut with a single movement. The waist cord came next and was immediately followed by the sound of two pairs of heavy boots running. Their noise faded into silence as he wriggled furiously out of the sack and jumped to his feet.

He was in a stone barn with a wide double door. Rubbing his forearms where the rope had cut into them, he walked over to it and looked in both directions but there was no one in sight. In one direction the track ran out across the fields. The other led between trees towards the village. With a sigh he set off that way, hoping that his suitcase was still beside the table in the pub garden.

*

Four hours later, at Langford Hall, Dougal McCredie recounted the kidnapping to his hostess while sipping a brandy and soda in the drawing room before dinner.

157

'… so there you are, Lady Langford. I have to say folk in this part of the world have a pretty strange way of welcoming visitors,' he concluded, 'but no harm done, I guess.'

'Do call me Claire, dear. And the same with Piers.' She gestured to her son who was sitting in an armchair. 'So you have no idea why, or who it was?'

'One of the guys was called Bert. And I got a look at the other one, but I don't know his name. He was slightly built and not too tidy.'

The two Spenses exchanged a glance. 'Bert and Nobby,' Piers said. 'What on earth were they up to?'

'We will initiate enquires at once, Dougal.' His hostess turned to her son and added, 'Won't we, Piers.' As Lord Langford stood up and left the room, she gave her guest a gracious smile, and asked, 'Now tell me, how big is your ranch exactly?'

Five minutes later Colonel Dance was disturbed at his supper by the telephone. In a few short, sharp sentences, Lord Langford let him know that two residents of the village had taken it upon themselves to assault and briefly imprison a guest of the family. He also suggested he would welcome an explanation, if they wished to avoid an appearance before the bench. His bench, in fact, at Banbury assizes.

He concluded with a pithy observation about the general maintenance of law and order in Great Tew, which stung the colonel to the quick. Face grim he replaced the receiver and put a call through to Burrows at home. His remarks were less measured than the noble lord's and his sergeant was left in no doubt what his immediate priorities should be.

Muttering, and eyeing the venison pie his wife had just removed from the oven, he continued the general downhill trajectory of the bad news by telephoning Dixon. Ten minutes later he met her outside the police house.

'Right. Half past seven,' he said. 'Houses first, then the pub.' With that they marched across the high street and knocked on the door of Nobby's cottage. His wife answered but could only advise them that he'd had his tea and gone out.

An enquiry further down Rivermead produced the same response from Edna Williams. A brisk search of the pub and garden also produced no result. Returning to the bar, Burrows said, 'Have you seen Bert or Nobby today, Mr Tirrold?'

'No, I haven't, Sergeant Burrows,' replied the landlord with equal formality.

This exchange attracted the attention of the Reverend Tukes who was relaxing with a pint at the end of the counter. 'I saw them after lunch. They were running across the common.'

'Running?'

'That's right. They seemed a little preoccupied, if truth be told.'

Burrows grimaced. 'Right. If you see them, tell them I'm looking for both of them and it would be much better if they came to the police station before I find them.'

The news reached the recalcitrant pair later that evening and after communing between themselves, they arrived at the police station at eight o'clock the following morning. Having received the scarcely believable explanation, Sergeant Burrows telephoned Langford Hall and announced that the two culprits were ready to explain and apologise to the gentleman from Canada.

At half past ten they were marched into the drawing room where Lord Langford, Lady Langford and Dougal McCredie were waiting. Burrows brought them to a halt, and they eyed the quality in front of them with unease. Nobby pulled off his cap.

'Well?' said Piers Spense, eyeing them with distaste.

Remarkably, the pair had decided to tell the truth and Nobby had nominated Bert as spokesman. 'It all goes back to the night of the wedding,' he said. 'After the celebrations in the pub me and Edna went back to Nobby's for a nightcap and his missus got the talking board out.'

'We didn't want her to, mind,' Nobby chipped in. 'But she did it anyway.'

Bert took a deep breath. 'She got through to someone who told us to watch out for a red-haired stranger in the village as they meant no good. Bringing trouble to the hall, was the message.'

'To the hall,' Nobby confirmed, wide-eyed. 'So really we were trying to do you a favour.'

'Alright.' Bert gestured at him. 'We're very sorry to Mr McCredie for the trouble, but we meant no harm. We were just going to ask a few questions, then he said he had an invitation from you, my lady, and we realised we might have made a mistake, and let him go.'

'What about the sack?' Dougal said, having not forgotten the humiliation of his confinement.

Bert cleared his throat. 'Yes, I can see that you'd be cross about that, but we didn't know you were invited. As I say, the message was clear, and we thought the stranger was you.'

'Who was the message from?' Lady Langford asked.

Bert looked at her, and she saw real fear and desperation in his eyes. 'They didn't say,' he replied.

She held his gaze for a long moment. 'I see. Well, we have an explanation at least, Dougal. Will you accept their apology, if not their stupidity?'

He grinned. 'I guess I will, it wasn't malicious.' He stepped forward and shook both their hands. 'I still think I'd win a fair fight though.'

'I'm sure you would, sir,' Bert agreed, not believing it for a second.

Thus dismissed, they left the room and headed for the back door, but just as they were slipping into the freedom of the grounds, Lady Langford's base voice called out.

'Bert.' He stopped, his face a grimace of frustration. *So close.* She came up to him and said quietly, 'I'm keen to know more about this message. Come and see me in the bower by Hugh's grave at five o'clock. I'll ask Eve to be there as well, I think.' She gave him a nod. 'Off you go and try to behave yourself in the meantime.'

At the appointed hour he arrived at the airy spot with the wonderful view, and Lady Langford got down to business straight away.

'Who was the message from, Bert?' she asked.

He looked at her. 'I'm not sure I should say and that's the honest truth.'

'Why would that be? Was the messenger also significant?' Eve asked.

'Oh yes. No doubt about that.'

Lady Langford sighed. 'Just tell us, Bert. We're all grown-ups here.'

And so, with a deep breath, he did. 'Mr Hugh was there in that room with me and Edna and Nobby and Bridget. He said he had a message for Mr Edward and that he was to beware a red-haired man. There was no mistake. Bridget wrote it down. Well, we didn't know what to do. So in the end we decided to say nothing but keep an eye open. I know how you grieved for Mr Hugh. And what you did for him, I didn't want to bring it all up again.' He glanced at the gravestone as he said this.

'Hugh.' Claire glanced at Eve and their eyes connected, then she looked back at Bert. 'Thank you for telling me. As it happens, I would certainly like to be informed about any other red-headed strangers that you see in the area. Come to me directly. Do not raise any alarms or speak to him. Just tell me. Am I clear?'

'You are. Thank you, Lady Langford.'

'You may go then.'

As he made his way off down the hill the two women looked at each other again and Claire said hesitantly, 'You know it seems ridiculous, but I have a feeling that Hugh was referring to

161

the long-lost father of Jaikie. I've wondered about him sometimes, and he would be the source of the boy's bright red hair.'

Eve's eyes were troubled. 'I felt something a few weeks ago. Far to the north of here. Like a single beat on a distant drum. More recently I heard another.' She pursed her lips and stared out across the sunlit space to the summit of Green Hill. The standing stone was just visible in the haze. 'I'll try to find out more, but I agree, Claire, I think we must be on the alert.'

'It's hard to think how he would find us down here. As I understand it there was no exchange of addresses or anything.' Lady Langford's face creased into an agony of concern. 'Oh God, Eve. Surely the man isn't going to turn up here. It would be an utter disaster. Edward is over all that business, and he and Innes deserve a chance to settle down and be happy now.'

Seeing the palpable distress on her friend's face, Eve hugged her and said, 'Let's not get ahead of ourselves, Claire.'

But Lady Langford pushed her back, her voice rising into a panic. 'I mean it, Eve. The merest hint of the truth would be hideous for Innes. And for Jaikie, for that matter, to say nothing of the Spense family reputation. The villagers would have a field day for a start and believe me, the aristocratic set love a scandal. The poor girl wouldn't be able to show her face outside the hall grounds.'

Eve tried to placate her again. 'We really don't know if he's a threat or not. Or even if he's coming here.'

'Don't we? Hugh does.' There was another silence. Then Claire turned to her friend and said with quiet resolution, 'Langford women have guarded the Spense family for a thousand years. I will do whatever is necessary to protect my own. Innes is one of us now. She is the future here and woe betide any trouble-making chancer who threatens that.'

Chapter Fourteen

Two weeks after he had been attacked, Don Lang, the Dumfries postman, died quietly and without fuss in Dumfries hospital. He never regained consciousness and the doctor treating him remarked confidentially to one of the nurses that it was 'probably a blessing in disguise', although that was not the view of his devastated wife who, having lost her beloved only son at Gallipoli, now found herself facing a lonely old age.

The death attracted the attention of the *Dumfries Post and Telegraph* which reprised the original story on its front page and lamented the fact that no one had been brought to justice. And this article was read with interest by Mrs Edith Grange, an elderly widow who lived alone in a bungalow in Cambridge Close, opposite number twenty.

Early on the morning of the assault she had caught the half past six bus into town and travelled by train to Liverpool where her daughter and son-in-law lived. The young woman was due to have an operation and her mother had offered to look after the grandchildren while she recovered. By the time she returned to Dumfries, the fuss about the postman had been superseded by other news.

Mrs Grange wasn't much of a reader, but as she passed the newsagent she noticed the *Telegraph* sub-headline mentioned the road she lived in. Deciding it was worth the investment she bought a copy and carried the paper home where she studied it at leisure with a pot of tea and a biscuit or two.

And what she read gave her food for thought. So much so that she had a sleepless night and in the morning presented herself at the counter of the main police station and announced she had some information about the death of Mr Lang.

Ten minutes later she was sitting in an interview room with a large highland sergeant called Macpherson, who had a notepad in front of him.

'Now then, Mrs Grange, what is it that you wish to tell us?'

'I saw that Don Lang the postman has died. That's a terrible thing.'

'Aye, no doubt about that.' The sergeant nodded and waited.

'You're looking for a red-haired man, seen running away from the scene?'

'Yes, we are.'

'Well, I saw him. The day before, in Cambridge Close, where I live.'

Macpherson blinked at her. 'Really? Are you sure about that?'

'I am.' Well satisfied with the impact of her statement, Mrs Grange leaned back and folded her arms.

'What exactly did you see?'

'He came down the road and called in at number twenty, across from me. Where the Knoxes live. They're very nice,' she added, not wishing to appear vindictive.

The sergeant frowned. 'Called in? He entered the house then?'

'Oh aye, he was in there for a good fifteen minutes.'

'Can you describe him?'

'Slim with a tweed jacket, grey flannels and, as I said, red hair.'

'How old?'

Mrs Grange pursed her lips. Everyone under forty seemed young to her. 'Mid-twenties, I'd say.'

Macpherson was taking notes, head bent. 'And did you see him leave?'

'Aye, they were all in the doorway talking for a moment and then he gave them a wave and walked up the street.'

'Did it look like he knew them already?'

'I've no idea.'

He looked up. 'We made house-to-house enquiries, how did we miss you?'

'I went to see my daughter in Liverpool early the morning it happened. She's not been well.'

'But you're sure about the date?'

'Definitely. It was the day before I left.'

The sergeant continued to question her for ten minutes, then satisfied he had everything that she could give, thanked her and they parted. He went through into the office and called Constable Weston over.

'Remember doing house to house the day after Don Lang was attacked? Was there anything at all from Cambridge Close?'

The constable consulted his notebook. 'No reply from number eight. I saw everyone else. No one saw anything.'

'Do you remember calling at number twenty?'

'Sorry, sarge, not exactly. I did an awful lot of houses that day.'

His superior nodded. 'Aye, well we're going to call in there again. The woman from number eight says she saw a red-haired man visiting the previous day.'

'Really? Well there was nothing like that when I was talking to any householder.'

165

Macpherson looked at him. 'Someone's been fibbing. I wonder why?'

An hour later the two policemen knocked on the door of number twenty Cambridge Close. A man answered and opened his eyes in surprise at the visitors.

'Good morning, sir. Mr Knox, is it?' the sergeant enquired politely.

'Aye. Can I help you?'

'Would you mind if we came in for a moment. Just a couple of routine questions.' Macpherson was experienced enough to notice the slight hesitation before the man responded.

'If you wish.'

A minute later the three of them were sitting in the lounge where a pair of French windows gave on to a well-tended garden. The view extended to the River Nith and the Galloway hills in the distance.

'Very nice,' the sergeant said approvingly. 'On your own this morning, sir?'

'My wife has gone into town. What can I do for you?'

'You may recall Constable Weston here calling in the day after Mr Lang the postman was assaulted. Sadly he has died of his injuries, and it is now a murder enquiry.' The sergeant met his eye. 'Which is obviously a very serious business.'

The constable had his notebook out. 'I was enquiring if anyone had seen a red-haired man. Do you recall?' Mr Knox nodded, a sinking feeling slowly permeating through his body. 'My notes indicate that you said you hadn't seen such a fellow. Is that still the case, sir?'

'Yes.'

Macpherson stirred in his seat. 'We have received a reliable report that a red-haired man was seen entering your house the previous day. He stayed for around fifteen minutes and then left. You and your wife were observed standing in the doorway with him. Would you care to comment on that, sir?'

166

'I really wouldn't, beyond saying that your informant has made a mistake.'

'So, to be clear, you maintain that the man we are interested in did not visit you.'

'That is correct.'

'So what explanation can you give us for the information that we have received?'

'None at all.' Mr Knox paused and decided to add, 'A malicious time-waster, I imagine.'

The sound of the front door opening carried from the hall, followed by a woman's voice calling, 'That's me back, Rory.'

'My wife,' Mr Knox said unnecessarily, and all three men stood as she entered the lounge.

'Oh.' She stopped in surprise.

'These gentlemen have received a bit of nasty gossip, Elizabeth,' her husband said quickly. 'Apparently a mysterious red-haired man called at our house the day before that poor postman was attacked.'

She looked at the constable. 'I remember you came round. We'd seen nothing though.'

'That is not what our informant says, madam,' Macpherson observed, studying her closely.

She looked at him and visibly braced herself. 'Stuff and nonsense. No one came round that day.'

There was a silence in the sitting room that seemed to go on for a long time. Then Mr Knox said, 'Well, if there's nothing else…'

But Macpherson stood as unmoving as the Bell Rock lighthouse and stared. Finally he said, 'Mrs Knox, as I mentioned to your husband this is now a murder enquiry. Lying to the police is a very serious matter. I'm going to give you both the opportunity to reconsider what you have told me.'

'I can assure you there is no need for any reconsideration, Sergeant,' Mr Knox said. 'We will not be changing what we've told

167

you because it is the truth. Unless, perhaps, you'd like us to make something up? Is that how the polis operate in Dumfries now?'

Constable Weston's outraged intake of breath was audible in the still air of the room. 'No, that is not how we do things, sir,' Macpherson said evenly. 'But I will tell you openly that I have grave doubts about the veracity of your statements and will continue to pursue my enquiries.'

'Well good luck with those,' Mrs Knox said briskly, 'allow me to show you both to the door.'

She led the way but as the sergeant stood on the step he turned to her and said, 'I don't know why you're both lying to me or what trouble you're in, but I can assure you it is unlikely to be as serious as the trouble coming your way if you're shown to have lied during a murder enquiry. Think well on that, madam.'

Then he nodded. 'Good morning, you know where to find me.'

*

Burrows had lost no time in telling the chief constable that, according to Archie Deville, Lord Langford and Vaughan Pentire had been close friends before the latter's arrival in the village. But, to his frustration, his superior was not particularly interested in what the sergeant considered to be a major clue.

'I cannot really see the relevance of this, Burrows. What point are you making exactly?' he remarked.

'Well, sir, I'm wondering why he concealed their friendship from us. You'd expect His Lordship to have been a bit more interested in his death, wouldn't you? To come forward in some way, but beyond the normal condolences there's been nothing. Surely, he'd have called in or telephoned to ask for news – if Mr Pentire was a personal friend.'

'And what are you suggesting we conclude from the fact that he has not done so?' The colonel's voice was quiet, and Burrows recognised the signs. These were dangerous waters. He tiptoed forward.

168

'If it was a villager who had concealed his friendship with a murder victim, wouldn't we be a bit suspicious?'

'Are you saying that you think Piers Spense had something to do with the murder?'

There was a painfully long silence in the study of Marston House. Burrows couldn't bring himself to say yes and yet was also, with the honesty and grit that had marked him down for promotion, unwilling to say no.

So he stood there, in an agony of indecision, and said nothing at all.

The colonel was an intelligent man. When he spoke, his tone was conciliatory. 'Look, I'll be frank with you. No one is above the law of the land, but any investigation of His Lordship is likely to bring the wrath of God down upon us. Not least in the form of the Dowager Lady Langford. She looks after that family like a she-wolf cares for its brood. It is not a happy thought, Burrows.'

The sergeant made a decision and told his superior about the conversation in the rick yard. 'I realise I made a mistake in asking Lord Langford if he'd received a poison pen letter and apologised immediately. He denied it of course, but the thing is, he ended by saying he didn't lead the kind of life that would leave him open to blackmail.'

He looked at the chief constable and continued in a small voice, 'But I'm not sure that's entirely true, sir.'

'Hell's bells.' The colonel blew out his cheeks and indicated a chair. 'Sit down. Now tell me exactly what you are thinking.'

Burrows took a seat, and said, 'We know someone visited the Dower House the night of the murder, and that an attempt was made to conceal the fact by washing up two glasses. We don't know who it was, but Pentire had no known acquaintances in the village, and was a solitary man. Now we hear that His Lordship had an undeclared friendship with the victim. I'm asking myself if that was a factor in Mr Pentire – the unmarried Mr Pentire, I might add – moving to Great Tew.'

He met the colonel's eye and added, 'And that leads me to wonder if Lord Langford was his confidential visitor? Perhaps there was a row that night between the two men. A row that led to a terrible result in the heat of the moment – murder or possibly suicide as we first suspected.'

The colonel looked grim as Burrows completed this declaration. 'If by any chance you're right, the implications for the Spense family and, frankly, the rest of us are appalling. When I mentioned Lady Langford and the wrath of God, I wasn't joking.'

'I know, sir.'

'How's Dixon getting on with alibiing the people on the list?'

'She's nearly there, but it's taking time finding and interviewing them one by one. The estate is large even with the Matchless.'

'I'll tell you something. Before we start getting too interested in a peer of the realm, we need to be absolutely sure that every other avenue and possible suspect has been explored and rejected.'

'Right you are, sir.'

In spite of his unease, his sergeant's observations had struck a chord with the chief constable, and he decided further discreet enquiries through his own channels wouldn't do any harm. So later that evening, as he and Eve were getting ready for bed, and with the door firmly shut, he said, 'I'm interested to know what Piers Spense was doing the night Vaughan Pentire died. Is there any chance you might elicit that information from Claire, with the utmost subtlety?'

'Any particular reason?' she asked carefully.

'It appears he might have known Pentire in London. Just getting clear who was where, and so on,' her husband replied vaguely.

But she knew him too well. 'Oh, Jocelyn, you don't suspect him of something, do you?'

'I can't really say. You know how it is sometimes.'

*

The upshot of this conversation was that the following day Eve called in at the hall and invited Lady Langford out on a walk. After catching up on various items of interest she said, 'I suppose Piers will have to find a new tenant for the Dower House at some point.'

'True, although I haven't seen much of him recently. He's been up in town a great deal.'

'Did they know each other? Piers and Mr Pentire.'

'Not that I'm aware of. Mr Pentire wasn't a particularly social type and hadn't been pushing for an invitation up to the hall. I rather liked him for that and asked him to the wedding, and he did come for tea one afternoon, but Piers wasn't around. I don't really think they knew each other at all.'

'He was unmarried, I believe, Mr Pentire,' Eve remarked evenly.

'Yes. Like Piers.' They looked at each other.

'Do you think—' Eve started carefully, but her friend interrupted.

'I really don't know.' She stopped walking, her eyes fixed on the distant standing stone on Green Hill. 'At Christmas I said to Piers that I fully accepted he wouldn't marry and that I understood he had a circle of friends in London who he saw regularly. I told him I thought it was a pity that we didn't see much of that set and if he wanted to invite any special friends down to Langford, they'd be welcome. As long as all necessary discretion was observed.'

Eve nodded slowly. 'That was very decent of you, Claire, I'm sure he appreciated it.'

'I think so. Anyway, two months later, out of the blue, Vaughan Pentire moved into the Dower House.'

171

Unable to share her husband's confidences, Eve said, 'I see. But you said you didn't think they knew each other.'

'Perhaps that's what discretion means.' Claire looked at her friend and raised her eyebrows, and Eve realised they were discussing something that she had thought about a great deal. 'I don't know if I'm constructing a mountain of unjustified conjecture, or I'm missing something obvious.'

'You don't think he's involved in the death somehow though?' Eve said.

Anguish showed in her friend's eyes. 'What if it really was suicide? Maybe he and Piers argued, and he took his own life in an emotional turmoil of some kind.'

'Well, if Piers was at the Dower House that night things might get a little complicated, Claire. Have you asked him directly?'

'No. I'm just thinking out loud.'

'Do you know where he was that night?'

'I don't. I was out myself at the Mulfords' until past midnight. Fenn brought me home and I went straight to bed. He was in when I left, but beyond that…' She shrugged and stared at her friend, her eyes troubled. 'But what if he was there, at the Dower House. And what if it wasn't suicide. What if it was murder, Eve? What then?'

*

Later that day, spurred on by her frank discussion with her oldest friend, Lady Langford spoke to Dereham.

'Do you remember the last time I went over to the Mulfords' place? I returned rather late as is prone to happen with those occasions.'

A ghost of a smile passed over the face of the man opposite her. 'It is a house that is famous for its hospitality, my lady,' he confirmed.

'Yes, quite. Anyway, do you remember if Lord Langford went out at all that night?'

172

'It was the night before Mr Pentire was found, wasn't it, my lady?'

'As you insist on mentioning it, yes I believe so.'

'I served His Lordship with a brandy after dinner and left him with the decanter in the billiards room. He told me he'd look after himself from that point onwards and, if memory serves, told me to "put my feet up with a good book".'

'So did he go out or did he not?'

'Mr Stafford telephoned at nine o'clock and asked for His Lordship. I was unable to find him in the billiards room or drawing room. Having disconnected I checked his bedroom intending to pass a message, but he wasn't there either. I left a note on his bedside table. Beyond that I cannot say with any certainty, madam. I'm sorry.'

Lady Langford watched him leave, a pensive look on her face. It was clear that no one at Langford Hall could provide an alibi for her eldest son on the night of the murder.

Chapter Fifteen

The next morning was Burrows' day off, so he and Laura took the pram and went shopping in the village, although Matilda was more inclined to walk and made her preference very clear.

It had rained in the night and the gravel surface of Dell Lane steamed gently in the warm sunshine as they progressed rather noisily towards the market cross.

'The draper's first, Burrows,' Laura said above the din emanating from the pram. They stopped outside and she said, 'Wait here, will you, I'll just pop in.' But her mother's disappearance infuriated Matilda even more and finally, as people stared sympathetically, her father picked her up and joined his wife in the shop.

Xanthe Rudge was standing behind a polished wooden counter which had a brass measure embedded along its edge, and he heard Laura say, 'And a yard of the one-inch blue ribbon, please, Miss Rudge.' To the shopkeeper's right four wooden spools loaded with ribbon were attached to the wall. She reached out and pulled the end of the blue one towards her. It was slightly frayed, and she snipped it cleanly off, leaving a few strands of thread on the counter before measuring out the correct length, cutting the other end and popping it into a bag.

'That's a lot of ribbon,' Burrows observed, staring at the wall.

Miss Rudge glanced over. 'Yes, well, there's forty yards on a roll.'

They paid for the purchases and left the shop. 'Are you dressmaking again?' Burrows enquired.

'Yes, I thought I'd make something up for the Ploughman's Ball. It's coming up soon and as it's a rather special occasion I thought I'd make an effort. Or do my best anyway. In this condition.' She patted her swollen tummy.

'Special in what way?' he asked, rather foolishly.

Her reply had more than a touch of steel to it. 'If you recall, dear husband, it was at the ball two years ago that we decided that it was high time we started walking out.'

'Ah, yes, I knew that obviously.' Burrows attempted to regain the lost ground, but his nearest and dearest was not impressed.

'And thank heavens I decided I'd make the running. Because if I'd left it to you, I'd be well on the way to spinsterhood and you'd still be sitting in the police house in the evenings, looking at the walls.'

'Well, I might be in the Black Horse,' Burrows countered, not unreasonably, he thought.

His wife made a noise that managed to communicate her thoughts on that very clearly and they turned the corner into the high street. Nearly everyone all the way up to St Mary's looked up to identify the source of the howling, which continued unabated.

'Push her up to the common, will you? Let her have a run round up there,' Laura said. 'I'll take the bag and do the shopping and catch you up. You can give us a swing on the walnut tree branch.'

'Right.' He set off, leaving his wife to saunter behind him.

Eve Dance watched them with a smile from the other side of the road and gave Laura a wave before she too headed for

175

the draper's. For some time, she had been considering changing the curtains in the sitting room at Marston House and had decided to get on with it. And although she thought the Misses Rudge were unlikely to have the choices she was looking for, she felt duty bound to check before going to the larger shops in Oxford.

Sadly, her instincts were correct. Both the window display and the interior of the shop were rather tired and a little dusty, giving the appearance of a business that was ailing. And, although Xanthe Rudge was able to show her a bolt of dark crimson material, it was not quite what she was looking for, and she said she'd have a think about it.

Xanthe seemed unsurprised and the unacknowledged failure of the draper's to meet what would have been a substantial order created an awkwardness which Eve found gently distressing. She wondered how they managed if the shop was their only source of income.

Reluctant to just walk out, she lingered and asked, 'Any news?'

Amongst the women of the village this was the standard invitation to share a little gossip and Xanthe took her cue. 'It's been a bit of a shock, hasn't it, first the death of Mr Pentire and now these awful letters that the vicar was talking about in church.' Her kindly face creased with worry.

'I do agree, it's created an odd atmosphere in the village. People keep looking at each other and wondering who's had one.'

'Setting folk against each other.' Xanthe nodded and shivered. 'It used to be such a nice place. I really don't know what's happening sometimes.'

Eve nodded sympathetically, although as the wife of the chief constable she knew very well that the inhabitants of Great Tew were just as capable of jealousy, vindictiveness and revenge as anyone else.

'I suppose we all have our little secrets, don't we. Things we'd rather other people didn't know. It's just the way humans are.' She met the other woman's eye and gave her a warm smile as she said this, because, with her elevated sensitivity and abilities, she thought she had worked out what Xanthe Rudge's secret was some time ago. And in her view, it was hers to keep.

'I know I have,' she added confidentially.

A veil seemed to appear in the draper's eyes, and she said, 'Well I'm not sure I do. My sister and I lead very quiet lives, I'm afraid.'

Eve gave her a smile. 'A clean conscience, eh? Good for you, I wish I had one. Well, I must press on with my morning. Give my regards to Geraldine, won't you. Will you be coming to the Ploughman's Ball?'

Xanthe appeared momentarily distracted, then gathered herself and nodded. 'Yes, we usually do.'

'See you there if not before.' With that she turned and left the shop.

The bell rang and dust motes swirled in the rays of the sun that came through the window. In the ensuing silence a footstep sounded, and Geraldine appeared from the doorway that led into the back of the shop. She had obviously been listening from the other room.

They looked at each other. Then Xanthe said, 'You don't think she knows, do you?'

*

After lunch Laura went to visit a friend, leaving her husband in charge of Matilda, who was having a nap under the plum tree in the garden. But try as he might, he couldn't relax with the newspaper because a persistent mental itch was buzzing away like a fly at a window. He couldn't throw off the feeling that something significant had happened when they'd been out in the village – that he'd seen or heard something that was important regarding the death of Vaughan Pentire.

Had he been aware that he had stood and talked to the person who had pulled the trigger in the study, his frustration

177

would have been even greater. But as it was, he sat there turning events over in his mind, the paper redundant on his lap.

There had been the brief visit to the draper's shop where his wife had bought the ribbon, then they had parted, and he had made slow progress up the high street as nearly everyone had stopped to commiserate with the bawling child and her father. He mentally listed them.

Eve Dance, Hector Dean, Rosemary Kennedy, George Wishaw, the Reverend Tukes and then, as he reached the common and released Matilda from her confinement, he had exchanged a few words with Aiden Connors, who had advised him that he would be leaving the village to take up a new position. This was not unexpected because as the chief constable had observed, 'We can't keep him here for ever.' Beyond asking him to leave his new address at the police station there was little Burrows could do.

Then finally he had met Lord Langford over by the walnut tree. The aristocrat appeared to have decided to let bygones be bygones with regard to their previous conversation and was friendly enough, even going so far as to swing Matilda on the low hanging branch.

Burrows was tempted to ask him directly if he had known Mr Pentire, and if so why he hadn't made this fact clear early in the investigation. But without the protection of his uniform, he simply didn't have the nerve, especially as the colonel had told him to avoid any further confrontation. So, the conversation consisted of neutral pleasantries during which the noble lord confirmed that his brother and new wife had had a marvellous time on their honeymoon and asked after the health of the sergeant's heavily pregnant wife.

'You can ask her yourself, sir,' Burrows replied with a smile and pointed across the common to where Laura had appeared and given them a wave. The three of them had chatted for another five minutes and then he had departed, having ascertained that she had three weeks to go and 'frankly, my lord, it can't come soon enough'.

Burrows sipped his mug of tea and mentally went back over the list. Perhaps it wasn't what he'd heard but what he'd seen, he mused. But again, there was nothing in the high street or on the common that he could think of. Confusedly, he also found the image of the threshing machine and the steam tractor that powered it appearing in his mind. *What has that got to do with anything?* he wondered.

Then there was the business of the poison pen letters. The first letter that the Misses Rudge had received bothered him. His theory that Connors had sent them before the murderer had pinched the crib sheet fitted the circumstances well, but the man's very credible protestations of innocence had left a nagging doubt that ate away at him.

If he hadn't sent it, then who had?

Sadly, that promising line of thought was terminated by Matilda who suddenly stirred on the rug, sat up and said with unequivocal clarity, 'Drink, Daddy.'

The morning after his day off Burrows commandeered the Matchless from Dixon, drove into Oxford and called in at the address that the valet had left at the police station. Ten Elton Place was one of a line of fine Georgian townhouses about a quarter of a mile from Magdalen Bridge. Removing his helmet and goggles he knocked on the front door. As he had hoped, Connors answered but was clearly not pleased to see him.

'What do you want?' he hissed with a glance over his shoulder.

'Can you spare a minute?' Burrows replied.

Connors visibly hesitated, then a voice sounded from behind him. 'Who is it? Police, oh my word, whatever is the matter?' An elderly man wearing an oriental dressing gown over his shirt and trousers had appeared.

Burrows replied, 'Nothing to worry about, sir. Mr Connors was a witness to an accident and came forward to report it, which we're grateful for. I'm just here to take a brief statement, if that's alright.'

'I see, well of course, carry on.' He disappeared again.

Tight-lipped, Connors said, 'Round the back.' Then he shut the door in his face.

Burrows left the motorbike where it was, walked to the end of the row of houses and round to the alley at the back. Shortly afterwards he was standing in the kitchen where the valet did not offer him a cup of tea or invite him to sit down.

'I've told you everything. You've got no reason to bother me like this, it's harassment I reckon. I've got a good place here.'

The police sergeant held up his hands. 'I've come to ask you something man to man. It's off the record and I can tell you that you will not be prosecuted whatever your answer. I simply want the truth so I can rule other things out of my enquiries.'

Connors eyed him warily and said nothing. Burrows pressed on. 'As you know I believed that you wrote the poison pen letter to the Misses Rudge and then sent a further demand for money which they paid. Twenty pounds to be exact. But I'm starting to wonder if I'm right. So, my question to you, Mr Connors, is this. Did you or did you not send those letters to the sisters? Just between us, here in this room. What's the truth?'

'The truth is that I did not. As I live and breathe, I am not a blackmailer.'

Burrows gave him a long look then thanked him and turned for the door. With his hand on the knob, he looked back. Connors met his eye, and he was certain he was telling the truth. 'Thank you, Mr Connors. I doubt I'll be bothering you again.'

And with that he returned to the motorbike and rode thoughtfully back to Great Tew.

*

That evening, as dusk turned to darkness, Burrows let himself into the Dower House. It was the first chance he'd had all day to test an idea that had come to him.

His reasoning was that the weak points in the study had to be the door and the sash window. The chimney was too small and there were no concealed entrances in the walls or wooden floor. They'd checked thoroughly, to the extent of moving the desk and rolling up the rug. It was also impossible for the murderer to have got out of either when they were locked shut. So somehow, they'd managed to relock the window or door from the outside.

All this he knew and had discussed at length with Dixon. But riding back from Oxford he realised that beyond giving it a brief inspection they hadn't had a proper look at the ceiling. And he had an idea about that.

Opening the study door he switched on the overhead light and the lamp on the desk then left again, shutting the door behind him. He climbed the stairs in semi-darkness, the night glow from outside falling onto the half-landing, and then walked along the corridor to Vaughan Pentire's bedroom.

Inside the plain furnishings were as he remembered them. He rolled up the rug that lay between the bed and the dressing table and leaned it on the wall, then pulled the curtains closed and turned off the light. Giving particular attention to the base of the walls, he commenced a careful examination of the bedroom floor, looking for any sign of light showing from the study directly below.

Ten minutes later he sat up on his knees and sighed with frustration. He had been hopeful there would be some indication of a concealed panel in the cornicing that ran round the study ceiling, but no light showed at all through the boards. He descended the main staircase again but as he started down the flight that led to the hall, he noticed something. Something that stopped him in his tracks.

There was a narrow line of light showing above the study door. A very narrow line. Even with the lights on in the room and the staircase in darkness it was only just visible. No wonder they'd missed it in the daylight, he thought. Pulse racing he hurried to the kitchen and returned with a hard wooden chair. He put it against the door then climbed on and peered at the gap. Then he grunted to himself, climbed down and returned to the kitchen.

After five minutes searching in the drawers and cupboards, he had what he wanted – a bundle of butcher's string. Having cut a three-foot length he went back to the hall and into the study. He looped the string over the top of the open door then gently pushed it shut, and locked and bolted it.

One end of the string hung invitingly. Muttering a silent prayer he reached up and pulled.

'Argh!' He groaned in frustration. The string was gripped tightly and didn't move an inch. Thin though the string was, the gap was thinner. Wafer-thin in fact.

Defeated he sat down at the desk and stared gloomily at the window.

Chapter Sixteen

It was the day of the Ploughman's Ball, the last of Piers Spense's 'summer season' events in Great Tew. As ever, a huge marquee had been erected on the parkland between the high street and Langford Hall and a prime beef steer had been slaughtered ready to be roasted on a spit. Stanley Tirrold had set up a rack of beer and cider barrels at one end of the great tent and was happily anticipating a profitable evening. A wooden floor for dancing had been laid at the other and a twelve-piece dance band from Oxford had been booked.

Lady Langford, who sponsored the celebration and paid for it out of her personal funds, came to check on things before heading over to the ploughing match on the common.

'It all looks splendid, Dereham,' she said, eyeing the sea of tables with pristine white tablecloths and colourful chains of twisted paper ribbon that hung in glamorous loops above.

'Thank you, my lady, we've put individual lamps on each table this year, so it'll look nice when it gets dark too. The Spense family are in the usual place, if that suits.' He pointed to one corner where a reserved sign stood on a round table with eight chairs.

'I'm sure that will do us nicely.' She walked over to the publican. 'Good afternoon, Mr Tirrold. All ready?'

'I am, thank you, Lady Langford. Trixie will be here in a minute to help with the serving.'

'Well send your account as usual. You've got enough, have you?' She peered over the counter. Four barrels were racked up and a further two stood waiting.

'We have, my lady. Even by Great Tew standards.'

She gave a brief laugh. 'Quite. Well, I'll get over to the common and see how the ploughing match is doing. We'll see you later.'

As they watched her leave the publican said quietly, 'She keeps the whole show on the road, doesn't she, Mr Dereham. The way of life we all have here, somehow it all comes back to her.'

The butler nodded. 'True. I hear from friends that other estates have been badly affected by the war, with only sons killed and death duties tearing places apart. We're lucky that things seem to have gone back to normal by and large. And now with Edward and Innes marrying there'll be continuity and children. An heir at least, maybe two.'

'What about this murder though, that's still not been sorted out, has it?'

'No. Or the letters. Heaven knows who is sending those, or what their motivation can be.'

'Are they posted?'

Dereham nodded. 'Postmarked Great Tew, by all accounts.'

Stanley Tirrold remarked, half seriously, 'I'm surprised Sergeant Burrows hasn't got Mabel Dixon lurking in a doorway by the post box making a list of people posting letters.'

Dereham smiled back. 'There must be at least a dozen post boxes that feed into the post office here in the village. She can't cover them all.' He eyed the barrels. 'All set up?'

The publican reached for a pair of glasses. 'Perhaps we'd better make sure it's running clear, Mr Dereham. Just to be on the safe side.'

'You can't be too careful, Mr Tirrold.'

'Starting early, gents?' Beatrice Wray appeared through the tent door and walked over. 'They won't be long. The judges are just deciding over on the common.'

'You look well, Trixie,' Dereham remarked, observing her glowing countenance.

'I am, as it happens. Me and Ronnie Back are getting wed and I'm right happy about it.'

'Congratulations to you both. I hope you'll be very happy. He's a good man. And decent prospects too.'

'I reckon so. I'm going to be a solicitor's wife and I feel like I've got a kitten purring in my heart and that's the truth,' she replied with a wonderful smile.

'What's this?' The Reverend Tukes had also appeared and walked over.

'Beatrice and Ronnie Back are betrothed. She's just told us,' the publican said.

'Aha! Well, I'm delighted for you both. Come and see me next week and we can have a chat.' He nodded in agreement as Stanley Tirrold held up an empty pint glass. 'Yes, please.'

Shortly afterwards Dereham finished his drink and left them talking, and ten minutes after that a cheer carried from the common. Stanley Tirrold cocked an ear. 'Here we go then, Beatrice, they're coming. You pour ten pints of cider and I'll do the ale. We'll set them up ready on the counter.'

*

By mid-evening the ball was in full swing. It was dark outside, and the marquee was lit by intimate pools of light on each table and coloured spotlights on the band and the dance floor. Burrows estimated that there were two hundred people gathered together and the atmosphere was redolent with fun and gaiety as the

185

dancers whirled, and the band played. He was sitting at a table with Mabel Dixon and Hector Dean, and his heavily pregnant wife, who was doing her best to join in but was clearly very uncomfortable perched on the wooden chair.

'Not too much longer, Burrows, if that's alright,' she said to him, her hand on his arm.

He nodded. 'Yes, fair enough. I'll just have one more pint then we'll walk home. Twenty minutes tops.' He stood and strode through the crowd to where Beatrice was holding the fort as Stanley Tirrold guided his wife around the dance floor with studious concentration.

'One more then, Trixie, then we're off,' he said.

'She's done well your missus,' the barmaid replied. 'When's she due?'

'Next week.' He took the pint and sipped at it. 'Did I hear you're getting wed?'

She beamed. 'I am that. Me and Ronnie Back.'

'Congratulations. When'll that be?'

She smiled coyly. 'As soon as possible. You know how it is. The Promised Land and all…'

'Yes, I do.' He smiled back, remembering his own wife's whispered suggestion that they 'go and see what all the fuss is about' when they had been courting. 'Well, I'm pleased for you. I wasn't sure about marriage but I'm happy now. And Ronnie's a decent fellow. He'll look after you.'

But the barmaid wasn't listening. Eyes narrow she was staring over his shoulder towards the corner of the marquee where Laura was sitting. 'Is everything alright over there?' she said uncertainly.

Burrows turned. There was some kind of disturbance at their table. Laura had half risen and then collapsed back down onto her chair, her face anxious. Dixon and Hector Dean were both standing, and the WPC was looking around, concern clear on her face. Putting his glass down he pushed through the crowd. By the time he arrived Laura's distress had caught the attention of the people at adjacent tables and a little crowd was forming.

His wife met his eyes. 'It's coming, Burrows. The baby's coming.'

'Oh right, well come on let's get you home then.' He reached for her hand, but she waved him away.

'No, no. It's coming now. Right now.' She grimaced as a long contraction took her and she gasped, 'Bloody hell, Burrows, I mean it. Put me on the floor.'

'Find Innes Spense, Dixon,' he said shortly and moved to help his wife, but two of the village women were already beside her, talking and helping her to the ground. 'Don't worry, my love, here's as good as anywhere else,' he heard one of them say as they pulled at her dress.

'Let's have a bit of privacy then,' he roared to the captivated onlookers. 'Use the tablecloths.' Within a minute two tables had been cleared of glasses and willing helpers were holding up a simple screen. 'You men face into the tent, please,' he cried as Innes arrived.

Torn between staring in fascination and looking away himself, he watched as she bent down and took his wife's hand, smiling and clearly speaking words of reassurance, before kneeling between her legs.

'They do pick their moments, don't they, Burrows.' He turned to see Eve Dance standing next to him. With a shock he realised the band had stopped playing and a silence had fallen over the crowd.

'She's having the baby,' he called out. 'She's having it now!'

A prolonged scream and calm words of encouragement from the doctor sounded from behind the screen, then another moan from his wife was followed by prolonged panting and then suddenly a baby's cry.

He looked over the screen to see Innes handing the baby up to his wife. She said, 'Well, that really was quick. It's a boy, Burrows. You have a son.' Then she smiled and bent to her work.

'It's a boy!' he bellowed across the heads of the crowd.

Cheers and clapping exploded in the marquee as the tension dissolved. Hector Dean shook his hand. 'Congratulations, Dad.'

Even though he'd been expecting it, Burrows was stunned. He'd known the baby was coming of course, but seeing nature take its course the way it had, had knocked him for six. He stood there blankly as a pint of cider was pushed into his hand and the men of the village surrounded him. Then Innes was there, her eyes warm.

'Everything is fine, under the circumstances. We need to get her home and into bed as soon as we can, but I think you'd better meet your son, don't you?' She led him round the tablecloths. Laura was still on the ground, leaning back on Ada Dale who was kneeling behind her. Her dress was pulled back down, she was flushed, and her eyes seemed enormous.

'Here we are then, Burrows,' she said quietly and looked down at the tiny crimson baby cuddled into her chest. He realised he was wrapped in the cardigan she'd been wearing. He crouched next to her, staring in wonder, and then leaned forward and gave her a tender kiss.

'I love you, Laura Burrows,' he said simply.

She reached out and took his hand. 'And I love you. Sorry for all the bother.'

His eyes watered. 'It's no bother. No bother at all.'

The next half hour passed in something of a blur. Fenn arrived with the car and a stretcher brought from the cottage hospital, and Laura and the baby were carried through the beaming crowd and loaded into the Alvis. Then they were slowly driven home where Innes helped Laura to bed and checked her

188

over while Burrows heated a bowl of water and provided some towels.

Annie the twelve-year-old girl who had been sitting in as Matilda slept upstairs was astonished by events. 'You go off empty-handed and come back with that,' she observed. 'Blimey.'

Back at the hall, the villagers took the whole thing in their stride. As the stretcher disappeared and the sounds of the Alvis faded into the night, Piers Spense looked at his watch and said to his mother, 'Well it's only ten o'clock, we might as well carry on.'

He stood and walked over to the band leader's microphone and addressed the crowd. 'Ladies and gentlemen, as there is plenty of time left and the evening has only been further enhanced by the arrival of a new life, I suggest we continue the celebrations in our time-honoured way. Mr Tirrold appears to have a surfeit of refreshments on tap, and I'm told there's plenty to pick at on the beef steer outside.'

He glanced behind him to where the band waited and continued, 'I therefore think I can leave you in the very capable hands of Mr Jimmy Absolom and the Oxford Nighthawks.'

To cheers Piers Spense stood aside and, grinning widely, the band leader announced, 'Ladies and gentlemen, please take your partners for the quickstep, the quickstep.' Then with a swing of his arm he counted them in and off they went.

Eve Dance sat and watched as the villagers threw themselves back into the celebrations. 'Well, that's given them all something to gossip about for a day or two, thank heavens there weren't any complications,' she remarked to Lady Langford.

'Yes,' she replied. 'And we're not above a bit of gossip ourselves, are we?' She rolled her eyes and grinned at her friend. 'Look at poor old Tukes, lumbered with the waifs and strays as usual.' It was true, the vicar was sitting at a table with one or two notably single village residents and the Misses Rudge, both of whom wore outfits that were at least twenty years out of date.

'Those poor ladies,' Eve said. 'If they hang on for long enough those dresses might come back into fashion, you know.'

Lady Langford hid a smile. 'Oh, Eve, don't be cruel. Piers, go and dance with one of the Rudge sisters.'

He looked at her. 'I'd really rather not, if you don't mind.'

'Noblesse oblige, dear boy, off you go,' she replied blithely. 'I've lost count of the number of ancient milords who've squired me around the dance floor while their wives glared.'

'What about Edward? He's just loitering over there by the bar.'

'They also serve, who only stand and wait. Anyway, he's got a wife to look after. You do not.'

With a sigh he rose, and they watched him walk over. 'Which will he choose,' Eve whispered. 'My money's on Xanthe.'

'You are awful, but if pushed I think you're right. At least she's got a kind face,' her friend replied.

'Bingo!' Smiling they both watched as Piers leaned over the younger of the two sisters and escorted her out onto the dance floor. Moments later the Reverend Tukes and Geraldine joined them, and they were rapidly absorbed into the whirling maelstrom of villagers performing their own, well-oiled and highly personal versions of the quickstep.

'Do you fancy a bite?'

'Yes, I am peckish. Let's repair outside.'

Thirty yards away the charcoal fire still glowed under the steer, which had been raised high enough not to dry out. A footman was on duty and helped them to a portion and they added pickles and bread before walking over to a bench below a huge beech tree.

'I hesitate to mention it on a nice evening like this, but have you got to the bottom of where Piers was the night Mr Pentire died?' Eve asked between mouthfuls.

'In a word, no. I ended up asking him in a roundabout way, but he simply said he couldn't remember but may have gone

190

out for a walk. Then he asked me why I was asking, at which point I had to make a strategic retreat.' She stared back towards the marquee. 'I sense there's something he's not telling me, but it may be entirely innocent.'

Eve decided to cross the line. 'In confidence, Jocelyn has found out that Vaughan Pentire and Piers knew each other rather well in London, before he arrived in Great Tew.'

Her friend stared at her in the darkness. 'What?'

'Yes. It appears that when you gave him permission, he didn't just invite a friend down for the weekend, he moved one in next door.'

*

The day after the ball, Oxford station bore witness to the arrival of a second red-haired young man and, in a curious further mirroring of previous events, the same porter found himself being asked the same question.

'Can you tell me the best way to get to a place called Great Tew? Do you know it?'

The porter repeated his answer regarding the bus but decided not to mention hiring a car. His previous interlocuter had been noticeably well dressed and, while the young man in front of him looked tidy enough, he did not exude the air of a fellow who didn't need to worry about money.

'... so you've missed the last one for today,' he concluded. 'If you're looking for a reasonable hotel, the Empire a few hundred yards that way might suit you.' He pointed to his left.

Thanking him, Cameron Breck set off in the direction indicated and half an hour later was sitting on a narrow bed in a modest hotel room with a window that looked onto the back of some houses, and a shared bathroom some distance down the corridor.

After attacking the postman in Dumfries and discovering Innes's address, he had returned to Glasgow and spent some more time working on the ferry. But having now arrived in Oxford with money in his pocket, the big question occupying his mind was how to handle the meeting with Innes Spense, as she apparently now was. Up to this point his focus had been on following the trail, but now he was forced to confront the reality of standing in front of her again.

Would she even recognise him? And what was it he wanted? Money? Her company? The boy back? And how easy would those things be?

One frustration was that, try as he might, he couldn't really remember what Innes Knox was like. A vague impression lingered of a forthright personality, and she'd certainly been pretty enough, her mother's eyes had reminded him of that. But beyond those simple memories there was a grey mist that he simply couldn't penetrate.

One answer would be to travel to Great Tew and spy out the land, but he was hesitant to do this. His experience of small communities in Skye meant he was well aware that a new arrival getting off a bus was noticed straight away. And his red hair was like a beacon in the night. His humiliating experience in Dundee had been the result of rushing in and he'd learned his lesson.

Then an idea occurred. The newspaper archive in Glasgow had served him well. The library in an academic town like Oxford would have the same facilities. He could ask for back copies of the local paper and comb them for articles about the Spense family. Surely there would be the odd thing about them, even if they lived quietly in some modest country house.

Happy with the decision, he put on his cap, left the hotel and went off in search of a dram and some food.

The following day he enacted his plan. Making enquiries with the owner of the hotel he was told that Oxford central library was located in part of the town hall in St Aldate's and was no more than a fifteen-minute walk away. He found it without difficulty and presented himself at the reception desk. A man wearing wire-framed spectacles and a well-worn flannel suit

192

looked up as he approached. His forehead was disfigured by an ugly transverse scar, and he wore a patch over his left eye.

The war. Breck's thought was instinctive and accurate.

'Good morning, sir, may I be of assistance?' the man asked.

Breck smiled back. 'I was hoping to look up some information on a family called Spense. They live in a village called Great Tew, I believe.' Encouraged by the recognition in the man's eyes, he added, 'I was thinking I'd have a look in back copies of the local papers.'

'You're not from Oxfordshire, I'm guessing, sir,' the man observed. 'And I think we can do better than the papers. If you'll follow me.' He came round the counter and led the way past an elderly couple to some shelves in a far corner of the high-ceilinged room. Lowering his voice he said, 'This is the local history section and if I'm not mistaken, we have…' he paused and scanned the upper shelf before grunting in satisfaction and reaching upwards, 'yes, here we are. A history of the Spense family from 1066 to 1910. Written by some chap from the university. They say the archives at Langford Hall are quite something. I wouldn't mind having a look myself, to be honest.'

He passed the slim volume to the young Scotsman, adding, 'If you're not a member you cannot take it out of the library, I'm afraid, but we have reading desks over there.' He gestured towards a row of tables where various people were sitting. 'The family are in the papers fairly regularly for one thing or another, so if you're looking for something more recent, that'll be the place to look.'

Slightly nonplussed, Breck took the book and said, 'Thank you. I'll have a look at this first anyway. Then I might come and see you for the newspapers.'

'Very well, it'll be the *Oxford Evening Echo* probably, although they're in the London *Times* from time to time as well.

There was a big wedding up at the hall earlier in the year and it was all over the society pages.'

'Oh really? Who got married?'

'Edward Spense, the Dowager Lady Langford's youngest son. To a Scottish lady, I believe.' He nodded and smiled in recognition of Breck's own accent. 'I'll leave you to it.' With that he returned to the counter, and Breck heard him greet a young woman who had just come in.

He took the book over to the reading area, found an empty table and settled down to read.

An hour later he closed the book, pushed back in his chair and rubbed his eyes. It was an academic tome, much given over to family trees and the finer details of strategic marriages, but one thing came through loud and clear. The Spense family were not like the lairds on Skye, impoverished aristocrats living a dwindling existence in a crumbling family pile. Oh no, not at all. They were entwined with the very history of England and had been present at every significant event for nigh on a thousand years. And they were still going strong before the war.

He returned the book to the shelves and crossed to the counter, where the attendant asked, 'Was that useful, sir?'

'Oh aye, most informative, thank you. I'll have a look at the papers now, if that's possible.'

In answer he was presented with a single copy of the *Oxford Evening Echo*. 'I took the liberty of digging this out for you. It's the report of the Spense family wedding from earlier this year. There's a four-page spread in there.'

Breck took it eagerly. 'That's ideal, thank you.' He returned to his seat and opened the paper. For a moment he did a double-take and hissed with shock, causing a woman at the far end of the table to glance over.

Under the headline *A Joyous Day at Langford Hall*, the front cover of the centrefold was dominated by a full-length photograph of Innes and the man he assumed was Edward Spense standing in

194

the doorway of a great house. The sight of her was almost like a physical blow. He'd remembered her being pretty, but the photographer knew his business and the light reflected off the planes of her face in a way that emphasised her startling beauty.

Next to her, and impeccably dressed in formal wear, her new husband grinned from ear to ear at the camera. Breck's eyes narrowed as he stared at the tall broad-shouldered figure.

No wonder you're smiling. But you weren't there first, pal. I wonder if you know that. And who else does?

Turning the page he read on, hungrily consuming the photographs and words like a starving man presented with a laden table. And what rich fare it was. Picture after picture of the bride and groom, Edward Spense's mother and elder brother, and the great and good of the land drinking champagne in the most opulent of surroundings. There were also plenty of people in highland dress and he recognised the Knoxes of Cambridge Close in the formal line up.

But it was two photographs on the back cover of the spread that caught his attention the most. A small boy standing in a page boy's outfit with a suit of armour behind him. A girl in a smart maid's uniform was holding his hand and they were both looking past the camera. In the other image the boy was with Innes Spense. They were in profile and there was no one else in sight. She was kneeling down in front of him, her eyes full of love and he was staring back.

Underneath, the caption read, *Mrs Innes Spense with four-year-old Master Jaikie Knox, her deceased sister's son, who has been welcomed into the Spense family and will live at Langford Hall.*

Cameron Breck's mouth tightened. So that was how she'd done it. He had to admit it was clever. And as he sat in silence staring at the pages two things occurred to him. Firstly, any vague ideas he might have of a reconciliation or future with Innes were untenable. He didn't have a chance.

The other thought was much more interesting. This was an immensely wealthy family with a reputation to lose. Eyes narrow and a gleam of avarice on his face, he stared sightlessly out of the window and wondered how much they'd pay to avoid a scandal.

*

Burrows' suggestion that WPC Dixon would find the task of alibiing the suspects on the list easier if she used the Matchless to get around had been greeted with surprise and delight by the constable.

After an initial and ill-fated attempt to straddle the bike while wearing her uniform skirt, an incident which had reduced her sergeant to blushing semi-hysteria, she had obtained a pair of male uniform trousers and made the necessary adjustments. Thus equipped, she had taken to it like a duck to water and her helmeted, goggled and gauntleted figure was now a familiar, if rather intimidating, sight in the quiet lanes and dusty byways of the Langford estate. The villagers had nicknamed her 'the flying frog'.

A few days after the Ploughman's Ball, she finally completed her interviews and was able to report to her sergeant with reasonable confidence that all sixteen of them could account for themselves on the night of the murder.

She tapped her notebook. 'But I'm certain that some of them were shocked or frightened by what they heard from Mr Pentire. Rosemary Kennedy was very tight-lipped and tense, and Lizzie Midding actually burst into tears, but they wouldn't admit anything. And I've double-checked each alibi.'

'So where does that leave us, Dixon?' Burrows mused.

'It leaves us with the names of the people the chief constable crossed off the list, I'm afraid, Sergeant.' She hesitated, well aware of the significance of what she was about to say.

Burrows saw the indecision on her face. 'What is it?'

196

'When I was doing the alibis Captain Perry's name came up as he was hosting a rural planning meeting in Banbury. It appears Mr Stafford from the Langford estate was also there. Out of interest I checked up at St Mary's. The night Mr Pentire died was choir practice so the Reverend Tukes would have been in attendance, and he always goes to the public house afterwards. So all three men are alibied for the period before Connors returned to the Dower House.'

The sergeant's blood ran cold. 'What are you saying?' Although he already knew.

'What I'm saying is that there's only one name left on the list. Lord Langford.'

Chapter Seventeen

Innes, Eve and Lady Langford were in Oxford on a shopping trip. Nominally Claire Spense was in pursuit of a new winter coat, but the main objective was to spend some time together and enjoy a pleasant gossip. They had repaired to the tearoom at Boswells, the oldest department store in the city, and were enjoying a delicious selection of cake and scandal in equal measure, when the talk turned to Innes's honeymoon.

'Tell me, did you prefer Paris or Rome?' Eve asked, before delicately forking a piece of chocolate gateau into her mouth.

'Paris, I think, but it was all rather wonderful. And the last week we spent on Capri was just idyllic. We had a cottage by the sea and a cook and a maid, but otherwise we were just left to our own devices.' She smiled at the memory. 'I think that was when we really got to know each other.'

'And no nasty surprises?' her mother-in-law enquired in her base voice, aware as only a parent can be of her son's faults.

'We had a couple of little rows, but nothing serious and we're both rather strong-willed people so I suspect those will crop up from time to time. As long as I win my fair share of them, I'm sure we will be fine.' She picked up a piece of sponge cake.

'Yes, I'm sure too. And you are looking quite beautiful, my dear, you really are. Edward is a very lucky man.'

'Well perhaps this is the moment to tell you that you're going to be a grandmother.' Innes smiled back.

Lady Langford's shriek of joy briefly silenced the tearoom but seeing that it was clearly good news of some kind or another, the other customers returned to their own business, leaving the aristocrat with tears in her eyes, grasping her daughter-in-law's hand.

'My darling, that is wonderful news. Quite wonderful. Does Edward know?'

'Not yet, but I'll tell him tonight I think.'

'Yes, do. That's marvellous. Things are just looking so good for us all now. You're settled and an heir on the way. I really couldn't be happier.'

Their conversation continued for some time and then they paid and slowly descended to the ground floor. Out on the pavement they separated. Eve wanted to pick up a book she had ordered from Blackwell's, while Innes had decided to buy a new toy motor car for Jaikie and Claire said she would come along too, before they went to look for a coat.

'Fenn will be here with the car at half past four, so we'll see you then,' Lady Langford remarked as they departed.

Suddenly uneasy, Eve watched them go, arm in arm. She felt detached from the busy street. Present but somehow not there. It was a familiar feeling and as she waited, the drum beat that she had felt getting closer and closer sounded again.

But this time it wasn't distant. It was here. Now. And it was deafening. She looked around and a thrill of horror pulsed through her body. Across the street a red-haired young man in grey flannels and a tweed jacket was standing in a shop doorway, staring after Innes and Claire. He looked shocked. Then, as though feeling her gaze, he turned his head and met her eye.

And she knew, she just knew. It was like looking at an adult version of Jaikie.

Appalled, and barely aware she was moving, she crossed the road and came up to him. He watched her silently and by the time she arrived in front of him a thin smile had appeared on his face.

'Can I help you?' he asked in the soft accent of the outer isles.

'I noticed you staring at my friends. Do you know them?'

'You might say that. Innes and I knew each other once, although I get the feeling she's gone up in the world since then.' He was openly smirking now.

Eve thought quickly. 'I see. And is it your intention to renew your acquaintance?'

'Aye, it might well be.'

'To what end?'

'You're a one for questions, aren't you. What's your interest anyway?'

The petite blonde stared at him, and he was taken aback by the sudden power that seemed to emanate from her. 'Innes is a friend of mine. A close friend. If your intentions are malign, and I have a strong feeling that they are, you should know that she is well protected. In ways I doubt you would understand.'

'Is that a fact? Perhaps I'll just head over to Great Tew in the morning and knock on the door of Langford Hall. That would put the cat among the pigeons, wouldn't it? You see, I've seen pictures of the boy. If I stood next to him there'd be no doubt who his daddy is, would there? A few words from me and that whole sneaky story of a dead sister would be blown out of the water like a Hun submarine.'

He saw the shock on the woman's face. 'Oh aye, I know all about that. And the society wedding. It seems to me I can turn a profit from the cards I'm holding, so don't threaten me with a load of blather about protection. What's your name anyway?'

'My name is Eve Dance, and I am the wife of the chief constable of Oxfordshire.'

He was momentarily silenced at this, then leered unpleasantly. 'So that's your protection, is it? The coppers? I've broken no law, so they can't lay a hand on me.'

'What's your name?' Eve asked.

He hesitated, clearly wondering whether to tell her, then apparently deciding there was no harm in so doing replied, 'Cameron Breck.'

'Well, Mr Breck, as you mentioned profit a moment ago, I can imagine the way your mind is working. Where are you staying?' He told her and she continued, 'Your arrival is inconvenient and the Spense family will not welcome it. But I would advise caution if I were you. I will speak quietly to the people who matter and see what is to be done.'

He grinned wolfishly. 'Aye, Eve Dance, you do that. I'll wait for two days. If I've heard nothing by then I'll be on the bus to Great Tew. I'll just sit in the local pub and let everyone have a good look at me. That should do for starters. Then maybe I'll have a wee word with one or two of the villagers about their squeaky-clean Innes Spense. Two days, with an offer. And it had better be a generous one. You scurry along and speak to your betters.' With that he turned and strolled off.

Aware that the Spense family were facing a major crisis, Eve watched him disappear, her face grave. But as she turned to cross the road the situation got even worse. Innes was standing under the portico of Boswells, completely indifferent to the blockage she was causing. All colour had drained from her face and she was staring after Cameron Breck.

Horrified, Eve dashed into the street, nearly got run over by a delivery lorry, but made it to the other side in record time as the driver shouted after her. Without saying anything she took her hollow-eyed friend by the arm and pulled her out of the doorway and along the street. Thankfully they came to a row of railings and a gate that led into a little urban park with a group of trees and a lawn. Benches were arranged in a circle around it. They sat down at the first empty one.

And at that point Eve paused. Her actions in removing Innes from the scene had been instinctive but now that immediate objective had been achieved, she simply didn't know what to do or say next.

In the event Innes looked at her and said, 'I left a glove in the tearoom and came back for it. It's him, isn't it?'

'Yes, it is him.'

'Cameron Breck,' she said distantly, eyes on a pair of toddlers gleefully chasing each other round a tree. 'How did he find me?'

Eve shook her head. 'I don't know, he didn't say.'

'What does he want?'

Her friend opted for the truth. 'He knows about the deceit regarding the dead sister. I believe his intention is blackmail. I'm so sorry.'

Tears appeared in the young woman's eyes and her haunted expression gave her beauty a fragile quality that lifted it beyond normal humanity. As though an angel were weeping. Cheeks wet she turned to her friend and whispered, 'It's the end then. Just when everything seemed so perfect.'

'It isn't the end. Not at all. It's not good news, I'll grant you that, but we will prevail.'

'But even if we pay him off, he'll always know. He'll always be there in the background,' she whispered.

Eve was silent. This horrible truth was all too apparent. Successful blackmailers rarely stopped at one demand, especially when their victims had deep pockets. She made to speak but Innes continued, 'Jaikie's the spitting image of him. He only has to turn up in the village and people will start talking.' The thought broke her, and she raised her hands to her face as great sobs wracked her body.

202

Eve could do nothing except hold her. But as she sat there, she realised one thing was absolutely essential. Cameron Breck must never, ever reach Great Tew.

'Everything alright, ladies?' A police constable was standing looking down at them.

'Yes, fine. My friend has just had some upsetting news.'

'I'm sorry to hear that.' He looked at her and added, 'Begging your pardon but is it Mrs Dance? I was introduced to you at a police function last year. Constable Fish, madam.'

Eve nodded. 'I remember,' although she didn't.

'Well, I'll press on then. I hope you feel better soon, miss. Good afternoon.' And with that he resumed his stately progress around the park. As Eve watched him, she saw Lady Langford on the far side of the railings, clearly looking for them. She waved and saw her raise her arm in recognition and head for the gate. Two minutes later she was sitting on the other side of Innes and looking across at Eve with raised eyebrows as her daughter-in-law continued to sob, her face hidden below the wide brim of her hat.

'What on earth is the matter?' she asked.

Eve said quietly, 'Jaikie's real father is in Oxford. I met him by chance and Innes saw us talking and realised who he was.'

Shock showed on the aristocrat's face. 'Good God. Why is he here?'

'I fear he is intent on causing trouble. Unless some settlement is reached.'

Claire Spense's eyes narrowed. 'I see.' She leaned into Innes and gently raised her face. 'Come on, my darling. You are not alone, and we will deal with this…' she glanced at Eve, 'what's his name?'

'Breck. Cameron Breck.'

'This Mr Breck. Look at me. Dry your eyes, people are staring. Eve, I think Fenn normally bides his time in the Turf Tavern while in Oxford. Do you know it?'

'Down the alley off Holywell Street?'

203

'Yes. Go and get him, will you. We'll wait here.'

Eve set off without further discussion while Lady Langford ministered to her daughter-in-law.

*

Later that evening a telephone conversation took place between Claire Spense and Eve Dance. Because of the danger of an operator listening in, either by design or accident, it was coded but the required information was exchanged.

'I have made a decision about our unexpected visitor and will make him an offer,' Lady Langford said.

'I see. Have you told anyone else?'

'No. And our young friend will also keep her mouth closed at my suggestion, even from those closest to her.'

There was a brief silence as Eve considered the implications of Innes keeping Cameron Breck's presence secret from her husband. 'Well least said, soonest mended, I suppose,' she concluded.

'That is very much my view. By this time tomorrow I intend the matter to have ended. Which hotel is he at?'

'The Empire.'

'Yes, I know it. Very well.'

Eve heard the resolution in her voice. 'Do you want me to come with you?'

'Thank you, but no. I will deal with this alone.'

'And you intend to settle with him?'

'Difficult though it is, I have reached that view, yes.'

'Are you confident that will be an end to it?'

'I will ensure he understands the implications of any further actions on his part.' The steely tone in Lady Langford's voice was unmistakable and in spite of her feelings, Eve felt a brief moment of pity for the man she had met earlier. He was undoubtably an unpleasant chancer, but he had no idea of what he was taking on.

'Well please do let me know how it goes. What have you told our friend?'

'Simply that she can rely on me to make the issue go away. And I am intent on achieving that.'

With that they concluded their conversation and Lady Langford replaced the receiver before heading to the drawing room. As she disappeared round the corner Innes stepped into view on the half-landing. She quickly descended the stairs and walked over to the telephone and looked at the two words scrawled on the notepad in her mother-in-law's distinctive writing.

Empire Hotel.

Chapter Eighteen

At ten o'clock the following morning Cameron Breck was just preparing to go out for a stroll when he heard a tentative knock on his bedroom door. He crossed the room and opened it, paused briefly in surprise, then addressed the young woman who stood there.

'Innes Spense, as I live and breathe. What a coincidence.' He smirked and opened the door wider.

'Everything alright, madam?' A voice sounded from down the corridor where the manager, uneasy at the remarkably attractive young woman visiting a single man in his room, had ascended the stairs with her.

She turned to him. 'Yes, I'm fine and will not be long. You may leave us.' With a shrug the man descended to the reception, satisfied that he had done his duty, although the sound of the bedroom door shutting firmly caught up with him on the half-landing.

'What can I do for you?' Breck asked as they stood facing each other in the room, five feet apart.

For a moment Innes took a deep breath and said nothing. The sight of him had brought back a tumbling kaleidoscope of buried memories that threatened to overwhelm her. The noise and busy chatter of the hotel bar in Oban, the unwelcome attentions of her fellow student, the easy smile and charm of the man now standing before her, and, much later, the whispering, giggling and drunken ascent to his bedroom. And the fateful half hour that had followed.

'Cameron Breck,' she said finally. As if confirming the matter in her own mind.

'Aye, you know it's me, Innes.'

'Why have you come? And how did you find me?'

'Through the university. I realised you must have been a medical student.'

She nodded slowly, seeing the sense in that. 'Why?'

He laughed. 'I think you know why. My great-grandmother had the sight. The night she died she told me I had a son. I worked out it must be you.'

'And now you're here, what are your intentions?'

This time it was his turn to pause. The woman in front of him was extraordinarily beautiful. The wedding photographs did not do her justice. A sudden wild desire pulsed through him. Was it insane to consider romance? He said, 'I've never forgotten you, Innes. That night was special. I've always wanted to see you again.'

He grinned tentatively and gave a little shrug, as though embarrassed by his feelings, then continued, 'During the war the thought of us being together kept me going. If I survived I hoped that we could have a life together. Then my great-grandmother told me about the boy and, well, I've been looking for you ever since. The three of us together and Jaikie with his real dad. You're the only girl I've been with. It's what I want, Innes.'

The young woman's eyes narrowed. 'I'm told your motive is blackmail, not a shared future.'

'No, no. That's not the plan at all. I want us to forge a new life together as a loving family.'

She wondered at this for a moment, then said, 'It is too late for that. You should know that I am happily married now. Jaikie has been accepted into my in-laws' family. I'm sorry,

207

Cameron, but there is no chance of us rekindling…' she hesitated, 'whatever it was that we briefly had.'

He knew she was telling the truth. The way she was standing, her expression and her tone of voice all formed a picture that said, *You're not coming back into my life.* And a slow, deep anger began to burn inside him.

'What about Jaikie, doesn't he deserve to know who his real father is? What have you told him anyway?'

'That his daddy was a soldier who died during the war and his mother was lost to Spanish flu. He's young and he knows he is loved. That is sufficient for the moment.'

'But when he's older and starts asking difficult questions. What then?'

'We'll cross that bridge when we come to it.' Aware of the increasing belligerence in his tone, Innes added gently, 'The die is cast, Cameron. There will be no change to what he has been told. I'm sorry but you can play no part in his life, or mine.'

It was her attempt to be kind that infuriated him. The ultimate condescension. He sneered at her. 'What makes you think you're the one deciding? There's nothing stopping me coming to Great Tew and telling everyone I'm his pa. Or that you're his mother and the child is a bastard, born out of wedlock. That would knock you off your pretty perch, wouldn't it. Once the villagers realise you've told them a pack of lies.'

Shock showed in her face. 'I was only protecting the boy. If you care about him at all, you won't do that.'

'Why should I care about him. Or you? You've just told me there's nothing for me here. I tell you, Innes, truly, I've a mind to catch the bus to the village today and let the cat out of the bag just for the pleasure of seeing your lies exposed. You were happy enough to creep up to my bedroom that night, but you're far too high and mighty to bother with me now.'

A tear showed on her cheek, and she said quietly, 'That night was a terrible mistake and I've regretted it many, many times. Please, Cameron. I beg you. Don't come to Great Tew. Please.'

A surge of excitement at the power he held over her coursed through him. 'Begging now, are you? Perhaps you'd better get down on your knees then, lassie. I'd like to see that.'

*

Returning to his bedroom after an excellent lunch, Cameron Breck had his second visitor of the day. A firm knock on the door sounded and he opened it to see a well-dressed and refined-looking woman with grey hair standing there.

'Mr Breck, I presume. I am Lady Langford.'

'I know who you are. I saw the wedding pictures in the paper.' He stood aside and gestured her into the room, adding, 'I'm quite the popular fellow with visitors from Great Tew today.'

If this surprised the aristocrat, she gave no sign. 'Is that so? And who else has been here?'

'Innes of course. Pleading her cause.'

This time Claire Spense could not hide her shock. 'Innes was here. This morning?'

'Oh aye. Very tearful and pleading with me to keep my mouth shut. But it's her that's the liar not me, isn't it?'

Distain on her face, the woman replied, 'Yes, your speciality seems to be blackmail.'

Breck ignored this and remarked, 'She's all high and mighty now, but it turns out she's no better than any other Glasgow girl.'

'She's a girl who made an unfortunate mistake. But her greater misfortune is that she made it with you.'

'No, her great misfortune is that she lied about it. That's her problem now, isn't it?' He laughed. 'You should have seen her face when I said I might pay a visit to Langford Hall and let the servants have a look at me. Oh, dear lord, that put the wind up her and no mistake. She literally got down on her knees and begged. I must admit, I enjoyed watching her do it.'

209

He leaned into the woman standing opposite him and added, 'She gave it a good long go too. Although it didn't make any difference.'

White-faced, Lady Langford came as near to striking a fellow human being as she had ever been in her life, but somehow she regained control and said icily, 'Understand this, Mr Breck. The estate is on guard. If you attempt to visit the village you will be seized within ten minutes. And you will never be seen again. The Spense family has killed to protect its reputation many times over the last thousand years, and I would have no hesitation in doing so again.'

She saw his expression tighten with shock at this direct threat and pressed on, her voice a vicious hiss. 'Do not doubt me for a moment. There are many loyal men on the estate who are inured to extreme violence by the war. A knife across the throat and a remote woodland grave are what await you in Great Tew. Think well on that, Cameron Breck.'

She paused and assessed his attempt to conceal his shocked expression, before continuing in a more normal tone. 'The alternative is five thousand pounds, which is enough to set you up for life. I would recommend Australia or Canada. I have a cheque in my pocket and will offer no more. Accept it and you save your life, decline it and I doubt you will see out the week. What is your decision?'

The young Scotsman struggled to maintain his composure in the face of this verbal assault. There was a compelling clarity to the woman's remarks that had hit home. *She means it*, he thought. *She is prepared to see me dead.*

'Let me see the cheque.'

She withdrew it from her pocket, unfolded it and placed it on the table, then stepped back, as though unwilling to be too close to him. He picked it up. It was for five thousand pounds, drawn on Coutts bank in London, made out to Cameron Breck and correctly signed and dated. His heart leapt, but he made no sign.

'There is a branch of Coutts on St Giles' in Oxford. They know me there. I will telephone them to expect your deposit. From there you can move the funds wherever you want.'

'Alright.' He put the cheque deep in his pocket.

'Then our business, such as it is, is concluded. Go away, Cameron Breck. Go far away, take your ill-gotten gains with you and forget this matter entirely. If I see or hear reports of you again, I will send men to deal with you. Many of my ancestors would have knifed you already, and worried about the consequences later. Not that there would have been any. Not with the likes of you. Take heed of my warning, it is real.'

With that she turned and left the room, closing the door quietly behind her.

Left alone, Breck slumped into a chair. The powerful energy of the woman lingered in the room like a firework and he felt as though he had taken a physical beating, but slowly the feeling subsided and after a few minutes he stirred and removed the cheque from his pocket. Five thousand. It was enough to buy a decent farm in the soft Perthshire landscape or maybe as she had suggested, a ranch in one of the more civilised colonies.

And there was more. A man in such a position would come to the attention of mothers looking for suitable husbands for their daughters. He could anticipate marriage to a pretty girl from a good family with a bit of money behind them too. And if he employed a manager, he could settle down to the life of a gentleman farmer.

As the memory of Lady Langford's furious contempt faded, he smiled to himself. He'd pulled it off.

*

When she got back from Oxford Lady Langford sought out her daughter-in-law who was outside in the garden with Jaikie. Her husband was out so they were able to have a private conversation as they watched the flame-haired boy kicking a ball on the lawn.

'The matter is dealt with,' Claire said. 'I went into town and met Mr Breck this afternoon and we have reached an agreement. He will not bother us here in Great Tew.'

The relief in Innes's eyes was obvious. 'Really? Are you sure?'

'Yes, I am.' This was not strictly true, but she saw no reason to reveal her innermost thoughts to the young woman who had the most to lose.

'Did you buy him off?'

The aristocrat nodded. 'Yes. He is a vain man and money will give him the status he wants. And the Spense family is rich, as am I personally, Innes. The settlement has come out of my private funds and is solely a matter between me and my bank manager. There is no reason for anyone else, within or outside the family, to become aware of it. And, for the avoidance of doubt, you owe me nothing and my opinion of you is as high as it ever has been.'

Traces of tension lingered in the young woman's face. 'Thank you. I am truly grateful, especially for Jaikie. But can we be sure he will leave us in peace now? Isn't there a danger that he will come back?'

That was not what was worrying Lady Langford, but she answered firmly, 'He understands the money is in full and final settlement of whatever grievance he has manufactured in his mind, and that any further attempts at blackmail will result in extreme sanctions.'

This observation was delivered with a chilling vehemence and, not for the first time, Innes saw the unflinching toughness that lay below the gracious and charming face that Claire Spense presented to the world. She wondered fleetingly if she had always been like that, or if it had been her role as the matriarch of the Langford estate that had forged it.

Claire saw this and smiled gently. 'Yes, there is steel in me, my darling, and there is steel in you too. That is one of the many reasons I wanted you here. Sometimes we have to dance and sometimes we have to fight. And when it is the latter, we fight to win.'

The football rolled over towards them, and Innes kicked it back to Jaikie who laughed and returned it towards her. 'Again!' he cried with the instincts of a child who senses an adult might be drawn into a game.

Innes picked the ball up and said, 'Catch,' then tossed it gently towards her son, who reached up and missed it, letting the ball land on his head. Both women laughed, and the tension of the moment dissolved.

Claire said quietly, 'It is over, my darling. Have your baby, look after your husband and we will run the house together. Starting with this young fellow!' This last remark was delivered in a rising tone, and she grabbed him by the ribs and started tickling him as he cried and wriggled.

Innes looked up at the late-afternoon sun glowing on the great red brick facade of the hall before swinging her gaze out over the gardens towards the parkland and the distant outline of Green Hill. Enormous relief flowed through her, and she realised something curious. Unacknowledged deep inside her, the thought of Jaikie's father finding them had always been there. And now it had been dealt with. The future stretched out before them all and it looked wonderful.

Although she gave no sign, her mother-in-law was less sanguine. She had put Innes's mind to rest but as she wrestled with the wriggling child, two problems remained at the forefront of her mind.

Wherever he goes, can Cameron Breck be trusted to keep his mouth shut? And, unthinkable though it is, did my eldest son murder Vaughan Pentire?

Before dinner she overheard Edward challenge his older brother to a game of billiards and decided to act on the second question. After leaving it for twenty minutes, she made her excuses to Innes and followed them across the hall and down the corridor. The clack of balls suggested that the match had started, and she pushed the door open to find her beloved sons sharing a joke.

Seeing them laugh together brought back bittersweet memories of the great gap that Hugh's death had left in all their lives, and she stood for a moment in the doorway, suddenly reluctant to begin a conversation that might bring more despair down on the household. But then Edward noticed her and said, 'Hello, mother, can we do something for you?'

'I'm sorry to interrupt your sport, but I wanted to have a word with Piers, if you don't mind,' she replied, glancing at her eldest son.

Catching her eye, Piers put his cue down and nodded. 'Of course, it's just a casual game. What is it?'

'Would you mind, Edward?' she asked, moving away from the door.

'Ah, private, is it? Well, I'll go and bother my wife then.'

'She's still in the drawing room, I think,' she said. And with a brief 'Cheerio' her youngest son disappeared through the door, which Lady Langford quietly closed after him.

Piers noted this in silence then said, 'Drink?'

'No, dear, thank you. Come and sit with me.' She crossed to where two leather chairs stood in a corner of the masculine room. When they were settled she continued, 'I want to speak to you about the night that Vaughan Pentire was killed.' She couldn't bring herself to say murdered.

'Again? As I recall you've asked me before, in a roundabout way, what I was doing that night. Were you not satisfied with my answers, your honour?' He smiled at her.

214

No, my darling, I wasn't. The thought flashed through her mind but keeping her tone light she said, 'Do you remember our conversation months ago when I told you that I was happy for you to invite friends from your London set down to Langford if you wanted. "Close friends" was the phrase I used, I believe.'

He nodded. 'Of course I do. And it was appreciated, even though you'll have realised that up until now, I haven't availed myself of the offer.'

'No? Well that's what I wanted to mention. Someone told me that you knew Mr Pentire in London before he arrived here. Knew him very well in fact. Is that true?'

He moved in his seat. 'Mother, I'm not sure where this is leading, but I don't feel it's something that you need concern yourself with.'

Claire's heart sank at his sudden, palpable unease. 'But is it true, my darling? Were you friends, close friends even?'

His expression tightened. 'As I say, I cannot understand your interest, I'm afraid.'

'And I cannot understand why you didn't tell us. Or indeed express any upset when he was killed. It seems to me that if you and he were close friends, as I have been told, then perhaps his arrival in Great Tew was more than a coincidence. It certainly would have enabled you both to see each other easily. And yet you appear to have kept your relationship secret.'

He eyed her, his face set in stone, and said quietly, 'What exactly are you suggesting?'

Well aware of the danger but committed now, his mother ploughed on. 'Did you go to the Dower House that night?' she persisted. 'Were you with him?'

'I beg your pardon?' He rose from his seat and looked down at her, then raising his voice said, 'Is that some sort of accusation?'

Fired by a range of conflicting emotions and increasingly sure that her son was hiding something, she stood up as well and raised her face to his. 'Were you there, Piers? I must know.'

Real anger showed in his face. 'You would do well to avoid listening to whatever tittle-tattle you have heard. I thought you were better than that. As to my relationship with Vaughan Pentire. That is my business, as it was his. And that, dear mother, is all you are getting from me.'

He stalked to the door before turning to glare at her. 'Just for once, do not meddle in things that are not your concern. No good will come of it. I say again, leave it well alone.'

With that he left the room, leaving his mother staring at the door, appalled by the implications of what he had said.

*

Upset by their disagreement Lady Langford announced she was going up early and asked for a supper tray in her room. She was reading in bed when she heard a quiet knock on the door followed by Piers's voice. 'It's me, Mother. Are you decent?'

'Yes, I am. Come in.' She put down the book. Lilly had drawn the curtains and the single bedside light gradually lit his saturnine face as he walked over to the bed. She patted the counterpane and smiled at him. 'I'm sorry we had a row. Sit down, my darling.'

He did so and turned to face her. 'Yes, me too. I've come to make peace with you and clear up the misapprehension under which you appear to be labouring. It's not every son whose mother thinks that he murdered a good friend.'

Claire grimaced. 'I'm sorry, it's just been playing on my mind. Perhaps I did allow my imagination to become a little overinflated.'

He raised his eyebrows and gave her an ironic smile. 'Yes, well, fortunately I love you and in matters of love, forgiveness is the most important quality, if also the most difficult,' he added pointedly.

She reached out her hand and he took it. 'I really do regret it if I've got things wrong. Piers. What is the truth then?'

'I did not visit the Dower House the night Vaughan Pentire died, although I did go out for a stroll in the grounds and ended up by Hugh's grave. I sat there for quite a long time thinking about him as it happens. With regard to Pentire, the whole thing is confidential and although I don't think you know the people personally, you certainly know their families, so discretion is required. Do I have your understanding on that?'

His mother managed to look intrigued and piqued at the same time, but her main sensation was one of vast relief. If Piers was here to explain, then he almost certainly hadn't killed his friend. Nevertheless, she replied primly, 'I'm not a gossip, Piers. And I'm sure I have kept many more secrets than you.'

'Quite possibly. Well, here goes then. Your informant was right, he and I were good friends and spent time together in London. And I did suggest to him that the Dower House might offer a place of refuge.'

'Refuge? Was he in some kind of trouble?'

'Yes, but of the heart, not of the law.'

There was a pause then she said tentatively, 'So were you and he not…'

'No, Mother, in the great lottery of life, Pentire was correctly wired, unlike myself. As is so often the case, the problem was a girl. Or woman, I should say. A married woman to be precise.'

She looked at him. 'Ah. The old, old story.'

'More or less, yes. Tamara Stevenson is her married name, but she was one of the Hampshire Jeffers before that.'

Claire consulted her mental notebook and brought the family to the front of her mind. 'Yes, I know of them of course. Shipping, isn't it?'

He nodded. 'That's it, they own a fleet of cargo ships. The banana trade, I believe. Anyway, twenty-one-year-old Tamara

217

Jeffers attended a hunt ball where Tommy Stevenson was present, their eyes met across the room and six months later they were engaged. They married quite quickly and settled down to a normal life, splitting their time between London and the shires.'

She nodded slowly. 'And?'

He sighed. 'That was all four or five years ago. There were no children and, as time passed, it became apparent to those that knew Tamara well that she was not happy. And one of those people was Vaughan Pentire. He told me he suspected that her husband was being unkind to her and perhaps even violent. There were occasions when he turned up alone at house parties and other social events, offering little by way of explanation for his wife's absence. And there was talk of concealed bruises. Women notice these things.'

'They do. Oh dear, what a shame. She wouldn't be the first woman to marry in a wave of joyful haste, only to have the time to repent at leisure.'

'Exactly. Anyway, Pentire and Tamara fell for each other. I'm not sure if there was an actual affair. Stevenson kept a very tight rein on his wife and frankly, I doubt if they'd have managed to arrange a tryst, but certainly they were in love emotionally. "Deeply and fully", was how Pentire described it to me and having seen them together in the same room I have little doubt he was correct. She came to life like a bloom opening to the sun when he was around.'

'How terribly sad for them. So what happened?'

'Well, her husband noticed. Or perhaps it was pointed out to him. People do love to stir the pot, don't they. At least one charming hostess deliberately invited poor Pentire to a soiree, knowing that the Stevensons would be there too, just to watch the barely controlled fireworks between them.'

'A classic ménage à trois then. Presumably a divorce was out of the question?'

'Yes, Stevenson made that clear. Anyway, things came to a head and Pentire told me confidentially that Tamara had written saying she was prepared to run away with him. They could go to live in the south of France. He had funds and she had money of her own as well, through her family.'

He nodded at a sherry decanter on a little lace-covered table in the bay window and said, 'Do you mind?'

'Not at all, dear, pour me a small one as well.'

This mission completed he resumed his story. 'I've no idea how the plan leaked out, perhaps she mentioned it to a friend or something. But anyway, it got back to her parents and the next thing Tamara's father is battering at Pentire's door. It appears that the Stevenson family were in a position to do the shipping line great harm if they so chose. Something to do with trade agreements in the Caribbean. Whatever the finer details, realising that her actions could bring down her family, and under the most dreadful pressure from her father, she called off the scheme and told Pentire it was over.'

'And in so doing broke his heart, I presume.' Claire sipped her sherry.

Piers nodded. 'Exactly so. He really was a shattered man. Stevenson was insufferable about it all, strutting about the London scene with Tamara on his arm even though she was clearly only just holding herself together. It was shortly after that the Dower House became vacant and I offered Pentire the tenancy. He badly needed a refuge and leapt at the chance. He asked me to keep our previous friendship under wraps so he could avoid any questions and have a complete break from the whole affair. The simplest way to do that was to leave him well alone, which I did.'

His mother's mind moved briskly forward, putting two and two together. 'So when Mr Pentire died, and you rushed off to London it was to tell Tamara Stevenson what had happened?'

'Exactly. I was desperate to tell her myself in the right way, rather than have her husband find out and crow over her.'

219

'Did you manage it?'

He nodded. 'Thankfully they were in town. I was able to get a pal to drag Stevenson out for a night's carousing and slipped round to their place once he'd gone. We sat and talked, and I explained that Pentire had taken his own life. She was utterly devastated of course, believing it to be her fault. I worried that she'd attempt to follow him. But very quickly, as more facts emerged, I was able to telephone her. It's ironic but the news that he had been murdered probably saved her own life.'

'Well, it must have relieved her guilt, I suppose. The poor girl. How is she now?'

He shrugged. 'They have some kind of working arrangement, I think. Mainly separate interests and so on. But she couldn't ruin her family and she knows that.'

There was a short silence as Claire finished her sherry and put the glass on the bedside table. Then she said, 'And Stevenson was definitely in town the night Vaughan Pentire died?'

'Good question, but yes, I'm sure of that.' He smiled. 'Enough speculation now, Mother. Alright?'

'I got hold of completely the wrong end of the stick. Will you forgive me?'

He nodded. 'You can see now why I needed to be discreet. The whole thing is damnably sensitive, and I was determined to protect Pentire's name, and of course Tamara's. I still am, come to that.'

'You're a good friend to have, Piers. Tamara is lucky, as are the other people in your life. Don't forget what I said about visitors.'

He smiled and stood up, well aware that his mother's raging curiosity would not be satisfied until he turned up one Friday with 'a good friend from town'. 'I won't. I'll leave you in peace now. Sleep well.' He leaned forward and gave her a kiss on the cheek then headed for the door.

220

But as he opened it, she said thoughtfully, 'There is one thing though.'

'What's that?'

'If you didn't kill him, who the devil did?'

Chapter Nineteen

Next morning, with the baby fed and fast asleep and Matilda playing with her father in the garden, Laura Burrows poked her head round the back door of Lea House and said, 'I'm just going out for a walk. I'll not be much more than an hour.'

'Fine,' Burrows called back. 'We're gardening.' He waved a trowel.

Smiling, she left them to it and within ten minutes was on the common. Wanting solitude she paused then, as a thought occurred to her, struck out for the Dower House, passed along its side and found the entrance to the ancient and rarely used track that led out across the upper Cherwell valley towards the Worcester road. Pleased with the idea of exploring somewhere new she set off along it.

The green lane was little more than a footpath in places, and quite delightful. For the first ten minutes it was sunken and mysterious, overhung with ash and elder, and with high overgrown banks that gave the impression it was buried in the landscape. *An old route*, she thought, her mind idly speculating on the others who had passed the same way over the centuries, and what their purpose might have been.

But the feeling of enclosure fell away as the path emerged onto the valley side and a dramatic view of the river below and to her right opened up. She stopped to admire it. On the far side of the valley the ever-present ridgeline of Green Hill prescribed a long line in the sky and below it she could just see the outline of farms dotted amongst the early autumnal countryside. A breeze stirred her hair, and she lifted her face to the morning sun, surrendering to a sudden and unexpected feeling of deep peace that enveloped her.

'Good morning.'

The call came from behind, and she opened her eyes in surprise, turning to look up the grassy slope. Fifty yards away Eve Dance was sitting with her back to a great black stone that rose for ten feet above her. She waved and called, 'Come on up.'

Like Laura, Eve had felt the need for some solitude that morning. She now knew that the curious drumbeats that punctuated her summer had signalled the approach of Cameron Breck. He'd said his great-grandmother had had the sight and when she passed Eve had connected with her, even though they were separated by six hundred miles. And that relationship had continued, in some oblique way symbolised by the drum. Its final pulse as she stood and stared at him across the street in Oxford had been overwhelming. But Cameron Breck had been dealt with by Claire's positive action and she assumed he would not bother them again.

Jane Meadenham was another matter, however.

The feeling of heat and flames had been terrifying during the rite in the centre of Creech Hill Ring, and she was not at all sure what would have happened if her fellow adepts had not been there to break her connection to the poor woman as she burned to death all those years ago. And although Eve tried to push the matter to the back of her mind it proved stubbornly persistent, not least because she knew such intense experiences usually had their basis in fact.

It was to try and work her way towards a next step in unravelling the mystery that she had walked to the stone she knew

223

as Yule that morning. Normally it was a winter stone, used in the dark half of the year and redolent with bright firelight on a cold night. She hoped it would give her inspiration, and she had indeed felt it would be easy to float away and perhaps explore some more of her connections with Jane Meadenham. But without the protection of her fellow adepts she had decided that would be foolhardy.

So she resorted to thinking. And when Laura appeared she had actually been wondering if she had been Jane Meadenham in a previous life, hence the intensity of her feelings. But no, she reasoned, during the civil war and Cromwell's subsequent reign, she had been Lady Olivia Spense, heroine of the defence of Langford Hall, wife of Sir Wyndham, and living in exile in France within the court of the man who would become King Charles II. Her deep connection to the Langford Ring confirmed that.

Am I being warned? And if so, what is the threat?

Only too aware of one obvious answer, she turned this uncomfortable thought over in her mind as Laura walked slowly up the hill and greeted her, then patted the grass companionably and said, 'Sit with me for a while. I saw you enjoying the view, it's rather wonderful, isn't it.'

Laura leaned back on the warm stone. 'Standing there, it felt for a moment as though I was being recharged. Almost as though I'd put my finger in some sort of therapeutic plug.'

'You had. This stone is part of the outer circle of Creech Hill Ring, and you were standing right in the middle of an energy line that runs across the valley. The stones were put here to mark where it crosses with another. It's a very powerful place.'

This observation would have been greeted with quiet derision by many city dwellers, but it was a measure of the curious nature of Great Tew and the people within it, that Laura accepted it without question. Instead, she simply said, 'Well it was certainly doing me some good. Babies are exhausting.'

'Ah, yes. Has everything settled down after his rather dramatic arrival?'

'All fine now, thank you, although it was rather public for my tastes.' She laughed briefly.

'Quite. And how is your husband? Over the shock?'

Laura shrugged. 'He's wonderful but rather preoccupied with the death of Mr Pentire. In fact, obsessed would be a better word. He still hasn't solved the mystery of how the murderer got out of the study and between you and me, it's driving him mad. And it's getting to me too. Divine intervention is needed, I suspect, but there's fat chance of that.'

Eve looked at her with a faint smile on her face, then said thoughtfully, 'Do you really mean that?'

Laura caught the veiled suggestion behind the other woman's words. 'Oh, no, Mrs Dance, I'm not implying anything. It was just a turn of phrase.'

'Of course, nevertheless, if you wanted, and he was amenable, I'm sure something could be arranged.'

Startled, Laura was silent for a moment, then before she could stop herself said, 'Arranged? As in…' She petered out, not sure how to phrase the words.

'It's quite possible I could help Sergeant Burrows along the path to discovery. He'd have to do the work himself, but I could take him to the right place to start.'

'Where would that be?' In the back of her mind, she recalled a sisterly gossip she'd once had with Innes Spense who had observed, *'You know, I'm sometimes astonished at the conversations I have with people on the estate. And of all of them, the ones I have with Eve Dance are the most remarkable.'*

How right you are, Innes, she thought. *In Great Tew normal is not the same as everywhere else.*

'I believe the vernacular in the village is "The other side", which is as appropriate as any other phrase. Doors may perhaps be opened that will allow your dear husband to see things that are currently obscured from him.'

The older woman looked at her with a twinkle in her eye as she said this, and Laura's mind boggled. Eve's prowess as a witch was well known, and when she had worked in the Black Horse she'd heard many stories about her activities on behalf of those who needed her. She swallowed and asked, 'Would he be safe?'

The witch nodded firmly. 'He would. There would be no threat and no repercussions. Just a new perspective on a tricky problem.'

'How does it work?' she couldn't resist asking.

The petite blonde glanced around. The hillside stretched away, and no one was in sight. 'Perhaps a gentle demonstration? Give me your hand and close your eyes. Don't worry, you will come to no harm.'

Curiosity overcame her reluctance and Laura obeyed. Eve's grip sent gentle sensations up her arm, and she heard her say, 'I'm going to use some words now, that you won't recognise. Let what happens, happen.' Her tone was both comforting and compelling and the young woman felt a dreamy complacency drift over her as the witch started to chant quietly and rhythmically.

The sensations faded in her arm, replaced by a steady powerful pulse that beat deep within her. At first she thought it was her heart, but as Eve's rhythmic words flowed through her she realised she was sensing something much more profound and powerful.

It's my essence, my life force. The thought came to her in a flash of intuition. *It's my soul.*

She became intensely aware of her body in a way she had never experienced before. As though, if she chose, she could focus down and explore its inner workings in minute detail. A curious weightlessness overcame her, and she felt herself gently detach

226

from the world she knew. And then Eve whispered, 'Open your eyes and keep hold of my hand.'

She did so and uttered a gasp of surprise. She was floating in the air thirty feet above the standing stone looking down at herself and Eve, hand in hand, eyes closed. She felt utterly safe and gently turned her head to explore this astonishing new perspective. In the distance she could see the tower of St Mary's above the trees that hid the rest of the village. But to her surprise, she could somehow see into the garden of Lea House. She smiled. Burrows had filled a bucket with water and he and Matilda were making mud cakes decorated with leaves and flowers for her to admire when she got home.

Laura felt as though she were being washed through with light and an ecstatic feeling of joy flooded her as Eve whispered, 'You will be alright. You will lead happy lives.'

Then she was back by the stone and Eve gently released her hand. Laura stared at her in astonishment. 'Was that real?' she finally managed to ask.

'I sometimes wonder what that word really means,' the witch answered, 'but in the context in which you were asking, the answer is yes. Your husband is making mud cakes and Matilda is helping. It turns out you're a natural.' The witch smiled with genuine amusement. 'I mean it. We should spend some time together.'

Her mind reeling at this offer, Laura struggled to stay on track but then asked, 'And you think you can help him?'

'I do.'

'Alright then.'

'Very well. This is what we must do…'

When Eve got back to Marston House a letter had arrived for her. It was postmarked Great Tew, and the address was typed, as was the single sheet of paper inside it, which bore a simple proposal.

If you want to know who is sending the poison pen letters, go to the old barn on Tan Hill at ten o'clock. Come alone, we know you can be trusted.

The petite blonde read it thoughtfully, her tea cooling on the table as she turned the thing over in her mind. The truth was she did very much want to learn who the source of the letters was, and after some consideration decided that she would attend as suggested. It was unfortunate that her husband had left early on police business and would not be returning until late in the evening, otherwise she might have discussed the matter with him. And had she done so, he might have insisted that the reassuring presence of Sergeant Burrows and WPC Dixon were secreted close to the barn an hour or so before the sun set.

But he wasn't there, and so the conversation did not take place, meaning that there was no opportunity to snuff out the appalling events which unfolded later that night and led to two further deaths on the Langford estate.

*

The last of the light had faded from the windows of Marston House when Eve went to the kitchen where Ellie and Mrs Franks were sitting together with a pot of tea. 'I'm going out,' she said. 'Jocelyn is expected about half past ten so please wait up in case he needs anything. And tell him he can lock up if I'm not back, I'm taking my key.'

'Yes, madam,' Ellie replied. Neither she nor the cook were surprised by the announcement as her mistress was well known throughout the estate for her nocturnal outings.

Leaving by the front door Eve walked down the high street and turned right into Stream Cross, then crossed the footbridge and set off up the steep track that led towards the summit of Tan Hill. Halfway up she paused to get her breath back and looked out over the Cherwell valley. The darkened scene was as familiar as the interior of her bedroom and she stood for a while letting her mind drift, watching the moonlight glinting on the river as it wound its way through the blue-black countryside. A breeze caressed her face and the hairs on the back of her neck rose as she felt a momentary shiver of anticipation.

There is danger ahead. I'll have to be careful.

Senses alert for any threat she resumed her climb, passed the great standing stone, and carried on towards Little Tew. After a further five minutes of walking the roof of the old barn appeared in the corner of a field away to her right. She left the track and slipped silently through a gate, then stopped with the hedge behind her so she was not silhouetted against the skyline.

Her objective was fifty yards away and, as she watched, her caution was rewarded when she saw a movement in the shadows and a figure appeared round the corner of the building and went inside. With the moon behind a cloud, it was impossible to tell who it was, nevertheless, encouraged that the note she had received was apparently bona fide, she cautiously crossed the field.

The door stood half open and she paused outside, listening. No sound emerged. Heart beating, she took a deep breath and moved round the door and into the barn. In the faint light from a single window high up on the end wall she saw the outline of a ladder and supporting posts leading to a platform above her head where hay was piled high. The sweet, aromatic smell filled her nostrils. At floor level the interior was in deep shadow.

Every sense screamed danger, and controlling a powerful urge to turn and run she said in a low voice, 'Hello? I saw you come in. Who's there?'

There was a rustling from the thin layer of hay on the floor and on the far side of the barn something moved, then a voice said, 'I am.'

Astonished, Eve recognised the voice, but she barely had time to react before there was a swift movement in the air behind her, followed by a great white explosion of light and pain in her head. All consciousness gone, she dropped like a stone to the floor.

The figure that had spoken moved into the light cast by the window and looked down at the prone figure. A distant madness showed in her eyes, and she said, 'She's a witch. And you know what they do to witches in Great Tew, don't you.'

From the shadows behind the door another replied, 'I do. They burn them.'

*

Fast asleep in his chair after supper, Burrows was dreaming. Laura watched him while keeping an ear out for noises from upstairs. From time to time he stirred and mumbled, his long legs twitching. She loved him very much and they were happy. And she trusted Eve – the potion she had given her, and which she had slipped into her husband's tea, would do no harm.

Feeling a sense of peace, she put the book down and reached for her sewing bag. There was just time to darn those socks before turning in.

Six feet away the slumbering policeman was not experiencing the same sense of tranquillity at all. In his dream he was walking uneasily up the deserted village high street at night. As he approached the churchyard he saw a shadowed figure standing under the lychgate. He stopped and stared as Eve Dance stepped forward into the moonlight. She smiled and cupped a hand to her ear, as though listening for something.

As if on cue, the distant sound of an organ drifted through the night. He looked towards the noise. A quarter of a mile away the lights of a fair showed on the far side of the common.

'*Shall we go?*' Even though they were thirty yards apart, her voice was inside his head, as though she were whispering into his ear. *'I think we should, don't you?'*

'If you want to.' He nodded.

Almost immediately the familiar boundaries of the common disappeared and he found himself standing slack-faced and disorientated, surrounded by a noisy kaleidoscope of rides and steam engines going at full tilt. He turned to look at Eve and she returned his gaze and touched his arm gently. Then suddenly she was gone.

And it wasn't just her. With a shock he realised he was completely alone; there were no customers or operators, and a chilling fear crept over him as he realised the fairground had no limits and stretched away over the horizon in every direction. Wherever he looked spinning drive wheels and long belt loops barred his way as the steam-driven machinery hissed and turned. Close by a great organ sent out a loud chorus of discordant notes that confused him further.

And then suddenly a bizarre caricature of Lord Langford was next to him. Only three feet tall, wearing a devilish grin and doing a little tap dance while repeating, *'Action at a distance, action at a distance…'*

He reeled around in the garish lights, entirely surrounded by machinery that seemed to be closing in on him, as though the fair were a single entity.

Trapped! He realised with a sudden, terrifying certainty, that he was going to get caught in one of the drive belts and pulled into the rotating gears of a roundabout or mechanical swing boat. Just as he opened his mouth to scream for help, Eve Dance reappeared at his arm, her skin red and yellow in the reflected light. She was pointing and calling something, but he couldn't hear because of all the noise.

He put his hand to his ear and leaned towards her, and this time he heard it.

'It's the belts, Sergeant. They're only thin, but their width makes them strong. Like leather ribbons.'

Stunned, he looked at her. But before he could react the fairground dissolved, and he was standing in the draper's shop on

231

Dell Lane, watching Xanthe Rudge pull a measure of ribbon off the roller attached to the wall. He heard himself say, *That's a lot of ribbon,'* then watched as she cut the frayed end, leaving a few strands of cotton on the counter. Strands like the one they'd found by the desk in the study.

'There's forty yards on a roll.' Her reply echoed in his head as a distant voice called, 'Burrows, Burrows,' repeatedly. Someone was shaking his shoulder and he stirred, reluctant to be drawn from the scene in case it could tell him more. But the words were persistent and finally he opened his eyes to see his beloved's face close to his.

'You were dreaming very deeply, Burrows,' she said, concern on her face. 'Is everything alright?'

Astonished by what he'd seen, he stared at her blankly for a moment then gathered his thoughts. 'It's the Misses Rudge. Bloody hell, Laura! They killed Vaughan Pentire, and they used a ribbon to get out of the study!'

'A ribbon?' she said doubtfully.

'Yes. And they've been writing the poison pen letters too.'

'What?' She stared back, her own mind moving quickly. 'But didn't you say that they had received a poison pen letter themselves?'

He shook his head, confused by the intensity of his dream and trying to catch up with his cascading thoughts. 'They showed me a letter. It's not the same thing.'

He leapt to his feet and glanced at the clock on the mantlepiece. It was half past nine. He kissed Laura and said hurriedly, 'I'm off to fetch Dixon. We'll go to Little Tew now.'

'Really? Can't it wait until the morning. They'll be at the shop up the road then anyway.'

He shook his head. 'No. This whole thing has driven me mad and I'm going to get to the bottom of it tonight. Then I can report to the chief constable in the morning.' And with that he went into the hall, hastily donned his jacket and helmet and left,

232

closing the front door behind him. It only took five minutes to start the Matchless and drive it the short distance up Dell Lane to the police house. As he entered the hallway the muffled sound of laughter reached him, and he called out, 'WPC Dixon, are you there?'

The giggling stopped abruptly and a silent pause followed, then he heard low voices and the door to the parlour opened. The policewoman appeared wearing a low-cut rose-coloured dress that matched the distinct flush in her cheeks. 'Sergeant?' she said, as Hector Dean's shirt-sleeved figure showed in the doorway behind her.

Burrows took in the scene, and it was a measure of the gentle education that he had received from his wife that he remembered to say, 'I'm sorry to interrupt your evening,' before adding, 'we must go out. Now.'

Dean said, 'That's alright, Mabel, I'll be on my way. See you tomorrow.' With a rather guilty nod to the sergeant, he collected his jacket, eased past him in the hall and left by the front door.

'What's up?' Dixon enquired.

'The Misses Rudge killed Pentire and have been writing the poison pen letters. We need to go and see them.'

Displaying the sangfroid which Burrows had come to expect, she received this astonishing news with raised eyebrows then turned for the stairs, saying, 'I'll put my uniform on then.'

Ten minutes later they were outside the police station looking at the motorbike and sidecar as the same problem occurred to them both. 'Are you planning to arrest them tonight?' the WPC enquired. 'Because we'll not all be able to come back on the bike.'

Burrows scratched his nose and considered the logistics. 'Let's go over there on the bike and interview them. If things are as I think they are, I'll arrest them there and then. You can bring the bike back here, then raise the colonel and he can bring his car over so we can get them back in one trip. One can go in the cell, while we get a statement from the other, so they can't collude out of our hearing.' He thought about this for a moment, then nodded, satisfied. 'Alright?'

'Yes, Sergeant. How did they get out of the study then?'

'They used ribbon from the shop.'

'Really? How did they do that?'

He smiled. 'Let's see if I'm right, shall we, Constable. Get in.'

But she ignored him and asked, 'But why kill Vaughan Pentire at all. What on earth was the motive?'

'It's as we suspected. Geraldine Rudge had her fortune told at the fete and Pentire must have said something that terrified her to the point they decided to shut him up permanently. Then they found the list that Connors had given his master. When I say they wrote the poison pen letters I mean they wrote all of them, including the one they showed us.'

'Really?'

'Oh yes. They fooled us good and proper. I should have spotted it was an outlier. All the other letters arrived after the murder. They put themselves in the clear by pretending they'd received one some weeks before and were victims too.'

'Blimey, that was smart. I wonder what their great secret is then?'

'I think Xanthe probably was involved in a scandal years ago and somehow Agnes Craig got to know. She must have mentioned it in a letter to her son when he was in hospital, and it ended up on Connors' list. Whatever it was they're obviously terrified of it coming out, even after all these years.'

'Family honour. Some people can be like that,' Dixon agreed, then looked startled as a thought occurred to her. 'There's something else. When Ronnie Back told us about hearing the gunshots a day or two after the fete, who did he say he met in the woods?'

Burrows stared at her. 'Xanthe Rudge! She claimed she was birdwatching.' He clicked his fingers in satisfaction. 'That settles it, Constable. I'm guessing we'll find the gun and a typewriter in their cottage and that'll be enough for a conviction once we've put the evidence together in the right order. Come on!'

He swung his leg over the bike and waited as Dixon folded herself into the sidecar, a process that took a minute or two if decorum was to be maintained. Then they were off. 'I'll take the track, it's much quicker than going round via Dell Lane,' he called out excitedly above the regular thumping of the engine. He enjoyed driving the powerful machine through the ford next to the footbridge and did it at every opportunity, fondly believing no one knew. In fact, the entire village was aware of his guilty secret because he invariably unconsciously uttered a schoolboy-like 'Wheee!' as the water splashed out to the sides.

The result of this was that even though WPC Dixon was covered in spray, she wore an amused smile as the bike emerged from the water and accelerated up the track towards Tan Hill, its headlight driving a beam of light through the darkness between the heavily overgrown banks and high hedges.

Chapter Twenty

Eve opened her eyes and raised her head sluggishly, struggling to comprehend what was happening. Her face was pressed against a wooden post and to her surprise and then shock she realised she was unable to move, a rope having been wound round her body multiple times between her chest and knees. She twisted her neck to look around and groaned as a deep ache made its presence felt at the back of her head. It was dark and she guessed the barn door had been shut.

'Hello?' she called. There was no reply and every sense told her she was alone.

Struggling to quell a rising sense of panic she tried to work out what had happened. She remembered entering the barn, but then nothing and with a start she realised someone had hit her on the back of the head. As she wondered about this, an arc of moving light caught the corner of her eye. She managed to shuffle ninety degrees round the post and then craned her head towards the end wall with the high window. A flickering light was coming from its base. *Firelight.* She watched in horror as another flaming brand fell through the window and landed next to the first.

Moments later the rich smell of smoke hit her as loose straw at the foot of the wall caught alight and flames began to spread. Appalled, in the growing light she noticed that someone had piled straw to waist-height all around the post and the full horror of her situation was revealed.

I'm going to burn. Like Jane Meadenham on the common. That's what the dreams were about and deep inside you knew it. This is how it ends for you.

She struggled, straining her body against the rope, but it was hopeless. The post moved slightly where it joined the platform above her head, and was clearly not in prime condition, but pressed up against it she couldn't exert any leverage and the knots that bound her were out of sight.

She stared stony-faced as the fire crept across the floor towards the post. *Twenty feet to go. Perhaps two or three minutes. Five at the most. I hope it will be quick.*

And then, as a last resort, she put her head back and screamed. A keening, summoning, cry of fear and anger that seemed to carry far across the night sky.

And throughout the county certain people stopped what they were doing and stood still, their eyes troubled.

*

The Matchless thumped up the track towards the summit of Tan Hill with the two police officers sitting in companionable silence. They both had things on their minds. Burrows was busy putting the finer details of the evidence against the Misses Rudge together in his head while making a note to take a length of ribbon over to the Dower House as soon as possible to test his theory.

In the sidecar to his left, WPC Dixon was considering the pros and cons of being married to Hector Dean and concluding that matters came out in his favour. Had her sergeant not appeared half an hour ago at the police house, she acknowledged with a quiet smile that the thing might well have been settled by now. What had started off as a lovely kiss and cuddle had rapidly progressed as Hector's ardent passion had aroused similar feelings in herself, and she had little doubt a proposal was in the offing. And yes, that would be very nice, she concluded.

It was with this warming thought in the front of her mind that they passed the standing stone and bumped along at twenty

237

miles an hour towards the start of the slope that led down towards Little Tew.

Then Burrows suddenly pulled the machine to a halt, turned off the engine and stared to his right. 'Did you see that?' He glanced down at the policewoman who replied in the negative, the bulk of the motorbike and her sergeant contriving to block any prospect on that side for the occupant of the sidecar.

'Over there, stand up, Dixon,' he said and pointed. She levered herself out of the seat, inadvertently grasping Burrows' thigh rather firmly as she did so. But his cry of 'Steady on!' was ignored as she squinted into the gloom. A gate gave onto a field and fifty yards away the shadow of a barn showed indistinctly against the woods behind it.

A light had been kindled at the foot of the end wall. After a moment's staring Dixon realised it was a small fire, and as the flame got bigger, she saw the vague outline of two figures. Female figures. Then, whatever was burning suddenly flew through the air and disappeared.

'Did they throw that into the barn?' she asked uncertainly.

'Into it, or behind it. Either way, we're going to have a look.' Burrows climbed off the bike and bellowed across the field, 'Oi! Police! Wait there, we're coming over.' In the darkness it wasn't clear if the figures had obeyed this instruction or not, but as they walked briskly over the cropped grass, a flickering light appeared in a window high up on the end wall of the barn.

'What's that?' asked Dixon.

'I think the answer to your question is inside. Someone's chucked a flaming rag or something through the window and it's caused a fire.'

And at that moment a chilling, almost inhuman, scream rent the night. It was so shocking that both paused momentarily. 'There's someone in there,' Burrows said in alarm, then shouted, 'hold on. Police, we're coming!'

238

With Dixon close behind, he accelerated over the remaining twenty yards as another piercing scream reached them. Its unworldly quality raised the hairs on the back of the policewoman's neck, and she wondered who or what it was.

Burrows hauled at the door then stared down in the dim light and cursed. 'It's tied tight, damn it, have you got a knife?'

'No.' The WPC could just see a thin cord wound round and round the handle and a metal ring in the door frame. Even in daylight it would have taken a minute or two to undo it. In the dark it would take much longer.

Another scream, loaded with terror came from inside, and a voice cried, 'There's no time,' before choking.

'The window!' Burrows was already running for the end of the barn. They dashed round the corner and paused. It was ten feet up and the barn wall was smoothly faced.

'Give me a leg up,' Dixon said.

It was a moot point who was the strongest, and for a moment it looked as though her sergeant was going to argue, but then he braced his knee against the wall and said, 'Start there.'

She put her foot onto his knee and stepped up as he bent forward and put his hands against the wall. 'Shoulders next,' he said calmly.

Reaching up with her left foot she placed it behind Burrows' neck and pushed upwards, hearing his muttered grunt as he took her weight. Wobbling horribly, she walked her hands up the wall until she felt the stony rim of the window and hauled herself upwards.

Intense heat hit her face as she reached the hole and gasped in horror. Patches of fire were burning across the floor and flames were licking up towards the hay in the gallery. In the centre of the conflagration where the smoke and flames were most intense, she could just see a figure, clearly unconscious, tied face forward against one of the posts that supported the platform.

Dixon was a brave woman, but even so she hesitated. But only for a second. Ignoring Burrows' shouted question, she reached forward, grasped the far side of the window ledge and levered herself upwards, only too aware of her sergeant pushing upwards from below, his hands on the obvious target.

Even in those desperate moments she smiled to herself. *Manhandled by two different men in one evening, things are looking up.*

Then she was in the window frame and, muttering a brief prayer, she jumped and hit the floor, smashing her elbow against the stone. Within a moment she was coughing violently and as she climbed to her feet, she realised she only had a minute or two before she passed out herself.

With a great roar she ran through the fire towards the post accelerating all the time and plunged into the sea of smoke and flames. She crashed head first into the post, feeling an agonising crack in her collarbone as it gave way and her momentum carried herself, the post and the unconscious woman clear through the other side and under the platform. Thankfully there was a space on the floor that was free of flames. Ignoring the pain in her shoulder she tore at the knots in the firelight, registering to her astonishment that the figure was Eve Dance.

She had no idea if she was alive or dead.

Coughing and dizzy from the heat and lack of oxygen she realised that she was going to pass out. With a huge effort she struggled to her feet, and she tried to haul Eve and the post towards the door, thinking she could charge it down from the inside. But instead, head reeling and unable to breathe properly, she sank back down to her knees. It was an unwitting gesture of surrender. She couldn't batter the door down in her weakened state.

Up above she saw the straw stored on the platform was fully alight.

I'm sorry, Mrs Dance, I gave it a good go. The thought drifted through her mind as the last moments of consciousness lingered.

She felt her eyes closing in the intense heat and then suddenly a pale oblong appeared in her vision. A pale oblong filled with Sergeant Burrows.

What's he doing here? she wondered, and even managed to dredge up a smile as he ran through the swirling smoke to her. *He's shouting something. What is it?* She tried to listen as he grabbed her arms and started heaving, but she shook her head sorrowfully at him. *I'm a big girl, Sergeant. Always have been. I'm not easy to shift.*

But something in his urgency got through to her and she suddenly realised what he was shouting.

'It's going to collapse! The bloody platform's coming down, Dixon. For God's sake crawl out, I'll get Mrs Dance.'

She rolled over onto her back and looked up as a flaming plank crashed onto the ground next to her. It was like looking up at a wonderful sunset that glowed and flickered as though it were alive.

'Roll if you can't crawl!' Burrows' voice collapsed into a paroxysm of coughing. But she knew she had to move and followed his instructions, rolling across the stone floor towards the open door. She screamed as her hair flared and hot flames ran over her face as she rolled directly through a burning patch, then Burrows was with her and hauling with superhuman strength.

Facing backwards she watched slack-faced, hair burned away on one side, as the platform collapsed with a great crash and fire and smoke exploded into every corner of the barn.

This must be what hell is like, she thought as she faded into unconsciousness.

*

The following morning accurate news of the events up on Tan Hill was at a premium and, as usual, the village fell back on speculation.

'Is it true the devil came calling last night?' Mr Willett enquired of the Reverend Tukes as he hurried down the high street towards the cottage hospital.

241

'Don't be ridiculous, there's no devil,' Tukes responded waspishly, only realising as he turned into Dell Lane that he'd rather given the game away regarding a cornerstone of Christian doctrine. However, that morning his priorities were temporal not spiritual, and he presented himself at the hospital and enquired if there was anything he could do.

Innes was there. 'Thankfully, I don't think your professional services will be needed, vicar, but we do have two very poorly people here. WPC Dixon is being taken to the Radcliffe or treatment for smoke inhalation and burns to her face. During the war they learned so much. We'll have to see what they can manage.'

Tukes nodded slowly. 'And the other person? Who is that?'

'Eve Dance. It's rather odd, to be honest. She's inhaled a great deal of smoke and is on oxygen but somehow or other she appears to have avoided getting badly burned. I only got a rather garbled explanation from Burrows last night, but from what he told me she was in the middle of a bonfire. I can't really explain it.'

'A bonfire? Good God. Will she be alright, do you think?'

'She's going into Oxford too, for her lungs. I've telephoned and they're sending an ambulance to collect them both. It should be here soon. The colonel's going to follow in his car.'

'What on earth happened up there?'

'A barn fire, I believe. Beyond that, you'll have to ask Burrows. I couldn't get much out of him last night. He's got a nasty burn on his hand as well.'

They both looked along Dell Lane as the Radcliffe ambulance appeared around the corner. 'Good, here they are. Excuse me, vicar.' Innes turned and went inside. Left alone, Tukes walked thoughtfully up to Lea House and knocked on the front door. After some delay Laura appeared.

242

'Good morning, Mrs Burrows. I gather there was an emergency last night and I wanted to offer any help that you might need.'

Her face tightened. 'If you can help keep my husband in bed that would be a good start, Reverend. Almost burned to death last night and smoke in his lungs, and yet he's upstairs putting his uniform on and muttering about the Misses Rudge.'

'The Misses Rudge? How odd.' But before he could speculate any further a series of grating coughs sounded and the sergeant appeared on the landing, then began to descend the stairs. He was, as his wife had observed, in his uniform.

'Morning, vicar,' Burrows said as he arrived in the hall.

'I was just telling your wife I heard about the emergency and wanted to offer my services if any help is required. I called in at the hospital on the way.' He briefly recounted his conversation with Innes.

'So, they're both off to hospital in Oxford. Good.' Burrows looked at the vicar. 'You want to help then?'

'Of course, anything I can do.'

The sergeant nodded at the Matchless through the open front door. 'Can you drive a motorbike, vicar?' He held up his heavily bandaged hand by way of an explanation.

Concealing a thrill of excitement, the Reverend Tukes admitted that he thought he could probably manage.

'Good. Hop on,' he paused and coughed horribly before adding weakly, 'I'll need a witness where I'm going anyway.'

Laura looked furious. 'You should be in bed.'

But he was already outside. 'Don't worry, love.' He climbed into the sidecar. 'Come on if you're coming, parson.'

Following a swift explanation of the controls from Burrows, Tukes started the powerful machine and, with a couple of false starts, guided them carefully down Dell Lane and round the corner.

'Where are we going?' he asked.

'Little Tew. The Rudges' cottage.'

'Yes, your wife mentioned them. What's so urgent?'

'What's so urgent is that they killed Vaughan Pentire, sent the poison pen letters, and last night tried to murder Eve Dance by setting a barn alight on Tan Hill. And I am going to arrest them.'

'Are you sure?' The vicar looked down at him in astonishment.

'I'm bally certain. And as I said, you can bear witness to anything they say. Who's got a phone in the hamlet, do you know?'

'Mr Edwards the butcher.'

'Right, once we get things sorted out I'll stay with them, and you can go up there and telephone Marston House and ask the colonel to come over in his car. Alright?'

'Yes, if you wish.' Tukes was rather enjoying the excitement. He opened the throttle on the bike, and they rattled and thumped their way towards the turn off to Little Tew.

Ten minutes later they drew up outside the cottage, about a quarter of a mile before the main street started. Burrows eased himself out of the cramped sidecar and stalked up the front path. Without preamble he thumped the door knocker and called out, 'Open up! Police.'

There was no reply, but he thought he heard footsteps on the stairs and assumed one of the sisters was descending to answer his summons. But nothing happened for a long three minutes and finally he banged again, repeating his call.

'I think someone's in,' the vicar said from the road. 'I just saw the curtain move in one of the upstairs rooms.'

With a grunt of irritation Burrows tried for a third time, giving the knocker all he could. The door shook and dust descended from the overhanging porch.

'They're not coming out,' came from the road, Tukes being a great believer in having things nice and clear.

244

'Right, I'm going round the back. You wait here and call if you see them.'

'You are sure about this, are you, Sergeant? I mean, they might just be terrified of the noise you're making. And they do seem like unlikely murderers.'

Burrows glared down the front path to where the vicar stood by the Matchless and at that moment a gunshot sounded above them. Tukes ducked down behind the motorbike.

'I may perhaps revise my opinion,' he called from cover.

Ten seconds later a second shot sounded. Pressed against the front door Burrows thought frantically. 'Any windows open up there?' he called in the ensuing silence. With agonising slowness, the vicar's head appeared above the seat, and he cautiously surveyed the upper floor.

'No,' he said on completion of his inspection.

'Stay there. I'll try the back door.' Burrows ducked down past the front-room window and walked cautiously down the side of the house. When he gently pushed at the door it opened without any restriction. He leaned in and eyed the view. The door led directly into the kitchen and beyond a corridor led down the hall. He could see the front door. The building was utterly silent.

Taking a deep breath, he called out, 'Hello, Miss Rudge? Are either of you there.'

'Any sign?' The voice in his ear almost gave him kittens. Furious, he turned round. 'For heaven's sake, vicar. I said stay on the road.'

But the man of the cloth was unrepentant. 'I think something's wrong. Very wrong.'

Burrows had reached the same conclusion and summoning himself he pulled his jacket down and said, 'Right, let's have a look then.'

And with that he led the way inside.

It took them less than five minutes to find the bodies of Geraldine and Xanthe Rudge. They were lying side by side on a

245

bloodstained double bed in the main bedroom, which looked out over the road. Both had gunshot wounds to the head.

'Murder and suicide, I'd say,' the vicar said quietly as they surveyed the scene from the doorway.

'Two suicides, more likely. Although you're right, technically the first one would be murder,' Burrows confirmed. 'I'll go in and have a look, just wait there for now, please.'

The metallic smell of blood reached his nostrils as he approached the bed. Xanthe was lying on her back, arms by her sides. Two feet to her left, closer to the door, her elder sister was half on her side and a gun was close to her shoulder. He leaned over and peered at it, seeing the word 'Mauser' on the butt. 'This is the weapon that killed Vaughan Pentire. I'd bet my life on it,' he said. Looking round, he added, 'You can come in now, Reverend. If you want to say a prayer or anything.'

'Thank you, I will. Whatever they did, there's no denying the tragic nature of these events.' As he approached the bed a hail from outside sounded. 'Miss Rudge, everything alright? I thought I heard a shot.'

Burrows looked out of the window. It was one of the farmers who lived locally. A steady man. He descended the stairs, opened the front door and beckoned the man over. 'There's been an incident. Would you find a telephone and call Marston House. Ask the colonel to come here immediately. If he's not in, ask them to telephone the police house in Leyland and tell the constable there to come. Have you got that?'

'Yes. What's happened then?'

'You'll know soon enough. For now just carry out my instructions if you would. There's a telephone at the butcher's, I believe.' With that he turned and retraced his steps without looking back.

When he re-entered the bedroom, the vicar was standing by the bed holding an envelope.

'There's a letter,' he said.

246

Chapter Twenty-One

To whom it may concern,
24th August 1921

Geraldine will be cross with me for writing this, but if circumstances turn out for the worst it will serve as a record of what happened, if nothing else.

The truth is that we are not sisters but have been the closest of companions for many years and moved to Little Tew in the hope that we could live a quiet life in each other's company. And so it proved. The masquerade was accepted by everyone, and our time here has been happy.

When Geraldine went to get her fortune told, she thought it would just be a bit of fun but the man's allusions to the real nature of our relationship terrified her. After the fete she followed him to the Dower House and realised it was Mr Pentire. When she got home she told me and even the faintest prospect of exposure, and the ensuing scandal, was too much to contemplate. After much soul-searching we decided to act.

My father left me a Mauser pistol and a box of ammunition he brought back from his travels in German East Africa. It had lain in a box in the attic for as long as we could remember, but he had taught me to use it and one afternoon I took it into the woods and practised by firing a few shots into a bank. It came back to me straight away.

As our plan developed, we realised that a brief reconnaissance would be needed and visited the Dower House when we knew Mr Pentire had gone into Oxford and Mr Connors had nipped out to Ada Dale's. In common with most residents, he had not locked the back door and as Geraldine kept watch, I spent five minutes in the study, checking two things. It was all that was needed and confirmed our scheme was viable.

On the night in question, I waited until Mr Connors had gone to the public house and then paid a call on Mr Pentire. Over a drink I told him that he had caused great upset to my sister Geraldine, when telling her fortune. The stupid man could barely remember her and insisted he had just been acting for people's amusement. Nevertheless, when I asked him to write a note apologising, he agreed, and we went into the study where I stood over him at his desk and dictated the words.

Whilst he wrote, I removed the Mauser from my bag and as he signed it, I shot him in the temple. Geraldine was waiting in the garden to warn me if anyone heard the shot, but it was a breezy night, and nobody came. I let her in by the back door. We were very careful about fingerprints, wiping the gun clean and wrapping Mr Pentire's hand around the pistol. Women are just as clever as men when it comes to crime! We even washed the glasses up and put them away.

With the note on the desk and the gun on the floor, we were sure that suicide would be assumed, providing we could leave the room shut from the inside. It was the steam engine at the fete that had given me the inspiration, the way the belt stretched across a distance.

We unrolled a full spool of ribbon, doubled it up and, with the light turned off, reached between the curtains and looped it around the brass knob on the sash window casing. A steady pull brought the catch forward from its open position parallel to the frame so that it was under the locking bar and pointing into the room, leaving the window securely locked and the curtains closed. It worked beautifully! Then we moved Mr Pentire and the desk back a foot or so, meaning the rear of the desk was level with the door.

At this point Geraldine left via the back door of the house and I settled down to wait with the light switched off. I needed darkness inside and outside to complete my escape. I heard Mr Connors come in and go upstairs to bed. Half an hour later I got cracking.

First, I crept out to the kitchen and unlocked the back door. Returning to the study, I pushed the window catch to open again then extended the doubled ribbon into the room and around the corner of the desk. From there it was another straight pull to the door. That's why we moved the desk. Opening the door, I draped the doubled ribbon over the top of it, before locking and bolting it from the inside. There is a wafer-thin gap at the top, you see. It's too narrow for string, but two flat strands of ribbon lying side by side

248

would fit in and move when pulled. That and the brass knob on the window catch were what I checked when we called in unannounced.

Then I lifted the sash window and after a careful look around outside, climbed through, closed the curtains and gently pulled the sash shut. Going round to the back of the house I let myself in and went to the study door. Both strands of ribbon were hanging there. With my ear on the door, I slowly pulled both of them. They were tight but ribbon is strong, and I heard the faint noise of the catch engaging.

Leaving them dangling I slipped round to the front of the house again and used my torch for a moment to check that the bolt was properly under the locking bar. Then I returned to the study door and pulled on one strand only until all the ribbon was out of the room.

And it was done. Hey Presto! The only loose end was that I was obliged to leave the back door unlocked, but I thought Mr Connors would, if he noticed at all, assume he had forgotten it while under drink.

But there is something else to mention. When I was speaking to Mr Pentire, he explained that his valet had given him a list of gossip about some of the people living on the estate. While I was waiting for Mr Connors, I found the list in his desk drawer and took it.

When Geraldine and I looked at it properly the following morning we were astonished. It wasn't gossip, but secrets. Real secrets, including our own. As we had now embarked on a life of crime, we decided to see if we might supplement our income a little bit. Business at the draper's shop has been poor for many years and we barely scrape by. The prospect of some extra money was irresistible to we two church mice.

So, we started writing letters. Twenty pounds here, twenty pounds there. And fifty pounds from Lord Langford. Very nice! And our masterstroke was to report that we, ourselves, had received the first one, and well before the fete. How we laughed after Sergeant Burrows and Constable Dixon had earnestly studied a letter we said we'd received weeks earlier, when I had typed it myself on our own typewriter only the previous day! We even made up a little story about putting it in the bin.

So there we are. I confess to the murder of Vaughan Pentire, but I doubt if I'll hang for it, because if you're reading this both I and my darling

Geraldine will be dead already. We've already decided we'll go together rather than face a scandal.

> *Yours faithfully,*
> *Xanthe Rudge*
> *P.S 10th September. I am adding a brief note to say that we suspect that Eve Dance has guessed our secret. She will have to go the way of witches in Great Tew, and we have a plan.*

With a heavy sigh the chief constable put the letter down on the desk. It was late afternoon the day after the barn fire and he and Burrows were sitting in the police house. He looked at the sergeant. 'Astonishing. Quite astonishing. And all because they feared exposure. Murderers and blackmailers they might be, but something about this is desperately sad as well.'

'You're right,' the sergeant agreed. 'But at least they had a long and happy life before it all collapsed. She says that in her letter.'

'Indeed. On many occasions in Great Tew, the whole truth is only revealed anonymously or posthumously,' the colonel remarked dryly. He handed the letter back to Burrows. 'So what is there to do now?'

'I'll write up a report for the file, but beyond that, very little. This confession would stand up in court but of course there will be no trial. We know who killed Vaughan Pentire and I don't doubt that the coroner's finding will be a murder/suicide, especially once the Reverend Tukes and I have given evidence. Were they alive they'd also be standing trial for the attempted murder of your wife. But that will not happen either.'

'No, you're right on that.'

'How is she, sir?' the sergeant asked.

'Remarkably, given what you've told me, she's not too bad. A number of her, er… friends, have come calling, enquiring after her. It's very odd because they started to arrive from all over the county early this morning. When you were at the Rudges.'

'Really? But news hadn't spread outside the village then.'

Colonel Dance raised his eyebrows. 'Quite. And here's a strange thing. Some of them had what appeared to be facial burns and two had badly singed hair.'

They looked at each other, then Burrows said, 'To be honest, it's a miracle that Mrs Dance wasn't very badly burned, at best, sir. Dixon caught it and I didn't escape unscathed.' He gestured with his bandaged hand. 'If you'd seen the inside of that barn…' He tailed off, then added uncertainly, 'You don't think her friends protected her, or shared it out in some way, do you?'

The older man stared out of the window for a long moment then said, as if thinking aloud, 'Sometimes my wife jokes with me that she has friends in high places. It's possible that we've just seen the proof.'

'She is a very special woman, sir.'

Her husband nodded and smiled. 'She is that. I spoke to the hospital about Dixon too. She's lost a lot of hair and her face is not good, but the chap at the Radcliffe is cautiously optimistic. He thinks she rolled through the flames quickly and they've not gone too deep. And her broken collarbone will heal.'

'Thank heavens for that. She displayed considerable courage in going through that window.'

'That is undoubtably true. She is a credit to the service.' Colonel Dance looked at Burrows assessingly. 'It must have been hellish. I went to look at the barn and it's completely destroyed, some of the walls have even come down. Not a scrap of wood left. You both did well. In the finest traditions of the Oxfordshire County Police.' He nodded approvingly.

Burrows glowed with pleasure. Although the chief constable had promoted him young, direct compliments were rare. 'Thank you, sir. I must admit when I managed to get the door open and ran in, I wasn't sure I'd be coming out again. And leaving the pair of them up in the field while I rode back down to the village to fetch help was a worry.'

251

Colonel Dance nodded, then said, 'The Rudges were clever, weren't they, with the poison pen scheme.'

'Yes. Very clever. They must have worked out that once they started blackmailing people, word would get out about the letters. Pretending they'd also received one, and being the first to report it, was an inspired idea and put them in the clear in my eyes, sir. They were very convincing, but it was a failing, I'm afraid.'

The chief constable nodded thoughtfully. 'And once they'd convinced you they were victims too, they were out of the running for Pentire's death. Because you were sure the letter writer was also the murderer.'

Burrows grimaced painfully, aware the colonel was right. 'When you're looking for someone who's cold-bloodedly put a bullet in a man from six inches away...' he shrugged, 'well, two spinster sisters in their late sixties weren't uppermost in our minds, sir.'

'For what it's worth, they wouldn't have been high on my list of suspects either. Take a day or two off and have a rest. I'll telephone Bull and Riley and tell them to cover here if needed.'

Well aware of the domestic crisis this would avoid, Burrows expressed his thanks and with a brief further exchange the two men parted.

*

Two weeks later Mabel Dixon was collected from the hospital in a police car and driven to Great Tew with Innes sitting next to her. Eve Dance had arrived back in the village a week earlier and was convalescing quietly at Marston House. After discussion with the doctors, it had been arranged by Burrows and Colonel Dance that the WPC would stay at the police house and Edna Williams would come in every day to cook and clean, and generally keep an eye on her.

The morning after her arrival she received two visitors. The first was Eve. Edna met her in the room with the counter and showed her through to the parlour where Mabel was sitting. Although she had prepared herself, the sight of the policewoman was a shock. The left side of her head was denuded of hair and her neck, cheek and forehead on that side were covered with scabs.

'Good morning, how lovely to see you back,' she said, sitting down next to her.

'Hello, Mrs Dance.' Her voice sounded different, Eve thought. Flat. As though the confidence that had been such a strong presence in her character had taken a knock. And it was hardly surprising.

'Tea?' Edna enquired.

'That would be lovely.' Eve gave a nod to Bert's wife who disappeared, and they were left alone.

Faced with her graphic injuries Eve decided not to beat about the bush. 'What have the doctors said?'

'They think my hair will grow back in the main and I'm told there's new skin forming under the scabs. It'll be a while before they know for sure. They gave me a mirror before they let me out.' Voice breaking, she said quietly, 'I look like a bally lizard.' A sob sounded in the still room.

Eve took her hand. 'But the prognosis is good, they've said that at least. I'd be surprised if there's much to notice at all by next summer. Your hair will be back, and the scabs will have gone.'

'And Hector Dean will have married someone else by then.'

'Ah. That's your worry, is it? Well if he's the chap I think he is, you may be mistaken there.'

'He didn't come and see me.'

'I'm not sure he was allowed. They only let next of kin and Jocelyn in.' Then she said, 'And how does it feel to have saved someone's life?'

253

'I don't know about that.'

'Yes you do, Mabel. I'd have died if you hadn't dived through that window and rescued me. I owe you a debt and at some point I will repay it.'

The policewoman looked at her. 'You don't owe me anything. Anyone would have done the same.'

The older woman laughed briefly. 'I'm not so sure. But anyway, I am here to thank you and say that I am Eve to you from now on, and you have a friend for life in me. And I have to say Jocelyn is pretty grateful too.'

Edna bustled in with a tea tray, her eyes alight with interest. 'You've got another visitor.'

'Who's that? I'm not sure I want to see anyone else, looking like this.'

'You might want to see Hector Dean, I'm thinking. He's in the office.'

'No, not like this,' Mabel wailed in distress, her hand at her scabbed face.

Edna looked at her sympathetically. 'He'll have seen a lot worse in France and I'd say you might as well get it over with. Keen on you he is, and you're not going to be looking like that for ever.'

Eve said, 'I know what you did, Mabel. You're a brave woman. Now's the time for a bit more courage.'

Without waiting for an answer, Edna left the room, saying, 'I'll get him.'

Eve stood up. 'That's me away for the moment then. I'll pop in tomorrow.' With that she melted away and moments later the large frame of Hector Dean filled the doorway.

'In you go,' Edna said firmly and shut the door behind him.

He stood there and they looked at each other, concern in his eyes, embarrassment in hers. In the silence Eve's voice calling goodbye to Edna Williams reached into the room.

'Here I am then, Hector. In all my beauty,' she said.

He crossed the room and sat down next to her. 'I'm just glad you're safe. They're saying in the pub you went into a burning barn and saved Eve Dance. You're a heroine. That's the talk.'

He nodded and Mabel saw his eyes drift to her scabs as he continued, 'I asked for time off to come and see you, but the hospital said no. Otherwise I'd have been there the first morning.' He met her eyes again. 'I was right worried about you, Mabel, and that's the truth.'

She asked, 'And now you see me, are you still worried, Hector? Because my remarkable good looks may not return completely.' She ventured a wry smile. It was the first since her injury and she felt the scabs on her face tighten. Somehow just having this strong and straightforward man in the room was a tonic.

He gave her a grin. Big, open and full of warmth. 'I'm not God's gift myself, Mabel Dixon. As you well know. But I like you, I know that. And I hope you do to. It wasn't so long ago we were having a nice cuddle on this sofa, and I wouldn't mind having another when you're feeling better.'

There was a silence. She looked away, aware of his eyes on her, then there was a quiet knock on the door and Edna appeared carrying a cup. 'Just in case you fancy a drop, Hector,' she remarked, then added, 'everything alright?'

In spite of her worries, Mabel smiled again. The desire to be the one with the news transcended all other considerations in Great Tew.

She reached over for Hector Dean's hand and felt a thrill run up her arm as he enclosed hers in his strong, warm grip.

'Thank you, Edna. And yes, I think everything will be alright.'

Eyes gleaming she cackled and said, 'I'll leave you lovebirds in peace then,' and went back to the kitchen.

Chapter Twenty-Two

Three hundred miles north, in Dumfries, Mr and Mrs Knox caught the bus into town and walked to the central police station. The simple truth was that they couldn't stand the lie any longer. After a brief wait, they were shown into a meeting room where Sergeant Macpherson joined them, notebook in hand.

Rory Knox took the lead. 'It's about Don Lang. I'm sorry to say we haven't told the truth.'

The policeman eyed them and nodded slowly. 'Alright. Just wait while I get Constable Weston.' When they were all settled, he said, 'Right then, Mr Knox, let's have it.'

'Your informant was correct; we were visited by a red-haired young man. He came looking for our daughter, claiming he'd been up at the university with her. He said he wanted to get back in touch.'

'What was his name?'

'Cameron Breck.'

'And had he been at university with your daughter?'

'No, we think he was lying.'

'Did you know him? From before?'

'We didn't know him, but we knew of him,' Mrs Knox observed carefully.

Constable Weston frowned in concentration at this distinction. 'So, you hadn't met him before. But your daughter had mentioned him?'

'Aye, that's right.' She nodded.

'You didn't like him, did you, Mrs Knox?' Macpherson said quietly.

She shivered slightly. 'It was just that sense you get with some people. You know.'

'I'm guessing you weren't keen on the idea of him getting back in touch with your lassie?'

'Not really. He wanted her address, but we fibbed and said we were waiting for it, and suggested he leave a note that we would forward. Which he did.'

'A note? Do you still have it?'

'No, I'm sorry. We sent it on with a covering letter that afternoon.'

'A letter addressed to her which I assume you posted in the box at the end of your road.' Macpherson glanced at his constable and continued, 'The box that Breck then robbed and in the act assaulted an innocent man so violently that he is now dead.'

Horror appeared in Mrs Knox's eyes. 'The letter. He was after her address.'

'We've been wondering about a motive. You have just supplied it. Have you heard from her?'

'No. They've only recently returned from their honeymoon.'

There was a significant pause as Weston made a note and his sergeant stared at the unhappy couple on the other side of the table. Finally, he addressed them.

'I'm glad you've seen sense and come in, but you haven't yet answered the two most pressing questions. One, why did you lie to the police about a straightforward matter like this? And two, why did Cameron Breck want your daughter's address so badly he robbed a post box and killed a postman?'

Mrs Knox turned to her husband, tears in her eyes. 'I think we better tell them.'

257

Rory Knox stared at the sergeant. 'Can we rely on your discretion?'

'Our priority is finding the man who caused the death of Mr Lang. If you have information that is pertinent to that enquiry my strong advice to you is to disclose it.'

'Some years ago, our daughter made a foolish mistake. This man may well be involved, and we see no merit in allowing him to find her.'

Constable Weston looked up in surprise from his notepad. 'Are you saying she might be in danger? From this Breck fellow?'

'He is certainly in a position to cause her great distress and upset. And now we know he is violent too. We are trying to protect her.'

'Where is your daughter now?'

'In Oxfordshire.'

'And Breck will have had her address since the morning he robbed the post box.' He gave them a steely glare. 'Listen, the pair of you, I want the whole story, chapter and verse. And I want it now.'

Rory Knox looked at his wife, who nodded tearfully at him. Grim-faced, he leaned forward and began to speak.

*

Cameron Breck sat in a corner of the Eagle and Child public house in Oxford with a dram in front of him. It was late on Friday afternoon and apart from two middle-aged men sitting at a table on the far side of the room, the place was empty. He was smartly dressed in new clothes and was deep in thought.

Part of him was well satisfied. He had taken the cheque to the Spenses' bank and arranged to have the funds transferred to a new account in his name at their main Glasgow branch. It would take a few days, the assistant manager had advised him, but things should be in place by the end of the following week. In the

258

meantime he had been happy to advance a hundred pounds in cash to the young man who seemed to be in favour with the Spense family. And Breck, full of the optimism that solid financial backing gave a young man, had chosen to stay in the city for a while, exploring the delights that Oxford could offer.

And yet, something rankled. In his moment of triumph, he should be feeling only delight and satisfaction that he had outmanoeuvred the Spenses and extracted a sum that would set him up for life. He was realistic enough to know that he was never going to be welcomed into the arms of a noble English family such as theirs, so it was as good an outcome as he could expect, he reasoned.

But something was missing and sitting there he realised what it was. The Spenses didn't just dislike him, they disrespected him. In their eyes he was a chancer and a blackmailer. A man who had taken advantage of a single woman on holiday. The lowest of the low. It was infuriating that they should sit in judgement over him when the saintly Innes had been a willing and enthusiastic companion on that fateful night in Oban. She had emerged covered in glory, her secret safe and married into a rich and influential family, yet they despised him.

His expression tightened. In spite of the money, he owed them nothing, including his silence.

'Everything alright?' A voice with a rich Oxfordshire burr interrupted his thoughts. He glanced to his left. A lean man in country clothes had taken a seat at the next table. 'Only you look as though you've lost a pound and found a penny.' He dipped his head and gave him a sympathetic man-to-man smile.

Breck nodded back. 'Just thinking about life's ups and downs.'

'Well, I've had plenty of those myself.' The man supped his pint reflectively and added, 'You're not local?'

'No. As you might have guessed, I'm from Scotland.'

'Down here for work?'

'In a way.'

The man drank again. 'Lucky you. Not much work for me since the war. They wanted us badly enough then, didn't they? The people in charge. But it's been thin pickings since they took my rifle and sent me home.'

Not really interested in another man's problems, for sake of saying something Breck asked, 'What's your line?'

'Farming and general labouring. I live in a tied cottage and get some work off the estate but it's piecemeal stuff, a day here, a day there. My family has been in Great Tew for generations, but we've always lived hand to mouth.' He grinned at the Scotsman. 'Maybe it's time for a revolution. Get some of your radical friends from the shipyards down here, eh? Start a union.'

Breck stared. 'Great Tew? That would be the Langford estate then.'

'That's right. Know it, do you?'

'I've heard of it. Let me buy you a drink.'

This suggestion was received positively, and he returned shortly afterwards with another dram and a pint of beer. Putting the drinks on the table he sat down and extended his hand. 'I'm Cameron Breck.'

'Bill Hays.' They shook and the man thanked him for the beer, then Breck continued. 'You know the Spense family then, I assume?'

'All of us in the village do. I've done plenty for them over the years, in the gardens and out on the farms they run directly.' He lowered his voice and added, 'Lord Colin who died during the war was alright, but I can't speak highly of his current lordship, Mr Piers.'

'He's not so good then?'

'There's plenty that think he's the bee's knees, but he's done me no favours. Then there's young Mr Edward. He's newly married of course. She's a fine-looking girl but if you ask me, she's taken on a lot of airs and graces since they got wed. I reckon it's moving into Langford Hall that's done it. She's just a Glaswegian teacher's daughter but look at her now. Footmen at her beck and call and a lady's maid to boot.' He paused and stared across the room as the two men at the other table prepared to leave, then turned to Breck and added, 'Alright for some, ain't it. Her living high on the hog and me searching for a regular day's work. I'm poaching rabbits to keep food on the table some weeks.'

Realising that fate had done him a good turn, the young Scotsman thought quickly. 'I'm sorry you're down on your luck. As it happens, I've done a good piece of business while I've been down here. How about I treat you to a bite to eat at the chop house round the corner?'

The man looked at him. 'Well, if you're buying, I won't say no. Thank you.'

They finished their drinks and twenty minutes later were sitting facing each other in the window of the little restaurant. They were the first in and once the waitress had taken their order, they were left alone.

'So, am I right in thinking you're no great admirer of the Spense family?' Breck asked in a low voice.

Hays met his eye as though assessing him and then said, 'I'll speak plainly. I'm of the opinion they could do with being taken down a peg or two. Especially that Innes Spense. Just because you've struck lucky doesn't mean you can lord it over everyone else. People should remember where they came from.'

Breck smiled. 'You're speaking my language, my friend. As it happens, I may be able to help you. In fact, I'm certain that I can.'

'How's that then?'

'I'm in possession of some information about the Spense family. Something from the past that would be very embarrassing for them if it got out.'

His dining partner looked sceptical. 'Mr Breck, perhaps you don't know these families. They've all got secrets and they have a way of keeping them.'

But the red-haired man held up his hand. 'Believe me, what I know is a scandal that would have a huge impact on the estate and the village, and far beyond. And most of it would fall on Innes Spense. You think she's got airs and graces. What I know would destroy that illusion once and for all. The woman has a history.' He was leaning forward, his tone intense, and the man opposite realised his new friend was serious.

'What sort of history?'

'The sort that destroys reputations. She isn't what she says she is, I can tell you that.'

The countryman thought for a moment and Cameron Breck saw a flash of cunning and intelligence in his eyes. *He really does hold a grudge, well met indeed*, he thought.

'So, what is it that you know?'

'We'll get to that. Let me ask you something first. You are a long-time resident of Great Tew and reasonably well liked in the village?'

'I am that. I've got plenty of good mates. We were in the war together. That builds up a bond.'

'Yes, it does. So, if you were to tell them something the chances are it would be believed? And passed on?'

The man laughed. 'You don't know village life, do you, Mr Breck? Gossip is the lifeblood of the place. They say a lie is halfway across the county before the truth has got its boots on.'

It was the Scotsman's turn to smile. 'Well as it happens what I know is the truth. And it's all the more potent for that. How's that bairn of hers? Jaikie, she calls him I think?'

'He's up at the hall now too. The talk is that he'll be adopted as a Spense by Mr Edward, although he won't inherit the title. She arrived in Great Tew with him in tow. He's her dead sister's boy.'

Breck looked at him long and hard, then said, 'Oh no he isn't.'

*

Forty-five minutes later the men parted outside the chop house. Cameron Breck walked down the street in a buoyant mood. The niggling itch had deserted him, and he felt that his time in England was coming to a close in a highly satisfactory way. His new friend had been astonished at his story, and Breck realised that the lie regarding the dead sister had been accepted without question on the estate.

It had taken little persuasion to get his dining partner to agree to seed the rumour in the village that Innes Spense was Jaikie's mother. His face creased into a cynical smile as he imagined the impact the news of her deceit would have across the area. Her twin moral failings in falling pregnant out of wedlock, and then lying about it would be discussed at length –opinions would be heard, judgements made, and the tale would spread like wildfire.

His friend had thought that her decision to lie to the village would be considered a greater sin than falling pregnant, but whatever the ins and outs of it, the news would fall on Langford Hall like a shell fired from a howitzer and the repercussions for Innes Spense would be unbearable.

Another thought struck him. Did her new husband know? If not, the marriage was unlikely to survive. He walked on towards his hotel with a warm glow of triumph. It was time to leave Oxford. He had the money he needed, and his Parthian shot would wreak havoc with Innes Spense's reputation and the life of ease she had manufactured for herself.

All in all, it's been a fine day's work. Very fine indeed.

*

The following morning a telegram arrived at the police house. After one look Burrows walked to Marston House, where the colonel read it out loud as he stood in his study.

263

'*Oxfordshire police Great Tew. Urgent. Cameron Breck believed in Great Tew area. Wanted for murder of postman Don Lang in Dumfries. Description: age 24 approx., red hair, slim build. Believed travelling alone. Langford Hall may have information on whereabouts. Arrest on sight and advise. Inspector Baker Glasgow Police.*'

The chief constable looked at Burrows and said, 'We'd better have a walk up the road.'

By coincidence, the man with whom Cameron Breck had dined at the chop house the previous day knocked on the back door of Langford Hall at precisely the same time that the chief constable and Burrows arrived at the front.

'See who that is, will you, Mrs Sutton,' Dereham said as he headed up the back stairs. Five minutes later he announced the arrival of the police officers 'on an urgent matter' to Lady Langford, who was writing letters in the morning room.

She met them in the entrance hall.

'Good morning, Lady Langford,' the colonel said formally. 'Sorry for the intrusion but we are seeking a young man named Cameron Breck. He's wanted for murder up in Scotland. There's a suggestion he's known here at the hall.'

Claire Spense was a woman of great experience but even she could not conceal her shock at this news. 'Murder?'

'So we are told. I'm guessing from your reaction that you do know him?'

She hesitated. 'I know of him.'

'Might I ask how?'

'No.'

This flat refusal was so unexpected that Jocelyn Dance was briefly flummoxed.

Burrows said, 'Our main concern is to locate him, my lady. Do you know where he is?'

She looked at him but said nothing.

'I do.' A voice from behind them broke into the loaded silence.

They spun round to see the man from the Eagle and Child standing by the back stairs door. Mrs Sutton was with him.

'And where is that?' Burrows asked.

'He's catching the sleeper from London to Glasgow tonight. You'll probably get him as he boards, if not they can get him at the other end.'

'How do you know—' began Burrows, but Lady Langford interrupted.

'Well, there's your answer. I will leave you to it.' Making a mental note to telephone the bank just in case the cheque hadn't cleared yet, she looked at the man by the door, said, 'Come with me,' and disappeared down a corridor.

He followed obediently, leaving Dereham and the two police officers staring after them in a little frozen tableau.

'Sir…' said Burrows quietly, after a moment.

The colonel looked at him. 'Yes, to horse, Sergeant. Come on.'

Lady Langford led the way into the morning room and sat down at the table. The man walked over and joined her, uninvited. She looked at him and after a moment's silence said, 'Was I right?'

The man nodded. 'Oh yes. He gave me twenty quid to spread the word.'

She looked at him, her face unreadable, and asked, 'And what word would that be?'

He scratched his head. 'Do you know, he said it so quickly I struggled to catch his meaning. And I can't properly recall it now.' He looked at her. 'Funny that. He thinks he's planted a bomb under Langford Hall that will blow up and take the Spense family with it. But he didn't reckon on you being smart enough to anticipate and defuse it, my lady.'

She nodded and stared across the room. 'A near miss though.'

'Well, that's true. Although it sounds as though he'll hang when the police get him.'

'And that'll be the end of that,' Lady Langford said quietly.

To his surprise she reached across the table, took his hand and looked him squarely in the eye. 'Not for the first time the Spense family owes you a debt of gratitude, Bert Williams. And not for the first time, you know our most intimate secrets. Is there anything you need? Anything at all that is in my gift you may have.'

He gently released her hand. 'We all rely on each other, don't we. In the end.'

She nodded. 'Yes, we do.'

'So you owe me nothing.'

'In that case let me just say thank you, from the bottom of my heart. Rest assured you have credit in the bank and may withdraw it at any time.'

He shrugged and added, 'Well, maybe next time one of your gamekeepers catches me out for a walk in the evening…'

Eyes warm with amusement, she said, 'For heaven's sake, Bert, I hereby give you permission to poach with impunity across the Langford estate. How about that?'

The lean countryman pictured the River Cherwell running silver and black on a midsummer's night as he crouched, pulse racing, in the shadow of the trees by Dipper Pool. He leaned back, met her eye and smiled.

'Oh, I don't know, Your Ladyship. Where would the fun be in that?'

The End

Printed in Great Britain
by Amazon

28577329R00149